ELDER TAPES

Xao

Kat

(Katherine)

from the
Author

16/12/05

signature

Best Wishes

ELDER TAPES

T R THOMPSON

Date of Publication:
2003

Published by:
Cambridge Publishing and Printing Ltd
PO Box 163
SG14 1XN

© Copyright 2002 T R Thompson

ISBN: 1-84446-001-0

CONTENTS

PREFACE

The reader needs to become acquainted with the following terms and descriptions which occur in Elder Tapes. Please read on:

Know thee well the 'Gates' and their 'Sigils', lest thee should fall prey thyself to the Haunters of Space.
Naasbite is a key, an anagram for him thee calls the 'Beast 666' and a Vampire Horror who purges the Spaceways seeking for the Infinite Essence. The Black Master whose many Legions gave birth to the Elementals of thy Earth.
The 'Incubi' and 'Succubi' of the night, and the Infernal Ones who haunt Man's unspoken dreams.

Was Krasshid the real Atlantis? And what of the reptilian race from the planet Vrom? There could be no turning back for Richard and Jefferson, their flame inside, their serpent power, would soon ignite.

The Abyssmal garden, the real Eden, where the webbed souls of the damned hang silently in awe of their 'Aeonic host' - The Spider Queen Of Space.'

The Revelations now revealed by Elder Tapes clearly gave cause for alarm. The two specials, Richard and Jefferson, had been given clear indication as to their planetary origin.

The Inplant Aeons ago into the then early Man had been performed by no other than a great Old One - who was an Elder God from Antiquity, Merlin of Old was no fantasy, no myth. The jigsaw was finally piecing together, now all that was needed was a Return to Earth. And that return was to defeat its greatest threat, that of the 'Mondemon.' The Monster Demon, brought into the world by two dying Aliens. It was their craft which had crashed into the Cornish waters, and their craft which had given Richard and Jefferson a Journey into Truth and Enlightenment.
Beyond the 'Shining Ones' lies the 'Abyssmal Garden, 'the haunt of the Spider Queen of Space.

ACKNOWLEDGEMENT

To Mother

THE BEGINNING

It was one of those cold crisp nights, the start of winter, when bacteria had flown and bitter winds showed their faces. The establishment's jeep parked precariously upon the cliff edge, and the discernible sounds of high waters hammered the rocks below us. Jefferson, a short but thick-set individual, peered through the binoculars at the object drifting towards shore. 'It is' he shouted, 'it bloody well is.' I stared at this unknown craft, its markings unusual, and yet vaguely familiar. Jefferson walked in my direction his face a fairground of delight. 'Look' I said, 'Maybe you had better keep an eye on it, and I will radio base.' Jefferson nodded in agreement, and quickly retraced his steps. From the position of the jeep, I could just see its geometrics, and I wondered about its creators. The hand-set was programmable for scramble code, which I now began setting. A bleep and a further bleep, then I could talk. An eerie foreboding fell upon me, and my message was somewhat garbled, but they responded with 'Roger, OK, observe, wait'. The jeep's windows began to frost up, and the cold now seeped into bones. Jeff stood motionless, transfixed by this Alien-intrusion upon our world. We had each been issued with a revolver and explosive cartridges, but I saw no need for weapons at this time, only stout nerves and a keen line for duty. I noted the time, ten past midnight. It had taken nearly one hour to reach this part of Cornwall, and it could take a further hour for the Scientific team to arrive. Perhaps we should take a closer inspection, a voice told me, my own willpower now taking command. I left the vehicle, donned a cap, and made my way towards Jeff. He had, by now, replaced the binoculars into their respective holder, and in a crouching position, motioned me to come next to him. Partly obscured by a large rock, before us lay this grey metallic-craft, no sign of movement, yet it seemed strangely alive. I again noted the time, thirty three minutes past midnight. We spoke little to each other, the next thirty minutes caught in a magnetic trance, given out by this thing.

'Richards, Richards, are you alright Man? answer me man' The Major and his team had arrived on queue. It had taken them just over the hour. The elderly professor, a Dr Marinett, now harassed myself and Jefferson with awkward questions, while the Major and a few specials took a closer look. About two hundred yards away, I saw troops erecting standard security fencing, with heavily armed guards enforcing security. Jeeps and helicopters, now invading the privacy of the Cornish people. Lights were everywhere, if anything was in the craft it was about to make itself known. The Major beckoned me and Jeff over to a makeshift tent and once inside announced his intentions. 'Gentlemen, my scientific team and certain top brass from other establishments, have decided to blow this object open, as there appears to be no apparent doorway. And secondly we cannot afford to waste time. The press and national media must be kept from this actuality, and road or air transportation will only add speculation to their reports.'

'Therefore at precisely midday today, a press release will ;announce the finding of a 'cache' of unexploded bombs, presumably hidden by some terrorist movement, and to be used at some future date. The authorities have decided to detonate these explosives at twelve thirty today February 8th 2015, at a undisclosed area around the Cornish coastline. I would suggest gentlemen, you find suitable accommodation until that time, and until we conclude this forgettable chapter.'

Jeff gave his encouraging wink to me. We had heard this crap before, on a similar mission in Arizona, investigating the disappearance of a whole family. Again the authorities covered the truth, by announcing a tragic gas explosion had wiped out an entire family. But the evidence clearly showed a UFO had landed outside their home, physical impressions in the ground and black powdered particles in the same report confirmed this. I glanced at my watch, a quarter to three in the morning, time to find a quiet place to talk. Jefferson bid goodnight to the Major, and without further words being spoken, we drove the jeep past security and down into Truro.

The Inn Manager, quite tired himself, showed us to a quiet back room, which overlooked a terraced courtyard, leaving us in front of a roaring fire and two heavy measures of local cider. 'That will keep the cold out,' he smiled, gently closing the solid oak door. Now alone, Jefferson began to view the options. 'Richard my trusty colleague, perhaps you and I should inspect this object, before any harm may befall it. Secondly there must be some known identification about it to warrant such decisive action on the Major's part.'

The little we knew about UFO's had been gained solely by co-operation with the Major, and to ignore his orders right now appeared mutinous. But, after seven years of building this jigsaw puzzle together, it seemed right for me and Jeff to finish the picture. The cider gave a healthy bite to our palates and after seeing the bottom of the glass, I proposed a plan. Jeff looked weary for his forty years, but his psychic abilities, and his determination put paid to any doubts I may have had.

'OK this is my plan, we take a small fishing boat, as close as we dare, then swim the rest, hopefully the doorway to the craft can be found submerged beneath it. Jeff smiled and nodded his willingness. He gazed upon the warming fire and concluded with 'If there's any life on board her, I hope it's friendly.' We spent a further hour drawing a sketch of the object, and where we assumed a hatch would be. Then without further talk, proceeded on foot via the rear room window out of Truro, and through the darkened courtyard, leaving the jeep out front in case we were being watched. It was six o'clock by the time a boat became visible for our use, the daylight now gradually appearing, and perhaps more fishing boats in nearby waters, would act as a cover. 'Let's get on with it then.' Jeff now clearly impatient, as he pushed the boat into the sea. I jumped and narrowly missed twisting my ankle on its hollowed bottom. Once accustomed to oars again the little vessel moved happily across the waves. We estimated a good half-hour's row, and then five minutes swimming, before boarding, if that's the word. A few fishermen waved at us, and we acknowledged their polite gesture, but being wise not to say a word. My arms now began to ache, and I was wondering was it really all worth the effort, when Jefferson interrupted my thoughts. 'Richard, just behind that rockface is the inlet, take in your oars and let her drift awhile and prepare yourself for a bloody cold swim.' Now within half a mile from our objective, I observed the scurry of special forces around the area. There was no doubt we would be shot if seen. My destiny was about to begin . . .

THE TIME TRAVELLER

It was a quarter to seven, and Jefferson was first to taste the cold salt water. He gave a wink, a quick handshake, and splash, two more specs of humanity dissolved into the endless seas. Neither of us having obtained a medal for swimming, we were nevertheless proficient in getting from a given point, to a finishing point, in the shortest possible time. Ahead of us a motor launch with a armed patrol, gave a discerning sweep, obviously spotting the now empty fishing boat adrift. To our left at about hundred yards, a small crevice in the cliff face, spewed out its waste, and filled the ocean with more toxic bacteria. Suddenly a shot rang out, the specials on shore had spotted us, there were three of them, two with rifles and one waving his arms. Jefferson shouted,'It's now or never,' immediately disappearing below the rough waters.

My last vision before joining him, being the craft, now only yards away. The dive was clear, and I could clearly see Jefferson beckoning me to the underside of the craft. With little breath left between us, and the obvious pursual of specials, time was now very valuable. I ran my fingers around a triangular kind of hatch, hoping to release some kind of mechanism. Whilst Jefferson occupied himself with a curious symbol. There was no physical levers of any kind, and it appeared fruitless. And then, as though fate had intervened, the triangular hatchway opened, it was an escape route so we took it. The expression on Jefferson's face said it all, our unknown aliens had saved us. The water chamber slowly emptied, and before us now, a gate to another world. I spoke in a hurried voice, more of excitement than nerves. 'Now they cannot get us from outside, I imagine they will put forward the explosion time, so let's waste no further time ourselves.' Jeff touched a blue crystal, which seemed to be the only means of activating our release. The internal hatch swung inward, a subdued green light echoed the stillness inside the ship. An array of crystal like switches neatly formed a control desk and about ten feet away, an aperture of triangular designs, possibly leading to some other room. My psychic friend grinned, and with the grace of an antelope bounded into the next room, via the triangular doorway. I felt no presence here,

4

besides my companion, we were alone. The lighting came from a tube embedded into the hull, and appeared to enhance any object with a strange luminous quality. The outside world seemed unreal whilst aboard this ship. The floor surface was very black, and its touch felt of plastic not of metal. Perhaps even a hard rubber synthetic. The only sound audible came from the adjoining deck, a soft humming, reminding one of a cold damp night, and the buzz heard from a street light. I now looked at the crystal switches, a different symbol accompanied each, they exhibited three main colours, red, blue, green. The indication here was apparently, levels of speed, drive, or indeed a preset time destination.

In front of this panel a blank screen, of transparent designs, seeming dormant awaiting some timely broadcast. And to its immediate right, a shelf containing numerous plastic-discs, but their mode of use was as yet unapparent. Besides this large panel of controls, the room was empty of any known comforts, whoever operated her obviously never intended a long travel. The humming sound permeated the entire ship, but was not too obnoxious. I gave one more quick glance at the empty screen, and then joined Jefferson. As I entered this second room the green light became even stronger, and my eyes took time to adjust to normal vision. Jeff seemed intrigued in a large crystal formation, in the centre of the room, and appeared entranced by its colourful display of light patterns. So much so, that my entrance went unnoticed. To the left of me, two transparent tubes, each enclosed a uniform, one piece suit that bore a bird like emble0m. To the rear of these further controls The rounded roof displayed the same blackness as the floor, and if it were not for the crystal display, would cast a fear upon me. I decided on breaking Jeff's trance, and called out to him, 'Hey buddy, what does your scientific mind make of this?'

He turned slowly, a smile on his square cut face and responded, 'Bloody fantastic, seems these UFOs use a magnetic-drive which can be accelerated or slowed down by the use of this wonderful crystal. 'What we are standing in can be termed as a Time- Traveller, by changing its vibrationary rate, one can enter other realms or dimensions. But up to now I considered its construction nigh impossible.' Jefferson was totally serious, he did not wink, nor give any other indication he was jesting, and as I stood spellbound he enlarged upon the matter. 'Gravitational fields exist in all worlds, be they matter or anti-matter, obviously vibration is a significant key to these worlds, and as vibration can be likened to heat, then the colour changes seen in UFO flight, indicate their propulsion mode. The metal or substance of this hull, must be very conductive for it can distribute particle acceleration beyond the light speed, and still remain a solid structure. The flooring and all of the inner shell made of an inert insulating material, not unlike rubber. The entire hull is permanently magnetised, hence the humming sound you now hear. If we can operate the correct sequence of switches, I'm sure we could travel space and its Time matrix.'

Again I looked upon Jeff's face and funnily he had me believing him, why shouldn't we be able to traverse time, it would explain many a strange phenomena. I asked the obvious question, where does the power come from? A long finger pointed to the radiant crystal and the circular housing about it, then a firm but polite reply followed. 'As the quarts crystal in your watch energises movement, so too the power within this form. When the crystal is lowered into the magnetic housing below it, its matrix, its geometric structure, accelerates the magnetic flow displaced about it. This magnetic flow interacts between the hull and the outside air, around the ship, causing gravitational changes. By increasing this flow, by lowering the crystal still further into the housing, electrical particles are then accelerated within the hull, and to a larger extent about it? One can change direction at any time by energising a magnetic pole, which passes through the ship's centre. The green light Richard is inevitably the rays given off by the dissipation of the ship's hull. I would presume this pure light force would change in colour, according to gravitational fields which the ship would encounter.'

At this point a sore subject was brought up, namely the approaching extermination, by explosives from outside. My watch face was now unreadable, as the magnetic strength around us affected such metals, it was time for a decision to try and fly her, if that was the appropriate word or return to humanity, and perhaps execution? I looked at Jefferson and then the crystal, perhaps too, I was caught in its hypnotic power?

CORRIDORS OF TIME

The Cornish coastline, now rested from its nightly battle of sea defence. Here and there, small channels and inlets had carved their character upon the face of the land. And the cries of gulls reassured the inhabitants that nature is a theatrical play, that at her best never ends. Some miles down from Truro, a large gathering of special forces were about to rudely awaken the quiet solitude. It was fifteen minutes to midday, and a cigar smoking sergeant now made his way to Major Rosie's tent. The Major was relaxing upon a cheap but adequate tent bed, shoes off and reading the latest forces bulletin. 'Excuse me Sir,' barked the sergeant, 'It's nearly time, the area has been cleared about the object, and the explosives attached.' :Putting aside his reading material, the Major swung his long legs across the bed, and slowly placed each foot into a cold army boot. His broad frame rose in the air, and his height bore the mark of command. 'It's raining Sir but the weatherman promises a warmer afternoon.'

'Thank you sergeant, I think we can provide a little thunder in a few minutes don't you?' Donning his beret and pulling on a Army overcoat, he followed the sergeant to the safest vantage point, and after acquiring a handset, gave his timely orders. 'Major Rosie Ansai speaking, in approximately fifteen minutes I expect that thing to be obliterated, no delays message over.' Borrowing the sergeant's binoculars, he took one last look at his companion's grave. He knew they were inside, spotted earlier from the shore. But orders were orders, and there was to be no evidence of any craft. The tide had risen, lifting the UFO closer to the rocks, it seemed different, perhaps the sudden rains clouded his vision. Nope, it seemed to be losing its density, something was happening. 'Quick Sergeant, give me that handset, I can't wait any longer, we must initiate the explosion now.'

Meanwhile back inside the Traveller, a new kind of initiation was about to take place. Fate and destiny now interwoven, locked the Karmic-cycle of both companions. Releasing the spiritual guides from their purpose, to facilitate the awakening of Cosmic truths!

'I've finished Jeff, how are you doing?' said Richard, putting down the last item of his underwear in an undignified heap. His friend came through the triangular aperture, with a smile and then a chuckle. His short stature lost in the blue uniform, the arms fitting well, but the leggings hung baggy and polished the floor as he walked. 'Are you sure we need these on buddy?' asked Richard, looking rather the part, taller than his companion, and much heavier all round. Jeff brought out a mask from within a zipped pocket,

'You must wear this too, these charming suits will protect us from vibration waves. hopefully,' he added. Pulling the mask down around his head and face, Richard now wondered about the disappearance of the former occupants. The plastic type eye pieces now gave a brighter vision, and the green hazy light became clear and distinct. Only the mouth and nose areas appeared to have any openings. Jefferson had begun pushing switches upon the panel housing the screen, and he appeared to know what he was doing. The humming was silent, in fact nothing was audible, the ears being covered by the mask. Jefferson motioned me across and pointed to the screen. I saw him push a square button with the distinctive sign of an asterix. There was a white glow in the screen's centre, then the picture became clear, a cliff face, then down below it some steady movement. It was some specials running away, but why were they running? Oh no, it must be nearly twelve-thirty out there, the Major was going to do it, and blow us up with it. Then again, perhaps the detonation time had been brought forward? A sudden tap on my right arm alerted me to Jeff's reaction. He pointed to the other room and leaving the screen on we moved swiftly to the other control panel. There were three buttons larger than the rest, without further thought Jefferson pushed the three. The light suddenly changed to a deep red glow, and the crystal was sinking fast into the magnetic housing, perhaps a little too fast. My hands began to shake violently, I looked again at the crystal, now deep within the circular housing. Rings of rainbow colours began ascending upwards and seemingly disappearing through the roof of the hull. I felt unable to move for a while, and yet transfixed by the sudden changes in colour, now engulfing the entire room A nauseating sickness came over me, and I fell into this sea of unknown depth.

Jefferson watched the vertical glass like tube, in the centre of the control panel. Along its length, numerous symbols, slowly flashing, as the clear fluid within began to rise. He was sweating, but dare not pass out, there had to be a connection, to this tube and the horizontal row of symbols displayed across the top of the panel? The crystal switches stood out, amidst the ever changing colours confronting his vision. But in a few moments he too would be captivated by such wonders, and join his partner in trance induced sleep. Then, as though awakened by a Telepathic Intelligence, the symbols gave forth their key. Moving from left to right, the thirty two signs showed their reflection in the symbols flashing upward on the tube. Jefferson pushed hard upon the sign donating a circle with a square within it, and awaited the result. There, upon the transparent glass tube, the duplicated symbol of a circle and inner square, stopped flashing, and the liquid also became stable opposite this sign. The array of colours about him now subsided, and his distorted vision and balance had corrected itself. A smile came upon him, he had found the crafts programmed destinations, but just where the hell were they? Jefferson removed his mask, but too early, and the resulting buzz began to tear his ears apart, so much so that he found it an effort to replace it. What had he forgot?

Turning his gaze upon his companion, he glanced at the crystal. It had stopped halfway. A return to the panel of switches provided the answer, three larger crystals still flashing, had not been released, but would he remember in what order he had first activated them? Was it red, blue, green, or green, blue and then red? They were the main switches, for engaging drive to crystal-alignment, and distribution of charged particles about the ship's hull. Assuming the 'green glow' which they first encountered on entering the ship was an indication of the crystal in its dormant position, he took a gamble. Then totally by chance, pushed down the red and blue crystal switches to disengage the drive and direction units. It was a good gamble, the soft green hue returned to permeate the craft, and the crystal now displayed its former colourful array of dancing light patterns. Whilst again removing his mask, Jeff made a mental note of the recent colour sequences, blue red, green, to initiate and green red blue to close down. With thirty two programmed time scales or destinations to choose from, the jigsaw was coming together, for amongst Jeff's psychic studies, the 'Kabbalah' or 'Tree of Life' remained prominent. Richard lay on his back, one of his long legs crossing the other, the steady raising of his chest ensuring life, and the REM diagnosing a deep sleep in progress.

Jefferson sat down beside his friend and after assuring himself Richard had sustained no harm, closed his eyes and thought of home.

THE WORLD OF PHYSICS SHAKEN

Major Rosie slowly opened his eyes, the scene remained the same, a scurry of specials frantically looking for any fragmentation of the vanishing craft. The explosion had gone off on queue, perhaps a tiny bit earlier than anticipated, but the target was somewhere else? His sergeant seemed visibly shaken and unimpressed by the sudden electrical storm flooding the skies. Rosie smiled, turned and left his companion alone on the clifftop. Inside he wished he was with them, and yet fearful of what they might find. The Professor and the other Zoo of primates would be relying on him for an answer, but could he give them one?

At 1400hrs that same day, a news bulletin confirmed the military had successfully destroyed a large cache of explosive materials, alleged to be the property of some terrorist organisation. And a small team of army personnel would be in the area for two or three days, to clear up anything which might be a danger to the public. In his office, Major Rosie Ansai began typing out his report on what would be known as 'The Cornish predicament'. His Superiors dismissed his two 'agent's by the same route, a tragic car accident whilst on holiday, presumably making the false bodies unrecognisable. Lighting a cigarette he began his story, making sure it detailed the 'two missing bodies', found in a local trawling net. (Three days before the 'Cornish incident'!)

On the 5th of February, I was called upon by a Prof Marinett to give my observations on a humanoid body, at the laboratories in a sensitive establishment near the Weymouth area. Because of my involvement with extra terrestrial phenomena, it was thought I may shed some light on their origins, and give valuable insight into the symbolic papers upon one of the bodies.

On the 6th February, a message was forwarded to two trustworthy agents, informing them to converge near a small inlet at a given time, somewhere on the coast of Cornwall. The autopsy by Professor Marinett provided some startling revelations! They possessed similar organs to us, and their build also resembled our own physical proportions. But their fluidical life or blood, bore no resemblance to any match on earth. The eyes were perfectly spherical, and their mouth also in our likeness, but they possessed no hearing apertures, which gave me every indication they were telepathic in conversation. Their fingers, of which there were four, ended in a pronounced circular fashion, without nails.

As the Professor will no doubt clarify the autopsy became expedient as a rapid decomposition of the cells and tissues bagan as soon as their uniforms had been removed. Within 24hrs they were of dust. The blue uniforms are now undergoing tests, and the results will be brought to your attention as soon as possible.

The gloves and shoes being of a similar material, they have been locked away for safe keeping. Found in a waist bag upon one of them, a folded document revealed a symbolic language. The language has been photocopied, and I have been trying to find a 'key' to its understanding. It bears resemblance to 'Runic' and 'hieroglyphs' from the ancient past.

As for the craft itself, I believe its origin to be dimensional, though the means of propulsion I have yet to understand. Its markings have been identified by myself and agent Jefferson, from an earlier sighting six years ago in the Arizona zone. This particular landing and abduction filed under AZ/AC 21 (Arizona-zone/Abduction Cse). The Cornish fishermen have been advised in their own interests to forget this incident, and appropriate action to rehouse them has been implemented. The vessel has been de-contaminated, and the nets destroyed, my questioning of the men involved now filed under SE/ABF/UC/155. (Southern England/Alien bodies found/Unsolved case). Testimonial of M Ansai this day 8.2.2015 1800hrs.

Rosie put the finished report on his desk, made his way to the drinks cabinet, and poured a heavy measure of whisky into a tumbler. He still had some time before the arrival of his Superiors. The cigarette tasted good, taken from a large box given to him from Jefferson. Richard never smoked, but he did indulge in heavy drinking sessions. It seemed strange he should lose them both in these unfortunate circumstances, but if anyone could bring some real evidence back on Alien worlds, it would be these two daredevils. He spoke aloud and in doing so raised a toast 'Whether you be in Heaven or Hell, good luck to you boys.' His line of thought suddenly broken by the ringing of an internal phone. 'Hello, Major Rosie's office, is there a problem?' A mild mannered voice responded 'Joshua Curtis here, I think you had better come down to the decoding section Sir, we have found a key to that unknown writing.' But he could not, the visitors would be there shortly, and orders were orders. 'Look Joshua, I'm pretty busy at the moment, give me a couple of hours and I will be down there.' The line went dead. The Professor, the Chief and Area Officer were making tracks towards Rosie's office, the maze of corridors within this establishment alphabetically coded. Hence Rosie's office of 'Saucer-Infiltration' could be located in the 19th corridor, room 9. Joshua's dept of 'Decoding-fac' corridor 4, room 6. Professor Marinett's 'Research Ops' found in corridor 18, room 15. X-ray Documents corridor 24, room 4, and so on. All of which proved a blessing, particularly for the transporter tube, which ran round in full circle.

The twenty six corridors, three levels below ground, could only be reached by way of this tube system, which enhanced the need for security. A control centre, positioned obviously in the centre of all corridors, could activate two emergency lifts, if the need should arise. Above ground the cover for this establishment, remained the same, a small disused airfield in the heart of England. It was amazing how many people went into the passport office, but never seemed to come out.

A sharp knock, alerted the Major's attention, and he quickly regained his posture behind his desk of command. 'No need for formalities my dear Rosie, you should know us all by now.' The Chief had spoken and he eased his rather large frame into one of the two armchairs. The Professor grabbed the chair nearest to the Chief, and the Area Officer tried to make the best out of the bare slimline stool left before him. Rosie pushed a button beneath his desk, it would ensure privacy by magnetically securing the door.

'Now then gentlemen, I have prepared a statement which you may now read. It is not fully explanatory but nevertheless truthful, and well accounted for.' The Chief looking somewhat older than his fifty years looked directly at Rosie and put forward a question 'Obviously, we are again unsettled by some 'Alien intrusion' upon our planet, and those above my position, are in need of satisfactory answers. It appears it is not enough, showing them actual bodies, nor is the disclosure of top secret film. What my Generals need Major is the how, and the where and reason they infiltrate our military screening.'

At this point the now agitated Professor leaned forward and reaching into his outer pocket produced a set of mathematical figures. 'I have Sir, the implications of a Non terrestrial visitation, indeed on the contrary, I fully believe as does the Major, we are dealing with forms from another dimension. Further, because their timescale does not conform to our physics or laws it is just possible our visitors are the same as those seen fifty or sixty years ago. I would hazard a guess the detaining of such would accelerate their molecular bodies to such a degree, they would die and decompose rapidly in front of our eyes. As happened earlier in the autopsy of two such bodies.'

The Major nodded in agreement and added 'On my visits to a factual landing site, the surrounding area has produced remarkable signs of accelerated growth, both in plant life and indeed in insects within the landing area. I therefore assume Sir, there are fields about us, that can, and are manipulated by some force, or displacement of being, causing changes in the acceleration of time. And by direct inclusion of geometrical patterns, these time zones are to a degree contacted. This feeling is influenced by my research into pyramidical geometry, and the power of ancient symbols, such as the cross, the swastika and the pentagram.'

For a moment the Chief and Area Officer looked puzzled, not by the scientific interpretation, but by their acquired knowledge. 'I shall reflect upon your views gentlemen, and be in touch within a short space of time, in the meanwhile good day to you both..'

The chair indicated a sigh of relief as the mountainous form of the Chief spread his weight to his feet. Rosie released the magnetic lock, and followed them to the door. He had not eaten for quite a period, perhaps the Professor would accompany him to the eating hall. A smile of wisdom caught his eye, as he turned towards the Prof 'I feel quite empty too Rosie, let's call it a day and head for corridor 5, room 8.'

Having lost his wife in an accident Rosie Ansai was pretty much alone, working in secret establishments left little room for finding suitable companionship, or making new friends of the opposite sex. Still, each day was different, who knew what the future may bring? Both men climbed into the four seater transporter and indicated their exit, a uniformed special pushed a button and the electric motor cut in. Stopping at every corridor meant another fourteen stops before reaching number five. This meant a travelling time of approx 42 minutes. But this rarely happened, and without stopping for passengers the time taken usually amounted to fifteen minutes. Rosie decided to miss out on the decoding-facilities block, and grab an early night, leaving a message for Joshua with his night relief.

As the tube approached corridor five, Richard and Jefferson returned to haunt his mind, perhaps this UFO business had began to take its toll?

NILREM TWO HAS A VISITOR

The Star Traveller had returned, but whom would they find on board? Surely not the two runaways, besides they had been infected. Commander Ranubis ordered the hatch to be opened, and cautioned his guards on using any weapons whilst on board. The ship's power source, the Inter-Stella crystal must not be violated by any external weaponry fire. A birdlike emblem upon the Commander's breast pocket indicated the field of work, and his command of Stella-ships in Nilrem Two. One of three bases, existing within a climatised shell, created by the 'elders' many aeons ago, his race the 'Nagosels' form part of the 'Brotherhood of the Trinity' which spans the 'Universal Pylons of creative forces'. Its member forms of life totalling thirty two.

The opposite negative forms of 'Chaos' united in the 'Brotherhood of Darkness' its members totalling seventeen, are the Anti-Bodies of cosmic essence, having the power to cross space/time without the need for dimensional craft, matter being at their command. The 'Nagosels' converse through thought transference, having no receiving organs at a physical level. Being in similar appearance to humans, they feed upon prepared 'Bacterial cultures' germinated by a substance found on their home planet of 'Geddonia', located in the star system 'Sirius' and close to the pylons of 'Sehad', the first gate of the Abyss.

Commander Ranubis watched as the bodies were carried out of the ship, and awaited his first officer's report. Officer Borcan smiled as he rejoined his commander, and relayed his telepathic communication. 'They are alive Sir and human, but suffering the effects of 'Vibrational distortion'. I have given instructions to house them in Alpha block, where they may be properly refreshed and adjusted for our environment.'

Ranubis nodded his approval, and replied 'Check the crystal-housing and the magnetic energy levels, and decontaminate the switches and suits, then when both humans are better, bring them to my rest area for questioning.'

The tall Borcan again smiled, then without further conversation made his way to Nilrem control. A large Star-map being the dominant feature in any Nilrem centre, gave a colourful view of planetary constellations and the 32 home bases of the 'Brotherhood of the Trinity'. Its webbed formation also showing the 'Pylons' or Gateways into the 'Dimensional-Realms' where Creative and Destructive forces hide their existence and nature. It is the communion or uniting with such forces, that confers the 'Knowledge' the 'Magic' of unnatural manipulation of the Rays of creative-essence.

Geddonia, Arballam and Shehashe are the 'Watchers' of the pylons or 'Towers of Sehad'. It is here the Els, the Nagosels Elders have cast their evil egos by using the time/shift formula in the symbol H. The Pylons or 'Towers' nearest the planet Earth, are watched by the planet bases of Sion, Amegon and Marattone, these are the 'Towers of Elsang', the Gateway to the winged forms of Knowledge and Guidance. (A full scale Map has been included, for References).

Borcan was worried, what if the two runaways had been found by the humans, and examined? It was possible their fluid could contaminate the human system. He liked the human species and was particularly fond of their female form. Perhaps he should ask for permission to visit planet Earth, and conduct tests in the entrance vicinity? He would ask Ranubis after the questioning was completed. After all two of the Star-Travellers were available for emergencies, was this not such a category?

A correlation officer, working in the control room, interrupted Borcan's thoughts, alerting him to the sudden onslaught of meteorite projectiles bombarding the outer shell of the base. Although the shell could stand anything forced upon it, it was necessary to renew the force field poles around it, as outside atmosphere sometimes drained their conductability and field strength. Borcan told the officer it would receive his urgent attention, but first he must visit Alpha-Block, and the two uninvited guests.

Richard awoke, confused and perspiring, from what he considered was a bad dream, his eyes smarting from some unknown agent. As he began to perceive his new habitat, the strange dream now became a reality. Beside him lay Jefferson, apparently still asleep. On the wall facing Richard some four feet from the bed end, a small screen flashed unearthly figures, followed by a script of unintelligible writings. It was all coming back to him now, the ship and the blacking out, wherever he was it sure wasn't Earth. The uniforms had been removed and in their place, a grey shirt and trousers with calf length boots, this completed the new gear. Upon the wrists of both men, a triangular instrument had been fitted, the same size as a wristwatch, but possessing only two holes about ¼ inch diameter, which appeared to be simulating contraction. Although not too obnoxious, these implants caused some concern. On a tray beside both beds, a number of transparent phials showed internal signs of movement, a sponge like substance, grey in colour almost filled one phial, whilst in another, red cells possessing fine thread like tentacles swam freely in the blood coloured liquid. With no syringes in sight, Richard could only speculate on their intended use, and as he and Jefferson had been re-attired any further operations seemed unlikely, so perhaps the gross substance was to be used at a later date? Two metallic collars prevented him from leaving the bed, one around his waist and the other firmly gripping both legs below knee height.

All Richard could do now was await his friend's recovery and the visit from their Alien hosts. The triangular doorway reminded him of that used in the ship, and as it was open he would hear any visitors approaching. Already having an indication of their appearance, from viewing the pictures on the screen, it would perhaps lessen the shock in first seeing them in the flesh. But how would he converse with them? And more importantly was their intentions friendly?

All these thoughts crowded Richard's mind, but the answers were about to arrive, the sudden echo of boots now made themselves known. The tall figure of Borcan now filled the narrow doorway, and except for the missing ears, presented no alarming qualities to Richard. A soft English voice now flooded Richard's head, assuring him that neither he Borcan, or any of the Nagosels would harm either Richard or his friend. That on no account should aggressive thoughts enter Richard's head, as the Nagosel race not only conversed at thought level, but freely picked up thought patterns which could be termed as malignant.

Borcan then smiled at Richard and pushed upon two buttons on a panel beyond Richard's reach. The restraining collars turned full half circle and disappeared into the beds. Borcan then suggested Richard should wake his friend, and help him onto his feet, for they must be questioned by the Commander. Richard looked hard at this strange being with spherical eyes, was this the pre-human race he thought, and was quite startled by a quick 'no' in answer to his thinking. Showing alarm from this invasion into his private little world, and having no wish for further prying, Richard immediately made his way to Jefferson's bed and proceeded to wake the sleeping beauty up. After considerable reassurance from Richard and a little enlightenment from their Borcan friend, Jefferson got to his feet and beckoned Borcan to lead on. The corridors to Ranubis' quarters were transparent and a rough hewn rock could be clearly seen behind the toughened glass screen. At intervals of fifty feet bright crystals gave out adequate lighting from overhead housings, and below their feet a hollowed channel carried cables of various diameter, presumably for distribution of the main power source.

They must have walked about a mile down the silent tunnel, before beginning to descend, and then Borcan conversed again, his strange voice entering both men's' heads simultaneously, and sounding not unlike an echo. A subtle speech, a form of ancient communication which transcends all known barriers, a bridge perhaps to the real mind? Focusing hard on the words now sounding within, Richard and Jefferson took note of Borcan's relayed voice 'At the bottom of this corridor lies our power complex, an enormous cut crystal brought to Nilrem Two, by a 'Galactic-Star-Traveller' the elite of our craft.

The crystal we use can only be found in the Star system of 'Imadogon' a region of darkness on the outer edge of space, and close to the walls of solid existence! Beyond which live the 'Shining Ones', they are the guardians of the threshold and great Void. Tomorrow I shall show you the Great Star Map, and teach the truths therein, but for now I shall introduce you to our Commander.' Jefferson looked at Richard in disbelief, what had they fallen into?

And why were the Nagosels giving out so much information, perhaps it was time to reveal their identity to the Earth, and what better way than using two known forms. Jefferson watched as Borcan keyed in a code on the panel of buttons next to the triangular doorway. A large section of the door descended below the ground, and for once a pleasing sight met both men's eyes.

Seated on either side of Ranubis, the bewitching forms of the Nagosel opposite sex, revealed their charms. The Commander laughed at Richard's thoughts and politely asked the two visitors to take a seat, his voice more distorted than Borcan's, but nevertheless distinguishable. He then continued, 'My name is Ranubis and these two are 'Amariel' and 'Sophiel', they are at your disposal if you wish. Being of similar attributes to human form, except of course speech, both 'Amariel' and 'Sophiel' should by union, unlock certain areas of your unconscious minds, therefore enabling you to comprehend our physics and purpose in the Trinity. We have adapted your breathing by using a modified pulse system, as our air lacks much oxygen and hydrogen atoms, our cellular growth rate is extremely slow compared to your earthly bodies. It has been necessary to slow your metabolic rates down considerably. These two impulse breathers therefore assist your heart pulse rate, though at times you may experience hallucinatory visions. But on return to earth's atmosphere, such governing instruments shall be removed. I do not wish to cause alarm my friends, but your digestive system has been given some of the bacterial growths, which were in your room, but I assure you it was necessary for survival. Now please feel free to ask your questions, bearing in mind Borcan is the science officer and he will enlighten you both tomorrow.'

Not used to thought transference, Richard began to speak normally, and quite naturally Ranubis had to remind him he was not on Earth, would he therefore learn to converse with his eyes and mind. Richard looked into the eyes of 'Sophiel' and asked if there were binding laws between the opposites, as was the case on Earth? A clear pronounced voice answered 'I speak for myself and others, our planet Geddonia is small, our population is also small. We can generate our species only once, after which, further union is used to increase awareness and enhance mental ability. The Elders taught us not to waste the essence within each of us, its power being creative, its flow should be directed to nourishment of the flame within, that which you call soul.'

Jefferson laughed, explaining he had heard every word. 'Sophiel' had conversed, but not a sound of Richard's voice, in fact he was beginning to like this form of conversation. He turned to 'Amariel' and asked his question! Amariel's bright green eyes held Jefferson's attention, her long flowing hair falling evenly about each shoulder, and the essence of a smile forming its grace upon her narrow lips.

Perhaps he Jefferson may find a inner-peace with this woman from another world? Quietly his thoughts drifted into the awaiting senses of 'Amariel's' form. 'I wish to know how you speak my language so readily.'

'Oh it's easy really,' responded Amariel. 'Upon your planet Earth are many tapes, located in a region of high mountainous ranges, where three valleys lead to a Temple complex built long ago by the 'Lemurian Race'. These crystal tapes record the vibration of your speech and can be relayed back to the Nagosels, via a series of patterns of light' beamed upon our eyes. The beginning of your race is recorded upon these tapes, and perhaps Borcan will given entry to our 'Crystal Library' so you may learn more about the 'Lemurians'?'

Both Richard and Jefferson sat silent, caught in a web of disbelief and confusion, only the interruption of Commander Ranubis bringing them back to their new reality. 'My friends I know there is much to learn, and some of this knowledge may frighten you, but it is a necessary part of transformation within. Before you both seek quarters and nourishment, I must ask if any life forms were found near the Star-Traveller, for it is of great urgency.'

Richard gave Ranubis a full account of their mission, including the briefing by Major Ansai, and as far as Jefferson and he knew, only two alien forms had been found. Ranubis excused Amariel and Sophiel, suggesting they might prepare a meal and comfortable resting place for their guests. After both females had departed, Ranubis again spoke, 'It would appear my earthling friends a lethal bacteria could be germinating rapidly within the area close to the proximity of the landing.

Two runaways, scientific personnel from Nilren One, became contaminated with a spore fungus obtained from a nearby planet in the Sirius system. It lives on the brain tissues and glands and then multiplies by dispersing a minute pollen into the air. Obviously our 'Runaways' were mentally unstable and unfortunately materialised upon your Earth.'

'Then we must return immediately,' interrupted Richard, 'and if possible with a antidote.'

'There is no antidote' came the chilling reply. 'But perhaps Borcan can provide an answer. Your earth timescale is helpful in such matters, as the rapid decomposition of the Nagosels bodies may have slowed down the fungus growth cycle. We can only survive upon your planet in protective suits, or by the use of prepared Impulse breathers, and if they are removed or our bodies pierced, the metabolic rate is accelerated beyond belief. Please go now and take rest, an attendant awaits in the corridor to take you to Alpha-block. Borcan shall tell you more tomorrow.'

Jefferson and Richard gave their thanks, and bid Ranubis a goodnight, but on rising from their seats both experienced an acute dizziness, the room began to spin and Richard nearly passed out, the Impulse Breathers would have to be adjusted.

PROFESSOR MARINETT BECOMES A MONSTER

The weekend proved miserable, Rosie Ansai quite content to lounge about watching predictable videos and consuming heavy measures of his favourite tipple. The rain continued to pour, leaving its signature upon Rosie's newly laid cement patio. Even his cat Diamond, cared little for a wet reconnaissance of her territory. Five weeks had passed since that incident, and the revelations extracted from the Alien papers caused such an uproar that even NATO admitted Defence vulnerability. Professor Marinett now showing signs of mental exhaustion had taken a long awaited holiday to America to visit his only daughter, leaving unfinished work in the hands of one Annabel Foster, a respected Nuclear physicist, single and in Rosie's eyes damned attractive. Using his remote control Rosie switched off his video recorder and made his way into the kitchen. A sandwich of ham and cheese topped with a tangy pickle seemed appropriate. Cooking a large meal tonight was out of the question. Diamond gave a loving claw at Rosie's trouser leg, presumably asserting her authority and expertise on fresh cream helpings. She was a greedy cat, never missing a chance to sample the larder's cuisine. But in contrast she was courageous, daring and formidable when challenged.

The workmen had left at two o'clock leaving a cover for the cement in case it should rain, but Rosie a little worse for wear, dropped off into a deep sleep and on awakening around five o'clock found the cover had been playfully removed by Diamond. Upstairs the old Grandfather clock announced the hour of ten, causing another rendering of 'Time gentlemen' from Rosie's ten year old parrot. A smaller portable television standing precariously between two wall shelves in the kitchen now made itself useful. Tuning into a suitable channel, Rosie picked up the latest news broadcast on the Pluto landings. America and Russia in a combined attempt had successfully landed a probe craft upon the planet's surface, and according to the latest reports there was some kind of life out there. Pictures of the great event would be sent out live at noon tomorrow Sunday 15 March. Other smaller news items were of little interest, the great ice barrier continuing to melt and major evacuation of the Polar region still in process.

Rosie was about to carry his sandwiches through to the living room, when a sudden barrage of knocks rained down upon his front door. 'Use the bloody doorbell next time.' shouted an agitated Rosie, suffering from the effects of an abused liver. The solid oak door swung open to reveal a distraught female, red-haired, slim, wearing spectacles and in her mid thirties. It was Annabel Foster, but why call this unusual hour, thought Rosie, trying hard to compose himself, still holding the plate of sandwiches in his free hand.

'Come in young lady, don't stand there getting wet through, give me your coat and wait in my living room, I will join you there in a moment.' Coffee, thought Rosie, must make plenty of coffee. Discarding the sandwiches he put the percolator on to brew, and after freshening up with a splash or two of cold water, quickly retired to the warmth of the log fire. Annabel had lit a cigarette and helped herself to a large dry scotch. She sat nervously staring at the photograph of Richard and Jefferson, which occupied a prime position beside another important facet of Rosie's life, his beloved late wife Harmony. 'I have put a coffee on Miss Foster, so perhaps you could explain your actions this evening?'

Annabel drew a last taste from her cigarette, and after stubbing it out in the already overflowing ashtray, she at last spoke! 'I am sorry to disturb your weekend Major Rosie, but as you can see, I am still wearing my lab gown and the entire autopsy block is now under strict quarantine. A number of personnel have been shot there, and about a dozen are being detained for further tests. Something horrible has begun to mutate in my colleagues' bodies and turns them into mindless monsters.'

Rosie poured himself another drink, his state of intoxication disappearing along with the hungry feeling experienced earlier. 'But I visited your lab early last week, and there was nothing to show alarm about. In fact we both took an extra lunch hour because things were going so smoothly' responded Rosie. 'Annabel, Professor Marinett did brief you on our Alien friends didn't he?'

No reaction, she looked confused, perhaps he should have watched his words, and yet she had passed security clearance. 'Look,

I will get the coffee and then you can tell me more,' said Rosie gaining his feet and making his way to the kitchen. Rosie's mind was now in turmoil, what the hell was going on he wondered? Surely there had been no contamination from the alien bodies? He remembered wearing protective clothing and breathing masks all the time the autopsy was being performed upon them, and the room was cleared of bacteria before he and Professor Marinett had left. He remembered too, how the suits and gloves worn by the aliens had been sealed inside protective chambers, and the remains of the decomposed bodies also sealed into special airtight flasks. No there was no relation between this incident and five weeks ago, after all, he was quite sane. Balancing two hot mugs on a tray with a plate of cake and biscuits on another, Rosie made his way back to the attractive Annabel. Diamond lay beside her asleep and seemingly quite content with her company. The fire had lost its glow and a further refreshment of logs would soon be needed. Once again comfortable in his favourite armchair, Rosie resumed the conversation 'So what do you consider is the cause Miss Foster? or should I say Annabel?'

'Annabel, will do nicely Rosie, thank you. I have been allowed to leave the area until midday tomorrow, when I must then also be scrutinised, and I thought it practical to inform you first, and to enlist your help on the matter. We have been experimenting on a sample of the material which constitutes the Aliens' suit. Johnson, the first technician to experience this madness, discovered a small bacterial growth on the inner portion of the sample. And after microscopic examination concluded it was rapidly multiplying its cells. It was just after this discovery that Johnson began to sneeze most violently, as though suffering from a very bad cold. I sent him home and told him to take time off, that was on Wednesday, 11th of this month. He returned expressing he was perfectly fine now, and carried on with his work. Later in the day he and other technicians went berserk. The sample is back in the sealed container, and I cannot imagine it could be the sole reason for this unknown virus, besides which I myself seem to be unaffected. The material by the way, also provided other intriguing information. It is impervious to heat, and therefore represents an ideal defence against any vibrational fields about it. It is also very resilient to sonic-waves or colour change, and probably most startling of all, one inch of this sample supported 1000lbs of weight before breaking like a brittle piece of metal?' Rosie seemed unimpressed with the scientist's revelations, after all his years of UFO investigation such information seemed pointless. Obviously Professor Martinett had not briefed her on the metallic robot found ten years ago on a crashed saucer near the Gobi desert, nor on the Maze of Parallel-Time. She was immature in the field of UFOs and such knowledge may switch her off all together. A further rendering of 'time gentlemen' from his beloved parrot Samson, brought Rosie back to the matter in hand. 'Annabel, I would suggest we both grab a little shut eye until seven, then I shall accompany you to the science establishment and together we may find some answers. The settee you are sitting on can be converted to a bed, you know where most things are, so I bid you goodnight.'

But there was to be no visit to the science establishment as Rosie soon found out. At precisely 7am a large explosion rocked the small village of Preston and smoke could be seen filling the sky with its veil of darkness. The blaze was a good one and little was left of the three new blocks allocated to the autopsy section. Reports of at least two dozen people being killed, quickly reached the news media, the Ministry of Defence claiming an underground gas main had exploded, at a defence establishment situated between Preston and Osmington. At precisely 7.30am Rosie's alarm clock gave off its Big Ben chime, the smell of bacon and sausages sizzling in the pan reminding him of the good old days of lazy lie ins, and cooked breakfast with Harmony. A small tear began to trickle down his eye. Missing his usual shower he pulled on a bathrobe and manoeuvred his way down the corridor stairway, and on into the kitchen. Annabel stood by the back door, looking out to the pond with its statue fountain, and humming some kind of nauseating tune.

'Good morning Miss, I see you have found some breakfast items.'

'I hope you don't mind, but I thought a good meal would start us off on the right track. Diamond woke me with her claws around 6am, and she is the boss I guess.'

A smile came across the big man's face 'I'm lost for words, perhaps I can repay this wonderful surprise by treating you to a candlelight dinner at a later date?'

'Yes that would be nice,' came the reply, from a thinly dressed woman, gifted with qualities Rosie could not match. They sat talking for a while, spending most of the time gazing into each other's eyes. The catflap opened and Diamond presented her gift for the morning, a small bird hanging lifeless between her teeth. It was her nature, how clever she was. 'Life can be cruel' remarked Annabel, but after some thought again remarked 'though none could compete with man.'

Diamond dropped her gift and ran off into the living room, obviously disgusted by the humans lack of interest in her find. 'Leave me to wash these, whilst you get dressed.' commanded Rosie. 'The shower is the second door on the left upstairs, clean towels can be found in the airing cupboard, just outside.' The slender shape of Annabel left little to Rosie's imagination, but perhaps he had seen too much to attempt another lasting relationship, only time would tell.

Whilst Annabel relaxed under a torrent of warm waters, Rosie rang his office to explain his movements, in case they required him. 'What, are you certain about that?' insisted Rosie, 'but why and what about Professor Marinett's replacement Dr Foster? Oh I see, well yes I will, let's say around midday should we, OK see you then.' Damn how can I tell her,' blurted Rosie, fumbling through Annabel's coat pockets. Pretty ruthless this ministry he thought. Wiping out a scientific group to prevent a spreading of disease.

Here it is, her security pass, well she won't be needing that anymore, not in Wonderland. The rattle of milk bottles on the doorstep told Rosie it was nearly nine o'clock, and the ride to the HQ would take at least two and a half hours, so time was the essence, so much for a relaxing week's break.

'I'm finished' shouted Annabel. 'I will change in your spare room.'

Rosie had just got time for a shower, though it would have to be a quick one. After giving Diamond her bowl of milk he rushed upstairs.

Mrs Shepherd watched through her bedroom window, as the E Type Jaguar rolled down the long driveway and then onto the busy road, and for once it appeared the Major had been enjoying himself, as she had observed a red-haired woman busily combing her hair in the passenger seat. They were obviously going out for the day, and in a rush too it would seem, as the Major had forgotten to take in his milk. Still, Mrs Shepherd had more important things to attend to, a relation had been injured by an explosion, whilst working at the government establishment near to Weymouth.

The traffic lights always tried Rosie's patience, he was more of an open road man, preferring swiftness to idleness. But at least Annabel had not questioned their new destination, in fact she rather liked the idea of visiting this secretive HQ.

Rosie spoke little for the next two hours and Annabel thought it best, particularly when they were travelling well beyond the maximum speed limit. But then just as they turned down a slip road off the motorway and into a quieter area of the countryside, Rosie broke his silence. 'Annabel, under your dashboard, you will find a plastic card with the name Alice Travel on it. Please attach it to your coat's breastpocket. It is a security measure. Once inside the airfield's hanger, we will be monitored and if the impregnated word on the card is not visible, our lift downstairs will not present itself.' The road began to twist and turn for a stretch of three or four miles, and after crossing over a small bridge, the airfield could be seen a mile or so on the right. It seems completely abandoned, thought Annabel, only a dirty looking hanger and bright windsock giving it any authenticity. The jaguar provided a smooth ride over the otherwise rough track around the airfield's perimeter. About twenty yards away from the hanger, they came to a stop. 'Be sure to keep close to me at all times, we walk from here on in,' said a confident Rosie. Without locking the car door, Rosie marched off towards the hanger, Annabel trying her best to keep up with his long strides. A strong wind blew its freshness upon her face as she surveyed the deserted runway, opposite the hanger, a small workshed housed a cessna bi-plane, its undercarriage showing a shortage of landing gear.

Rosie sat patiently inside the hanger's office, a broken window adequately ventilating the smoke from his rather large cigar. He liked Miss Foster, but at times she gave little indication of a sense for duty. There she was, lost in a world of her own, rummaging about in some filthy forgotten shed, which housed an equally filthy old plane. Damn it, thought Rosie, hurry up woman. He stretched his long legs beneath the office's only desk and tapped a few ashes into the ashtray, and in doing so observed a familiar cigarette-tip. Only one person smoked Russian blacks, Colonel Andy Peterson, Candy for short. Obviously, something big coming up for him to make his presence in Wonderland, thought Rosie, but what? His mind was diverted by the opening of the office door. At last Miss Foster had completed her reconnaissance. Rosie regained his feet and asked Annabel to accompany him into the old adjoining passport office. Annabel said nothing and followed the big man and his tobacco trail into the next room.

A sombre looking gentleman wearing a green beret dressed in a camouflage type uniform and carrying an automatic rifle asked the Major for the appropriate password. 'Two way Mirror!' barked Rosie, 'Level three urgent.' A steel door came down from the ceiling completely covering their only means of exit. At last Annabel was to view the place known as Wonderland. The floor slowly descended, giving the impression that the entire Passport Office was indeed a lift. Annabel looked at her wristwatch, the timing of the lift's descent would give some indication of the depth of this underground establishment. It was the smoothest lift she had been in, and the time element from top to bottom or level three, was exactly three minutes. From this information she deduced the levels were perhaps two hundred feet each, and if that were so the entire complex could cover two or three miles. The steel door lifted and two more green berets met them through the new exit. Rosie flashed his security clearance and explained the appearance of Annabel, and awaited confirmation by the internal phone link. 'OK Sir,' said one of the specials 'jeep four will take you to the service tube.' Three jeeps stood motionless outside a lengthy tunnel, each chauffeur driven, and each carrying armed escort at the rear. Annabel laughed at so much security, just what the hell were they guarding she inwardly thought? 'Come on

Miss Foster, this is the rabbit hole to Wonderland,' said a more relaxed Rosie.

The jeep sped off down the twisting tunnel and again Annabel nervously took note of the time element. They stopped at a corridor marked M. A small set of rails led off in either direction through spherical tunnels, whilst immediately in front of them a well lit corridor housed perhaps twenty to thirty offices. The jeep returned to the main tunnel leaving Rosie and Annabel alone. Rosie pulled a notebook from his breastpocket, and began to show Annabel the alphabetical coding of Wonderland. Pointing out the high risk areas of Bacterial-experimentation and Lazer weaponry, his voice now rather charming and without aggressive undertones of Military command. He even managed a smile or two, but the deep lines on his face characterised a man of little compassion. The alphabetical coding intrigued Annabel, it was clever and yet sinister, for what offices lay in the corridor of the 26th alphabetical letter?

She was hungry and using her newfound code she asked Rosie if they might go to corridor 5, room 8?

Rosie nodded in agreement, and slightly tapping his stomach he replied 'and thence to corridor 18, room 15.' (see coding pgs). They both waited for the next transporter, Annabel now feeling rather relaxed and with increasing confidence, showered Rosie with numerous questions. What had happened to Rosie's friends, Richard and Jefferson? And was there any concrete proof of Saucer Infiltration? Rosie answered Annabel in a roundabout fashion, for surely the information could be found in Marinett's notes, after all she Annabel had access to such information, being his temporary replacement. The tube's magnetic line now gave off the recognisable buzz of an approaching transporter. A larger than life figure hugged the two rear seats, sporting a dense beard and a balding headline, the Ex-special air service and mercenary, now commanded the entire ground defence operations. It was of course Colonel Andy Peterson, Candy for short.

The transporter came to a halt and Rosie and Annabel sat in the seats in front, giving the driver indication of their exit point. Candy explained he had been urgently called upon, because of the crisis in America, but by his friends facial expression it became clear to him they were not privy to this information. So he decided to illuminate them on this delicate subject. 'There is, as I am sure you know, a cover up of Bacterial invasion upon our Earth. That of the Weymouth explosion, nr Preston. And the events brought about by the Cornish predicament filed under SE/ABF/155. Also Professor Marinett, whom I had every ounce of respect for, has, how should I put it, been quarantined for the safety of all of us.'

Annabel frowned, she wanted to speak, but felt this was perhaps a ill advised moment to ask awkward questions, beside which the driver of the transporter would not hold the level of security clearance as herself. She would have to wait, and so would Rosie. Annabel looked at her watch again, there had been no stops, passing through 17 corridors, the time taken was 18 minutes, she could assume then Wonderland had a diameter of about 6 miles. Judging an average speed of 20 mls per hour by the transporter tube. She also noticed the double track at each corridor door, presumably to allow another transporter to overtake when one was picking up or dropping off passengers. 'Corridor E' shouted the driver, and the three then disembarked. Candy lit a cigarette, insisting this corridor was primarily a zone for letting one's hair down, and by the names of some of the rooms Annabel could easily believe that. The eating hall was room eight out of twenty in this corridor, opposite Earth-Studies, which appeared empty. A large projector could be seen standing on a rather old desk, and a weird map showing some tunnel formation with the word 'Pyramis' directly above it.

'Come on Miss Foster, there's a good curry on today, I thoroughly recommend it,' said the huge man-mountain stubbing out his expensive Black-Russian into a discarded food item. Rosie choose a wholesome soup and fish and chips, then made his way to a corner table with three empty chairs. Sometime past without a word said between them, each consuming their new found vitality with vigour. Candy was an old soldier and had seen the look of passion in Rosie's eyes before, and perhaps if he had been Rosie's age, he too may have wanted this attractive young thing himself. Lighting another cigarette he embarked upon a new discussion. 'Miss Foster, you are a good physicist and have collected your own patterns of thought on time and its endless doorways, please give me your personal belief on reincarnation.

Rosie shook his head and pulled out a well rounded cigar from his inside pocket, knowing only too well that Candy had experienced many past lives under hypnotic-regression. Annabel sipped some of her coffee, got up from her chair and proceeded to walk behind Candy. After which she then said 'As I stand behind you, so too your shadow, and it walks with you always, though in a different realisation of time. Your past and present are therefore linked, and each incarnation creates a new shadow, each with a will of its own, yet collective in experience and thoughts. Hypnotism contacts such shadows, for they are really our guides. And yes I believe it possible to traverse time and space, but such a time-machine must be capable of 'molecular-transformation' just like a rubber cube which can pass through circular, triangular and oblong doorways, by its ability to conform.'

Space is a progression of endless geometric-tunnels, which combine to produce the universal framework. Each tunnel a trapped time where many worlds exist, and are controlled by the gravitational and magnetic forces, held stable under the alignments of their relative geometric form. In other words we exist under the influence of circular time, and our souls revolve around this Karmic circle of Reincarnation, until our new life form is drawn into another geometric time tunnel.

Therefore I disagree with modern views on the Atomic evolution of expanding space. Other worlds herald weird but wonderful shapes in their planets geometry, the sphere type planet a mere grain of sand in a sea of unknown plankton. All UFOs are not craft, I am convinced of that, some may indeed be life forms.'

Annabel regained her seat, smiling and rather pleased with her small but impressive speech. Candy, rather taken aback, narrowed his eyes and gazed suspiciously at Rosie, his large right hand clenched and tapping in tune with some inward thought.

Annabel finished her coffee and suggested they make some movement towards the briefing room, as she was eager to hear of any further news on the Professor. Candy agreed, and without further comment pushed his bearlike frame into a vertical position.

Rosie pushed his chair under the table and whilst doing so took the opportunity to observe Miss Foster's delightfully long legs, her attire was perhaps unsuited for command HQ's, but who was complaining? Candy led the way to the transporter, his balding head quite prominent, providing a reflective base for the overhead lighting. His shoes as always lacking the lustre of a good polishing. But his uniform tailor made and accentuating the proportions of the man. A waiting transporter soon whisked the trio to corridor 2, room eighteen was at the left of the corridor, two doors up. Unfortunately it appeared the Chief had arrived well in advance, and as they were a few minutes late, it was a general view he would not be too happy.

'Nice of you to attend,' said the Chief, in a somewhat sarcastic manner. Annabel's first impression of the Wonderland Commander had got off to a good start. The three late arrivals were shown to their respective seats, and the Chief gave a brief talk before showing slides on Professor Marinett's condition. 'Gentlemen and Miss Foster,' he began 'We are now confronting a potential Armageddon, in the uncontrollable form of bacterial plague, brought to our planet, as most of you are aware, by unknown alien lifeforms. The following photographs were taken two days ago in the secretive nevada complex, the Professor heavily sedated to prevent any further spread of the airborne plague.

As you will see certain parts of his new anatomy have been photo-enlarged to show the spores which release a deadly pollen into the atmosphere. Lights please!' The Chief sat down beside Colonel Peterson, his overweight frame taking the width of two chairs. The lights were dimmed and the first projection shown. Not alarmed, but slightly nauseated, Annabel fixed a stare on the man she once knew as Professor Marinett. Crude glutinous bubbles had formed on most of his body, his eyes covered in some hideous spotted skin growth. Both cheeks badly blown outwards and tentacles or feelers now replaced what were once ears. A further slide showed the enlarged spores at the centre of his abdomen and again on his upper arms. A total metamorphosis was taking place, pubic and facial hair completely removed by some chemical reaction in the bloodstream, and replaced by blisters or surface bubbles of a dark green colour. Two more slides followed, taken some time before full transformation had begun. The Professor's face badly distorted, and his eyes resembling those of an asylum inmate. Sexual organs now a mass of congealed skin, having the colour of cancerous tissue. His anus completely grown over in a similar way. Body weight generally increased by two or three stone.

The silence remained as the projection assistant packed away his gear, nothing further being said until he had left the room. The Chief then regained his position in front of the darkboard and picking up a suitable piece of chalk outlined the emergency measures now in motion. Rosie made a rough note of these rather drastic procedures wondering if the Ministry of Defence could contain any localised plague without causing national alarm. Besides which men in space-type suits wandering about the countryside, carrying off dead humans on stretchers would need some explaining. However, before Rosie could raise this point, Annabel intervened with a profound statement. 'I am rather amazed Sir, you never mentioned the other possibilities of bacterial contamination, I speak of animals and plants, surely they too might be at risk to infection?'

To this Candy gave a hearty clap, and shouted, 'Answer that one Chief.' The Chief seemed puzzled for a moment, but then gave back an equally good reply 'Well Miss Foster, that is where you come in, we are counting on your background experience to ascertain if such an infection was likely, and further you have the freedom as did our late Professor, of our research labatories to find an antidote to this alien bug, if at all you can.'

Annabel said no more, Rosie put forward his question on containment of media coverage and prevention of mass hysteria. Again a firm but adequate message was replied 'My dear Major Rosie, because of your infinite knowledge of UFO activity, and expertise in the 'Cover-up' story, then perhaps you would be best suited in dealing with areas of unwanted intrusion. Finally before he too asks a question, Colonel Peterson has the exclusive task of removing unfortunate plague victims either directly or indirectly according to the situation. Two patrols of specials being assigned to his overall command. Further information on Professor Marinett's condition and the escalation of the Alien plague will be made available here every morning at nine o'clock sharp gentlemen, and I do mean sharp. Rooms have been billeted for an extended stay, and these can be found in corridor one, room 1A-20A. Good day gentlemen and Miss Foster.' The Area Officer closed the door as he and the Chief left, leaving the three remaining companions in a more relaxed mood. A coffee machine in an adjacent corner provided a refreshing much needed tonic.

A VISIT TO THE CRYSTAL LIBRARY

The Nagosel space station lay hidden, like an egg yoke in its shell. A complex of three living units, watching and assisting neighbouring star systems in accordance with the Space Trinity Laws. Underground tunnels linked the three units and their command centres closely together. Nilrem Two provided security and travelling stella ships. Nilrem One housed the scientific and research facilities. Nilrem Three however contained the 'Hall of Remembrance' a cavernous museum exhibiting the remnants of a former dweller of this space time.

The Nagosels 'Elder Race' the Giants of Time, builders of the great 'Gates' or 'Pylons' between the dimensional realms. The addition of a third eye gave them the ability to transcend the illusory worlds of matter, and penetrate the mechanism of time. Using this knowledge they created a formula known as Time-Shift H. 'The crossing of one universe into another by way of the Abyss'. 'The transformation of Aeon into Aeon, current into current'. Their travels then recorded onto the 'Great Star Map' and their secrets hidden in the Crystal Library. The Elders abandoned their Nilrem home and leaving behind a number of star ships crossed into Infinity.

A total of three hundred and sixty Nagosels lived within this climatised shell, selected from the elite of Geddonia's race. The symbol of a Circle and Square within, was the mathematical formula for Nilrem 'The Circle of Time' concealing a fourth dimensional world. Borcan, first science officer gave his thanks to Commander Ranubis, a return visit to the Earth planet would cleanse his mind with new vigour, and besides only he Borcan could prevent the annihilation of the human race. Only problem now was whom to take? The corridors to Alpha-block seemed endless, and Borcan found difficulty in choosing between Jefferson or Richard. Perhaps after their guided tour of the Crystal Library, and the teachings of the Star Map, one of them might prove himself worthy for the task, it was one way of choosing. A time limit of six mansions had been given for the human education. At least four mansions would be used in the Crystal Library, leaving only two for the great Star Map.

Borcan grinned, hoping his two friends would be refreshed and not tired from their night's experiences. Indeed if Amariel and Sophiel had awakened their inner egos, then he would have little difficulty in teaching Nagosel Science.

The tall mirror left little to the imagination. A slim nubile form graced the polished glass with subtle sexual imagery. Amariel gave thanks to her youthful magnetism, her long flowing hair caressing the firmness of ripened breasts. Whilst two taut limbs suspended a secretive vault of mystical essence. Green misty eyes surveyed the Nagosel temple, stopping only momentarily to analyse the marks of human love.

Jefferson lay asleep, the night's union playing rehearsal to countless dreams. The Nagosel act of love releasing the fire-energy or serpent flame of mystical essence, the Nagosel 'Gortani' and the human 'Kundalini'. Hidden chakras, flowers of untapped space, now bloomed and shot forth their rays of vibrational truth, enlightening and purifying the cells of man's reflective thought. A river of endless colour carried Jefferson on and on, through worlds of unknown depth and geometry. Fields of harmonic wonderment danced to the unplucked strings of universal sound, and here and there great walls of solid existence gave new course to his river of time, until all fell into the waters of life, the whirlpool of creation, the vortex of love.

A voice now broke the essence of his dream. It was Amariel calling upon him to awake and prepare for this new day. Weary eyes removed their lids of sleep, and bathed their senses within the bright light of her room. A small tray presented the morning nourishment, two brown phials of moving cultures and a third full of milky liquid. Ugh, how totally foul, thought Jefferson turning his attention to Amariel, now dressed in a one-piece rather tight blue uniform. Again she entered his thoughts, 'eat my love' Borcan is on his way, and there is much to learn upon this day.' Jefferson now accustomed to telepathic communication enquired upon the means of Nagosel cleaning? A quick response from Amariel assured him the transparent cubicle opposite would more than compensate for human bathing needs, and no drying of the body afterwards would be necessary. A short but stout frame edged its manly form off the oval shaped bed, and with some apprehension placed itself into the Nagosel cleaning unit. Immediately on closing the transparent door, a fine jet of fine coloured particles showered Jefferson in a warm embrace. It feels like millions of magnetic atoms are massaging my skin! thought Jefferson, and in some fashion removing unwanted bacteria by vibrational means. But at any rate, it sure feels damn good. An automatic sensor switched off the machine, and Jefferson hurriedly attired himself with the grey two piece uniform.

Amariel had finished her phials of nourishment and sat beside the mirror combing the long blonde hair that Jefferson had found so enticing. Perhaps one day, thought Jefferson, forgetting the Nagosel's ability to read one's mind. A sudden response from Amariel, reassuring him of her powers. 'Yes I would like to take you to Geddonia, I feel for you in like manner.' An outburst of laughter from an embarrassed Jefferson relieved the tension of a lovestruck man. Clearing his mind of further thought and taking a seat near the oval bed, he embarked upon the task of taking nourishment. Borcan waited outside Sophiel's door, his senses told him they were dressed and preparing their minds for combined teachings. Sophiel had done well, she had awakened Richard's 'Gortani'. Borcan could only hope Amariel had done similar with Jefferson. The two triangular doors opened simultaneously, and two smiling partners confirmed Borcan's hopes.

Borcan entered the earthmen's thoughts 'It is a time for learning my friends, your minds should now be opened to the level of receptive generation. The Crystal Library will impart many cosmic laws and long forgotten secrets of your earthly sphere. Relax in front of each Crystal tape, watch and digest its images of truth. We will spend four mansions within its learning facility, and thence onto the control area and the great Star Map. Richard agreed heartily to this new education, but asked if Borcan might first inspect his impulse breather, as at times his vision became impaired.

Jefferson watched as the science officer adjusted Richard's wrist breather with a pencil type tool. A pair of fine needles ejected from the pencil and Borcan slowly merged them with the two holes on the wrist breather. An audible buzz could be heard inside Jefferson's head, though this noise did not travel via his external hearing organs. The buzz reached a high peak then stopped instantly, and accordingly the programming of the impulse breathers had been completed, as Borcan now retracted the two needles back into his pencil instrument. The walk to the Crystal Library was brief, the transparent corridor walls seemingly darker and the rough hewn rock behind them changing its reddish hue to a dense blackness. Borcan read his friends thoughts, and in response assured them this change of colour, was due in part to the crystal emanations from the Library. 'Crystals' continued Borcan, 'Are responsive to all elements and the physics thereof. Their greatest virtue being 'Inter-dimensional-mirrors' and the power of 'Transformation' when manipulated by outside forces.'

The telepathic communication stopped, a circular doorway with the symbol of a great bird now confronted them. Borcan pushed a sequence of crystal buttons on a nearby panel, and the circular entrance opened in two halves.

'Come' said Amariel, her sweet voice once again invading Jefferson's thoughts. 'Sophiel will help Richard, and I shall assist you in Crystal generation.' Three spherical mirrors hung down from a concave roof, they appeared to reflect everyone and everything, though their means of suspension was not obvious to either man. Two seats of a giant's proportion were positioned directly beneath the three spheres. And to the left and right respectively, a five pointed star, a metre in height and breadth, pulsated in a white rhythmic glow. 'Know this is the Star of the five angels' spoke Borcan. 'It is your Pentagram but in truth it is the symbol of 'Elsang' the winged forms of knowledge and guidance. The crystal screens in front of these chairs will reflect images given by the crystal tapes, into the light channels you call eyes. There may be some pain experienced, but this is to be accepted. As the unused cells of your matrix are destroyed and regenerated by rays of knowledge and guidance, this is a time of trust between us and a test of faith within yourself. I shall be back in less than four mansions. Amariel and Sophiel will help with your teaching.'

Richard spoke to Jefferson using guttural speech, realising for the first time the power in vibrational sound. 'Jeff old buddy, we have come a long way from our first encounter with UFOs, and I reckon we would be foolish to throw in the towel now, so I say, let's take a seat to knowledge.' Jefferson held out his hand in a gesture of true friendship, but said nothing. Richard shook his hand and whilst smiling at Sophiel occupied the huge seat nearest to him, sliding rather like a baby into its parents bed. After both men had positioned themselves as best they could, the two Nagosel females began feeding in the first set of tapes.. The title of the first teaching was 'Earth's Awakening'.

A Holographic picture of a Solar System appeared on the crystal screen, and both Richard and Jefferson recognised it as Earth's planetary region, but the name given to this region was unknown to them, and with the images came a telepathic voice 'Know this is the 'Shunitree system' founded many Aeons ago before the building of our Nilrem base. Here in this world of ten spheres and one giant solar fire, a small scout ship named 'Ator' accidentally entered via a gate known as 'Elsang'. The propulsion unit on board momentarily affected by a rare 'high' energy oscillation' field, which unbalanced the flow of electrons and magnetic particles about its form. The 'Ators' home planet of 'Vrom' is a close neighbour of our own Geddonia, and therefore belongs to the time period of 'Sirius' near to the first Gateway of 'Sehad'. Vrom being a 'Reptilian sphere, contained large quantities of the element you know as water. The Nagosel term being 'Osiphiel'. The main source of nourishment for the Reptilians lived within this 'Osiphiel' and could be found in great abundance! These fish forms of life we call 'Mermdine'. But as the Vrom sphere or planet was growing in population, it was deemed necessary to implement a small task force of scout-ships to seek out more of this element. 'Water'. This unmapped region of space therefore now provided the answer!

The sensors aboard the Ator gave indication of a rich source of this wanted element, and other minerals useful to Reptilian culture. A small planet attracted their attention, large green land masses gave way to a wondrous quantity of this 'Osiphiel'. And sensors detected a life form at the beginnings of its evolution, offering no real threat to higher intelligent species. The 'Ators' Commander, 'Namiseon' gave orders to land upon a large barren rock between the deepest waters. Samples would be taken of Atmospheric gases, of the rocks physics and the life within the waters. After which time images would be recorded of the skies and any life forms within a pre-determined area.

The timescale within this Solar System had a greater vibration than that of Sirius, and therefore Commander 'Namiseon' considered perilous to maintain a static-position with his ship for too long. The magnetic field about Ator would ensure 'a freeze of molecular activity' for only a short period, and he would suggest to his superiors on the home planet of Vrom, to return in a 'Galactic-Traveller'.

Within sixty mansions! a Nagosel time period which you would call five days! a fleet of 'Vrom' star craft returned to Earth. Materials for constructing a Vrom star Base and organisms for producing Reptilian nourishment were gently lowered from the huge Galactic Traveller. Sea Domes were placed at intervals along the ocean floor, containing the early life cycle of Vrom Mermdine. After a period of incubation these fish forms would be released into the seas, thus providing a rich source of nourishment for the entire reptilian race. But the difference between Earth's 'time' and that of the Sirius system, brought about certain giant mutations, which quickly devoured the smaller mermdine. Some of these giant 'fish' were captured by the reptilians for nourishment and transportation to 'Vrom' but others escaped into the greater seas about your planet.

Tunnels linked the waters about the rock with the new Vrom base, whilst long metallic tubes drew the much needed 'Osiphiel' up and into transporting tanks, held inside the main body of the Galactic-traveller. The city base of 'Krasshid' transformed the once barren rock into a beacon of colour. At the four corners of the city stood 'towers' of pyramid-designs, each containing a crystal source from the 'Imadogon' system. By the use of these Towers a complex vibrational time-barrier was generated, enabling the inhabitants of 'Krasshid' to live in time conditions suitable for long periods of stay. The exalted position of base commander now fell heavily on Namiseon, and although a relief of personnel arrived every 'omion' he himself would remain until his timely death.

By way of some comfort therefore, a small temple was erected near the northern face of the rock. A still pool became a chamber for prayers, the writings and pictures of Vrom antiquity descending slowly into the pools depths. Edifices purposely cut out along its walls neatly tucked away the figures of past gods. About ten feet below the cool passive waters projected a platform for meditational purposes, here in silence Namiseon and a few selected others could leave their external thoughts behind and enter into the realms of mystical eternity. Here then were a peaceful race, living entirely upon the seeds from their magical Osiphiel, that which earthlings take for granted. Occasionally, small silver ships patrolled the land areas populated with the primates. The hair covered animal, quite content with devouring his fellow mates without conscious thought or remorse, making his retreat into weather carved holes in the rocks and mountains about the denser areas of your planet. Afraid of the darkness of night, they crawled amongst the whitened bones of numerous barbaric feasts.

A hundred of your Earth years passed, and the face of Earth began to take new shape. The bright burning Orb within your Shunitree system became more volatile, sending forth bursts of Elemental Fire. An increase of heat from this source dried up many waters of the earth, and the green belts became engulfed in flames. Only the high waters and the deeper seas about Krasshid remained safe, and many of the primates were lost in the inferno. Great trenches were formed on land and in ocean, and in places great geyers rose out from the crust of the earth, spewing hot melting rock and liquids into the air. The Osiphiel now appeared in strange form, drifting magically amidst your skies, actioned upon by the force you call wind. Great electrical and magnetic anomalies caused thunder in the skies, and the towers of Krasshid were struck by this dissipation of Raw Energy. An imbalance in the generated timeflow about the Vrom base caused the opening of a number of Dimensional-Portals.

Through which fell the anti-bodies of Chaos, those Dark shadows of Space, having the power to cross space/time without the need for Dimensional-craft. Literally feeding on the Cells of reproductive thought, they manifest their malevolent force by progressive transformation of living tissue. Below the bowels of your earth they went, hiding, waiting, until the arrival of one of their Masters, he whom is called 'Nassbite'. The darker subterranean caverns of your earth provided the Shadows with useful elements, And by their mastery of Matter, the Anti-bodies began to unionise with four creative energies. Those of fire, water, air and earth. And they gave themselves titles and formed themselves ranks of lesser spirit energy. And they called these four element masters, The Salamanders, The Undines, The Sylphs, and Gnomes. By using their matter to energy existence, the Shadows would manifest a visual form within an appropriate element. However, as we shall see, this unorthodox union with earthbound creative energy would trap these Shadows forever upon earth's time-scale.

Below the temple pool of Krasshid, a weary Namiseon found sanctuary, his troubled mind now pardoned, free for a while to venture into the Universal Realms of thought. Surrounded as he was by Reptilian god-forms, he was safe and the embrace of the silent waters touched the essence of his heart. These Awakening tunnels were not new, colourful bands of fire, undulating in the patterns of harmonic dance. Here and there strange faces formed their own landscape, fashioned by some spiritual karma now fully unwound.

A silver web flirts with the weary eye, as the Spider-Queen of Space surveys her threads of time, a doorway beckons, and yet another behind which lies 'Death' or Attainment. Each mind creates its own illusion, the cells are closed or opened by the few. Still deeper, still deeper, into the cave of Maat. Sight is lost for a while as the hands of Darkness remove the colours of the mind. Movement is sensed but yet unseen, as fear crosses the bridge of one's destiny. Below as above are the waters of all eternity, flowing with the memories of countless images of endless lives. 'She is here' hidden by the veil of all truth and knowledge. Her eyes are the gates to heaven, her bosom the bowels of hell, and her womenhood the wastelands of forever. She is Maat. Skilfully the colours are woven back into place, and with each vibration new images of sight are restored. A luminosity haunts this cave, and each cave beyond. Be it the Light of the Hermit, or the Light of a Soul, outside are the lights of many.

Namiseon returned, back to his awakening state of being, some peculiar unseen force had swept him from the tides of the deep. His mind not yet focused on external reality, he sensed the presence of some foreboding visitation sharing the waters about him. Darting reptilian eyes searched the many edifices that supported the gods of antiquity, and for a moment the reassurance of their benign protection showed signs of weakening, under some fearful apprehension of evil. The temple light which so aptly displayed the god-forms about him, appeared dimmed, as the filtered rays from its source showed signs of increasing movement.

Green reptilian eyes pierced through the clarity of the waters above, hoping to catch a glimpse of this unwanted intruder. They were suddenly rewarded, and such was the sight beheld that they froze, and the limbs of Namiseon also froze, for this was unprecedented horror. From the darker side of space he had come, called down by his minions, and now manifested by atomic-manipulation into the purest evil.

A multitude of eyes gazed balefully around the temple walls, there was no face and yet Namiseon sensed one. Four large tentacles fell away from this hideous mass, stopping short midway on the Beast's form. Along their length tiny worm like creatures could be seen burrowing in and out of the grey skin substance. And in their wake a vile fluid shot forth its reddish hue. It walked on two thick members, and from its feet came plumes of smoke, which danced and formed the shape of unknown speech. A soft hiss penetrated the waters and through the ears of Namiseon the Beast proclaimed its name!' Naasbite, Naasbite, it rendered Namiseon called upon his gods, though unable to move his body his thoughts were still free. He wanted to break away, to dive to the bottom of the pool and then flee along the carved channel to the outside seas, but he could not. He felt violently sick, and silently prayed for his soul, for this abomination was the eater of souls. And then worse, a friend a joyous friend had entered the temple, unaware of his fate. All Namiseon could do was watch, as the malevolence of evil unleashed its awesome powers.

Unable to move, mesmerised by the same fear as Namiseon, the Reptilian was easy prey, as the four tentacles wrapped around his tiny body. A once proud face became a filthy mess of punctured holes, and oozing liquid. The worm like creatures ferociously burrowing into the helpless victim, and with some form of extraction, the entirety of the body now dwindled away, as lumps of bone and flesh were seen to pass along the four tentacles in strange undulation and finally become as one with the Beast. The discarded remnants of skin lay like unwanted clothes in a bed of lifeless gore.

Refreshed by this display of gratification and enriched by a new life force, the Beast looked down into the still waters of the pool, and hissed his contempt to the ears of Namiseon. And such were the words he gave before disappearing into a dense cloud of smoke. 'Knoweth I, 'Naasbite' have come to cleanse this planet of all purity, and shall leave it in Chaos'.

Little broke the silence of the pool and the empty faces of his gods left him in bitter remorse. Perhaps the old wise one was right, the Vrom race would need the allegiance of another, to eradicate the darkest hand of power. The wise one had prophesied this would come to pass, but Namiseon had not foreseen how soon. He must be strong, for was he not the leader of Krasshid? The Commander of this base. His heavy frame now had movement, his arms and legs felt alive and his mind had banished the madness into a threshold hidden from any conscious thought. Only dreams would remind him of such horrors. With extreme difficulty he swam to the surface of the pool, it was fear that held him back. The dryness of the temple air gave pain to his amphibious lungs, for he had been submerged, for some considerable time. And although reptilian by nature, the Vrom race could not sustain too long a period underwater. The remains of his friend reminded him of reality, but now was too soon to administer them to their resting place. Namiseon would leave such a task to others. The intricate carvings upon the temple walls had been blackened by the smoke given off by the Beast. And here and there splashes of its foul substance left their permanent gesture upon the floor. Still feeling a numbness in his limbs he pulled open the heavy temple door, the outside air awakened his senses, and he left the temple never to return again.'

THE UNION OF MAN WITH HIS GODS

Two mansions had passed in the Nilrem base, and the first instruction tape had finished. The crystal projection screen became blank and two confused earthmen sat in silence, meditating upon this revelation. The soft gentle tone of Amariel's voice however returned them back to external consciousness. 'You must now take refreshment from one of the phials my friends, and this will relieve your pain about your eyes and forehead.' Richard turned to the little table beside him and partook of one of the phials, which tasted of the similarity to a strong sweet coffee, and yet its sticky substance remained in his throat. Jefferson did the same but his facial expression clearly indicated his dislike to the mixture. Again the telepathic voice of Amariel entered the heads of both men. 'Sophiel has gone for the Great tape of your race, you will then know why we understand your thoughts and speech so easily. After its instruction Borcan will show you the Great Star Map and by its enlightenment you will understand much. I must go now, for Commander Ranubis wishes to know of your progress. I shall see you later Jefferson.'

The slim youthful body caught the attention of both men, her long flowing hair and green misty eyes reminding Jefferson of a pleasurable union. Had he fallen in love with this alien woman? Only time would tell. Richard looked about the room again, which was rather awkward because of the immensity and depth of the chair he had acquired. The walls appeared ebony black, inconsistent with the walls to the rest of the complex. An open archway led to an adjoining room, this was the repository for all the 'Elders' Tapes. Here could be found all the Universal secrets and the maps and discovered areas of Interplanetary-space and beyond. Such a library would even contain pre-universal history, the creation of life as being.

The power and knowledge now held by the Nagosels was frightening, but at least they appeared to be of good intent and of benevolent mind. The white opaque floors were highly polished and in certain areas rather translucent. And the lack of furnishings in both rooms suggested a sterilised area, where hygiene and cleanliness were foremost. The tapes being guarded in this fashion from an unwanted intrusion of dust or bacterial particles. They were large tapes thought Richard, some ten-inches in diameter, and extremely heavy for their size. Not at all like those found on the Star-Traveller. And their very black composition fitted in well with their protective walls, or was there some link? Perhaps Jefferson may have an answer. He turned to where his partner was sitting, but his seat was empty.

Suddenly Sophiel came running from out of the tape depository, holding the next tape to be shown, but nearly dropping it in the process. Her words were even more alarming to Richard than her entrance! 'He has gone into the wall, did you see which one?' Richard answered in a confused telepathic state. 'Wall, gone into a wall, did you say, but how, what do you mean Sophiel?' Sophiel still looking rather alarmed replied 'It's my fault, I should of told you both about this place. The crystal tapes are well protected and secured by means of an 'Inter-dimensional-gate' that is why the walls look so black, for in real truth there is nothing there. But do not worry Richard we shall get Jefferson back by calling to him.'

Richard watched in amazement, unable to say anything else as Sophiel systematically stood at all four walls in turn, calling in telepathic silence to Jefferson. And then the impossible happened, first an arm, then a leg came through what seemed to be solid dense walls. And finally his somewhat dishevelled partner appeared in full form. Sophiel helped him to his seat beside Richard, and with calm reassurance told him. 'You can walk in that darkness forever, and still be lost. Without the breathing apparatus you now wear, you would indeed be forgotten. Please ask Borcan for further information on 'Inter-dimensional-gates' before attempting this again my friend.' Jefferson shook his head in reply, and whilst doing so mopped the sweat from his brow with a sleeve of his uniform. He said or did little else. Sophiel waited a few minutes for Jefferson to regain his composure, then fed in the second tape. Her voice now softer and less erratic drifted into the two earthmen's thoughts. 'Please observe carefully this tape, for it gives forth your true origins and fathers. When you feel pain I share that pain with you, for we are coming together as one, and the 'Gortani' will soon be felt within you both. Relax, for two mansions will soon be over!'

The screen again showed the system known as 'Shunitree' and the subtle voice returned to the Aeons past, to the beginning to the city of Krasshid and Namiseon.

'Within the Sirius system floating between the planets 'Vrom' and 'Porphos' lay the much larger planet of 'Geddonia'. Here were the beginnings of the Nagosel race, here were the forefathers of their culture. An advanced civilisation well versed in Sacred geometry and Universal doorways. These 'Masters of Space' called themselves the 'Elders' and indeed they are the Gods of Antiquity. Having discovered the formula for Ego-separation they quickly cast their Evil-egos into the realms of 'Sehad', splitting the positive and negative essence for all time. The development of a third eye gave the 'Elders' an insight into time and its hidden mechanism. Observing time as an endless corridor, with an infinite number of exits, each with its own dimensional shape and size.

'There were many Uni-verses, containing numerous 'Circles of Time' and between each Universe an 'Abyss' a crossing place of Non-time, each with its own guardian. But the exploration of Time/Space caused abnormal changes to the planets environment. The bacterial growths picked up from other 'Realms' of space, causing hybrid plants and vegetation to manifest. This and the acquired collection of other world life forms caused much alarm in early voyages. To house these 'strange oddments' and to protect themselves from unwanted intrusion, giant 'Pyramids' were built across the planet. This 'Configuration' this pyramid shape also contained the formula of 'A'. The conversion of a fourth dimensional world into a single dimension, which is an anomaly of Time levels. Using gravitational forces through Triangular manipulation of Atomic-mass. One such Pyramid stood out amongst the rest, the walls covered in the rich golden ore, mined on the planet 'Porphos' known as 'gamfray' to the 'Elders', it is perhaps best recognised by earthlings as 'Gold'. Being much used as an energy-convertor between the hulls of their Spacecraft, the outer of a 'Magnesium and Magnetite alloy, and the inner of the malleable 'Trilethium' a black ore of Infinite strength and which is impossible to melt. The propulsion system working primarily through a 'circular-trilethium-housing! being governed by the Crystal mass lowered or raised within its distributing field. By converting the hulls polarity, gravitational forces about the craft could be 'Engaged' A back up system was later introduced by releasing 'Anti-matter' through ducts built into the base of the craft. But such momentum for Time and System to system travel gave its use only in the large Galactic-Travellers.

A new area of exploration however, had unexpectedly presented itself. And the promise of rich minerals and a Space-Time suited to building a repository of knowledge, now commanded their attention. This little known region was called the 'Shunitree' System, by the neighbouring planet of 'Vrom'. But an Alliance would first be needed to defeat a 'Dark-force' now in control of a single planet. Because of its position in the 'Heart' of this System, and because of its polarity to closer planets, the Reptilians called this place 'Earth', an anagram for 'heart'. The oldest 'Elder' therefore, and one other, a genius amongst most, travelled to Vrom to initiate an attacking force. This 'Genius' was known as 'Nilrem' and one of his many inventions was a 'Dimensional-Mirror' an oval shaped stone, with a highly polished face. Suspended in mid-air by twelve even spaced conductive cables. These cables in turn supported by two pillars one to the left of the polished face, the other to the right. And by a 'positive' and 'Negative' current a 'field' would be introduced about the stone. Such a spacial doorway could be used for entrance or exit to inbetween worlds. But on this occasion Nilrem's skills would be employed to create a 'Portal' from this system which would lead to the outer Abyss. The 'Elders' were well aware of the 'Dark Brotherhood' they would help the Reptilians for a price.

Now said the strange unknown commentator, let us return to the planet Earth. To the City of Krasshid and to the Dark One, a 'Minister' of the 'Dark Brotherhood' his name like many others 'casts another spell of words'. The deep 'ways' of Earth lie underground, treasures from time and space bestow this Astral place with 'key's yet to be found! Listen then to truth as we join Naasbite on his throne.

They sat about his form, the elemental kings and their sub-ordinates. Shadowy incarnate spectres filling the underworld chasm with rapturous sounds. Black plumes of smoke danced and swirled with unspoken speech, manifesting a subtle grimoire of magical enchantment. His substance was putrefying, a constant transformation of cellular resurgence. The collected essences from countless primates now constituted his being. Any ghoulish remains from regeneration being quickly consumed by his legion of Anti-bodies nearby. This indeed was the true 'Sabbat' the Black rite of sacrificial convergence.

In this way a soul essence would be 'reborn' into the 'Light of Darkness', the flame of Immortality and Endless deaths, serving 'the Masters of Chaos' for Infinitum. With sexual congress a few primates had been given life, though filled with the evil substances derived from the unions with Shadows. And yet, continuing to be, even after death of the physical, by feeding upon the nocturnal emissions of suitable human consorts. Such nightly visitations are known by mankind as the 'Incubi' or the 'Succubi' Such beings are the remnants left behind by the Dark-Ones, and although not considered harmful, they can however trigger the latent cells which lie dormant in many universal races, reactivating past lives and astral-doorways.

Above as below, evil permeated the face of your earth. Strange apparitions appeared to the dwellers of Krasshid, and the minds of some could not cope, and madness was their way. The Temple to the north of the rock had grown a web of luminous roots, which slowly elongated and moved south towards the City. The removal of one of these green roots proved deadly. As its energy form escaped it entered the reptilians organism and caused immediate evaporation of his living tissue, leaving a petrified mass. There was no escape for Namiseon and his fellow companions, the only Star-traveller had succumbed to anti-bodies penetration. Its crystal drained of power and its hull badly damaged by matter manipulation. The time-barrier generated by Krasshid could not keep the anti-bodies or Shadows out, but did drain their energy patterns enough to stop full manifestation of their elemental body. Only their Master 'Naasbite' would be able to retain full manifestation for long periods, for his essence could endure the entire time continuum. Namiseon looked into the heavens, his message to Vrom appeared unanswered. Surely there was one race whose alliance would be welcomed? His thoughts were suddenly broken by the approach of Thal, the tallest reptilian in Krasshid, and the most outspoken 'Commander, good news, our space impulse-unit has picked up five craft. The leading ship is reptilian, but the others are unknown. Perhaps they are our Alliance?' Namiseon thanked Thal and accompanied him to the control centre. The impulse-unit showed the shape of a Vrom Galactic-craft, and also four larger vessels which puzzled him. Ships from 'Arballam' were of a much smaller class, for such a race stood only three feet tall. And ships from 'Shehashe' rarely showed up on any space detecting machine, because of the reflect shields used in propulsion-mode. The answer then must come from either 'Porphos' or 'Geddonia' the latter race considered as giants in evolution and Space-physics. Namiseon took a guess, and turning to his controllers remarked 'My friends I do believe we are in the hands of the 'Els'.' A broken message barely audible, relayed instructions to accept a 'large mother ship' in the command of one 'Nilrem', from the Geddonian planet.

The Time-barrier being immediately stabilised, a great ship landed amidst the rock. Its cylindrical shape being supported above the ground by a central pillar. At either end of the ship were spinning wheels of colour. Four in all, and aligned to rotate in reverse of each other. One of clockwise movement, and its opposite, a Anti-movement. The bluish corona first observed about the entirety of the ship had now dissipated, as the spinning wheels slowed down to a discernible pace, but never quite stopping. Namiseon and Thal moved cautiously towards a triangular aperture now visible to one side of the central pillar. It bore an emblem of some winged creature unknown to them, and in one of its claws it held a 'key' or a symbol of hidden meaning. It resembled a primate, with a head and two outstretched arms, but with only one descending central leg.

The crackling of static energy always proceeded the opening of a magnetised hull. The triangular aperture quietly sliding aside and revealing the presence of one of the inner occupants. 'Nilrem' was rather small compared to most 'Elders', but his genius of mind made up for that. The third eye, at a point of 45 degrees to the other two, had been covered up by a blue-headband. As its visual perception would interfere with the dimensional-physics now observed within the earthly framework. No external hearing organs were visible and the fingers being somewhat longer than usual ended abruptly with circular appendages instead of fluted or conical, no nails. The perfect circular-eyes met Namiseon's, and the voice of Nilrem manifested its speech inside Namiseon's head. Thal also heard the soft tones which form the Elders language. Nilrem continued 'All can understand us, for telepathic waves are translated and projected by image, rather than vibration.'

'Signals from one cell to another are recognised by their 'Twin' receivers and then constructed as speech. Visualise a circuit, made from millions of black dots or cells. A wave or thought form is bombarded upon this circuit, and the compatible dots-cells are illuminated and projected into the electrical-impulses causing a distortion, though very minute, it is heard or channelled as speech. 'Each letter or symbol is illuminated and formed by its allotted number of dots or cells. This is the word manifested, though not yet vibrated as in guttural speech. The 'Intelligence of any being' is assessed by 'the number of Illuminated dots/cells' within his circuitry framework or brain.

A single cell has its companion within a Universe. The secret of secrets is to 'permanently bridge' the dormant cells of Dimensional access. By this telepathic communication I have already bridged some of these cells within you both. Namiseon and Thal thought hard upon this new enlightenment, and began to perceive the Elders message. But such meditation would be left for another time, and their immediate thoughts reflected on ' Naasbite'. Nilrem stepped down from his craft, and after adjusting some wrist instrument walked towards the two reptilians. With telepathic conversation he assured them both this 'Naasbite' and the 'Shadows' or Anti-bodies would be despatched from this sphere.

A second 'Elder' left the cylindrical craft and gave his name as 'Oragonon', he carried a machine or weapon with both hands, and by his facial expression its atomic-weight was considerably high. Two transparent tubes of equal length protruded from a golden coloured box, which generated a tone not unlike a swarm of insects in flight. Nilrem pointed to the northern temple, and his fellow Elder acknowledged the request. 'Oragonon' raised the machine and directed the tubes towards the temple door, then depressed a button on top of the box. Immediately two beams of blinding light shot forth, striking the green roots and transforming their substance into coloured glass. Which in turn exploded showering any reptilians whose unfortunate presence was close by.

This demonstration was greeted with some degree of caution by Namiseon and Thal, for such was the power of Nilrem. Again the Elder spoke in this telepathic way, reassuring Namiseon that this glass was now of no importance, and not harmful to his reptilians in any way. but that it should however be gathered and melted down, for it possessed in small amounts a chemical agent known to the 'Elders' as 'Rozime' considered useful by some as an 'Inhibitor'. He further explained that the 'contents' of the Box were removed from the 'System' called 'Cyclon', the region nearest to the Vortex to Universe 'B'.

Here can be found the race known as the 'Lemurians' their realm of space is of 'High vibration' and their time level therefore is considered dangerous. Even a time-traveller with newly fitted Imadogon crystal would be cautious about its length of stay. The symbol of this Benevolent race is a 'Candle within a Serpent's Loop',. 'The light of Truth within the Circle of Concealment'. The Lemurians are a tall race, some seven feet. Having long blonde hair and pronounced cheekbones, eyes of brightest blue, and a nose and mouth similar to our own. Using only telepathic speech, they also have the ability to change atomic state of matter by thought power alone. Their star craft therefore uses no crystal or anti propulsion unit, its form is motivated solely by thought energy.

Nilrem looked deep into the Light of Namiseon, this was a strong essence of life, a light of purity, broken only by the waves of unconscious intervention. 'Come Oragonon and friends, and I shall show you the greatest of all weapons. 'The Arm of Geddonia', 'The Light Rod of Death'.' The three followed Nilrem into the craft, the Spinning Wheels at either end of the machine, alive with one revolution of colour, a vibrant red which bathed the perimeter of the craft with an eerie glow. Once inside the interior, Namiseon and Thal were given a helmet, quite heavy but effective in providing clarity and vision in the Dimensional Matrix now encountered.

'You will see' pronounced Nilrem, slowly removing his headband, 'there are indeed many doors within doors. Few forms have encountered what you now behold. Know then Time and Space are the Fabric of Each web, each web is a Uni-verse and she whom spins each web is the Mother of its Creation. Beyond this glistening domain are the 'Walls of Solid existence' and here resideth the Shining-ones', the Golden-helmeted Gods of Iniquity. My little time-machine transcends all levels of time within this great web, but outside its matrix, across the abyss into the unknown terrain, it dares not venture.'

'Perhaps the 'Els' that follow shall charter its nameless spaces?' Namiseon interrupted Nilrem's talk, and hesitantly asked about the 'Armafgeddon' ray. Nilrem smiled and apologised to his guests, being too eager to dispel his science. A stronger more emphatic voice now entered the reptilian's head. 'It is time to communicate with the other craft about this sphere, and create a pathway form this eternity to that of the forbidden Abyss. Such a Trans-dimensional doorway will drain the 'Evil-force now predominant upon this planet. Those shadows however, who have made union with the Elemental and Primates will be forced to remain. Time and its magnetic variants will also take on a new transformation, and new rays shall permeate this heart of the 'Shunitree-system' this anagram for 'Earth'.

The negative and positive matter being 'fused' into the composition. Now you may see 'The Light Rnd of Daath' but with a warning, touch not its girth or length in any fashion, or thou shall be as not.' The entirety of the craft reminded Thal of the ancient mystical mazes he had studied whilst at science school. The interchangeable corridors unnerved him a little, for the interior of the craft was infinitely more spacious than the exterior portrayed. As though the world outside were a trick Illusion. A haunting thought echoed a subtle truth, his body together with the three others had 'Dimensionally' altered, and was in comparison extremely reduced in size. Thal began to wonder if he might be lost forever down one of these many corridors, but the sudden intervention of Nilrem now calmed his troubled mind. 'My friends I speak to you both, fear little, for these helmets you wear prevent any misadventure into another parallel time. I have read your thought Thal with some amusement, for although they bear some resemblance to truth, the reality of Timeless Space and Space-Time is perhaps better understood by two words. One being 'Displacement' and the second 'Movement' the latter being secondary to the Rule of 'Time-Shift'. Always remember that *any* movement causes change, for each act of thought upon the physics of Matter and its Alias, displaces sub atomic particles and molecular forces into rearranged patterns. I shall say only this, before we activate the 'Light Rod!' 'Thought is predominant in Achievement of Desire, and achievement is the 'Creation of Something which was Not'!'

Oragonon stopped the party midway between two corridors, and bade them enter the spherical compartment with greatest caution, again reminding Namiseon and Thal not to touch the 'Light-Rod' in anyway. An orange hue bathed the senses of the reptilian sight and each experienced a feeling of intense joy and well being.

It is alive, thought Thal, an instrument of purest destruction and endless capabilities, yet inherent with an Intelligence beyond any comprehension. An opaque table supported the lengthy rod, its dimensions hard to ascertain, the yellow veil sometimes transparent sometimes protective, like a floating cloud which hides its nature within. Some device, with four cones escaped the veil's disguise, and reminded Thal of the forms of instrumental sound. At either end of the Great Rod he observed a movement, not of energy but of form, yet unclear in its shape or geometry. Occasionally such movement unsettled his mind, for at times these transient forms looked as numbers do.

Namiseon felt the presence of some other being within the spherical-compartment, a guardian entrusted with this Rod, or a Spirit unknown from beyond this Universe. Where Nilrem had acquired such a force he dared not ask, for the flow of energy now possessed Namiseon's reasoning. Visions of 'She' 'The Spider Queen' and her domain, high on the edge of space, gave haunting glimpses of the 'Shells' those unfortunate souls whom roam the 'Wastelands of Forever'. And lost for Eternity because of infernal dealings with the 'Dark Ones'. The pressure of Thal's hand upon Namiseon's shoulder, broke the spell of timeless-visions, the orange hue still bathing the space about them as they followed Nilrem and Oragonon from out of the compartment.

Oragonon remained outside the doorway, bidding the reptilians to accompany Nilrem back to control. He, Oragonon would now attire himself in a special suit, and after removing the great rod, position it into the focal point of amplification, a part of this craft which shares little of its Dimensional capability. Thal and Namiseon followed close to Nilrem, not wishing to disappear down some dimensional corridor, and cause further delay in the banishment of this Evil known as 'Naasbite'. Again the voice of Nilrem echoed forth its instruction to them both, but with much more urgency than ever before. 'Go now to the outside, to 'Krasshid', prepare yourselves and your inhabitants for a new world, some of you may age considerably, but this cannot be avoided, for the opening of such a 'Portal to the Abyss' will change part of time and its magnetic-current, bringing new rays upon this planet and those worlds within the 'Shunitree-system'. Namiseon and Thal returned to the Control centre of Krasshid, the energy field about the rock had weakened, and many reptilians had succumbed to the onslaught of evil manifestations. The Anti-bodies were now draining the last reserves of the Crystal power source, and soon Krasshid would be their's. The green luminous roots grew strong amongst the city walls, and the Temple again glowed with its new parasite. There were no further replies from the silver scout ships and the sea-domes remained silent, the links had been severed by the Anti-bodies.

The control room light had dimmed and Namiseon ordered all power to be switched to Astral-scope, to observe the four ships now in orbit. Namiseon and Thal now took a seat and with silent prayers to their Gods, waited for Nilrem to fire his Light Rod. The Astral Scope condensed light rays from its point of observation, its focal point, then by remagnification through a domed shaped crystal a picture appeared onto the prepared screen. As they watched the ship's movements it became clear a geometric pattern would be needed to obtain a portal opening into space time. The shape of a cross was therefore maintained by the four ships, and by using the magnetic flow on all four impulse units, a gravitational hole began to form.

56

However, the green belt now encompassing the four ships could not be maintained for an indefinite period. Yet because of Namiseon's observations on board Nilrem craft, the usual damaging effect caused by high oscillation fields and gravitational anomalies would be dampened or equalised by the ELS dimensional matrix fitted inside each craft. Only one ship would be threatened by implosion, that being their own Reptilian star traveller. As the time portal increased in size, so too did the intensity of the green belt. The amplification of the light particles now unleashed from the Geddonian light rod also carried the awakening vibration of 'Shawaiss' the 'Serpent current, a macrocosm of the microcom known to all as 'Gortani'. The flow of primeval energy, which when aroused moves freely through the unseen tunnels and creative framework of each Universe. The entire 'Shunitree-system' felt the presence of this newly created portal, the Burning Solar-orb undergoing a new manipulation as time and space drew closer together. 'Observe' cried Thal, as all in the Krasshid control centre watched in sensory abandonment.

The unseen fabric of space now unveiled herself, as the new cosmic rays and elemental forces bathed themselves and united with the Shunitree space time. Deep trenches as though cut with some purposeful plan, now unfolded their innermost secrets. An intricate network of conductive lines seemingly without end, like some connective tissue, pulsed their waves of light energy from one planetary body to the next. At intervals along this network rose 'Points' small needle like antennae piercing the skin of space. Soon a link was formed, a vibratory passage, from Krasshid to the Portal and beyond into the nether regions of the Abyss. Along its entirety swarmed the Anti-bodies sucked into its Vortex, caught in the magnetic current of 'Shawaiss' which alone can disperse their nature and atomic substance.

The Great Beast 'Naasbite' came out from the bowels of the Earth, his dark malevolent form covering the waters about Krasshid. Baleful eyes watched as Legions of Shadows lost their way into the Abyssmal tunnel. He, the Master would not leave without vengeance, and upon stone tablets he would leave a message of return. The dwellers of Krasshid watched his dissolution, as slowly his essence and manifested form lost its elemental and corporal density. Twelve granite stones bore his message, cut only by the power of his speech. And within the bowels of the earth he built thrones and palaces for those Shadows he must leave behind. He gave these Kings names and they would do his bidding until his return. Unable to rise against future earthly forms, they would nevertheless have the power to possess the weaker minds of some, and to distribute evil and chaos forever. The Dark Brotherhood would form its Church upon Earth and assist in Soul transference to the essence of Chaos. And the four Names he gave were: Choronsax, King of the Vampires, Baalmedon, King of Demons, Luvicerous, King of the Elementals of the Night, and Absilom Abhornis, King of the Walking Dead. The Great Beast bid his followers to transport the granite stones to a mountain range which forever exists in snow. And there to conceal the twelve stones deep within the caves, which hide beneath a frozen lake. And when an eternity of Aeons have passed, the destined human master shall acquire them, and through their workings and secret speech call forth Naasbite to return.

'Chant my name in high places, and I shall be forever near you, but Chant my name in fear, and I shall surely destroy you. For my name holds a hidden speech, and time and space can conjure by its call.' And thus were the last words uttered by Naasbite upon your world, as slowly the Multitude of Eyes which had crowned his fiendish form, relinquished their point of gathering, and by some strange transformation, made flight into the Abyssmal-Vortex like a swarm of bees.

Nilrem waited, for he knew of the Dark Brotherhood, he also knew of the Created Time Shift, and the permanent affect now triggered off. Strange new rays would bombard this tiny planet. Yet they would give a new benevolence upon its inhabitants, indeed, the primate species would now possess reason and perhaps it was time to interfere in their 'Magical Evolution'. The Dwellers of 'Krasshid' the Vrom race, were perhaps not suited to do this work. Therefore the ELS could easily manipulate the primates Cerebral-Matrix and introduce to that area two 'Extra' glands, much larger than the originals, and by this introduction eventually phase out the unwanted two, now predominant in the Primate's growth span.

One gland to create new 'Visions' within the Primate's framework and the Second to create a form not unlike the ELS themselves. But minus one eye, and the speech to reflect the ELS, but only to a degree, that is, to be used by guttural recognition, the spoken word rather than telepathic. He, Nilrem would return to this sphere, and implant prepared glands into the females of the species. He would embark upon this quest with vigour, and even stay for an unknown period amongst them, but in clever disguise. And although life threatening to his own form of being, have removed by surgical means his beloved third eye. Pondering for sometime upon this new venture, and whilst reviewing his 'Magical-mirror' he stumbled upon his new Earthly name. AHH, thought he, tis but simple, as the mirror reflects, so too shall my name. With this godly ambition in mind Nilrem now gave instructions to Oragonon to turn off the Armofgeddon ray, as there had been no further signs of chaotic essence passing along the Abyssmal Portal.

Nilrem attired himself for the outer world, replacing the blue headband, and covering his third eye, the dimensional matrix and Atomic planes of Earth somewhat disturbing to his own dimensional vision and realisation. Again the crackling of static currents echoed the opening of the Ship's outer door, but this time a new warmth permeated the air, the skies heralded a brilliant blue and the once turbulent ocean appeared calm and full of new wonders. The protective time barrier about Krasshid remained still, broken fragments of coloured glass made an uneasy path towards the city's interior. The odd vitrified mass lay silent amid the walled courtyards. Whilst pools made stagnant by dead reptilians brought forth new life. A piece of coloured glass caught Nilrem's attention, the actual shape or texture of the glass was not the image attracting him, but the reflection seen within its mirrored surface was. The change of time and gravitational alignments within the Earth's magnetic flux had 'Let in' some unusual visitors. But before embarking onto their origin, a voice shouting from a short distance away reassured him Thal was alive and quite well. Putting aside this new discovery Nilrem quickly joined his Vrom friend, whom had aged considerably within a very short space of time. Nilrem looked into his eyes, he had from a distance picked up Thal's voice, but the speech was not too recognisable. Now at close quarters the telepathic waves gave forth an understandable sound. 'Nilrem my friend, I and my colleagues have grown older prematurely, as you well predicted, but also poor Command Namiseon is with us no longer, his metabolic rate was very fast and now he is mere dust. I as the new Commander, have transmitted instructions to Vrom for new supplies and more Imadogon crystal. A new batch of reptilians will live here but perhaps not above the waters. Come into the control centre and let me offer some means of nourishment, for there is much to be done.' Nilrem followed his friend saying nothing of his recent discovery. Plans would be made to revisit Earth by the 'Els' and with agreement on both sides, the 'Els'' would be permitted to use the Silver-scout ships of 'Vrom' to research and carry out experiments on the Primate Species.

THE GREAT STAR MAP TEACHINGS

Darkness engulfed the mind, the screen in front of Jefferson and Richard now a blank, and the echoes of the internal voice of strange commentary, drifting into the subconscious memory, hidden in the vast storehouse of Terrestrial being. 'Oh my head' retorted Jefferson, wiping small droplets of sweat from his brow, and feeling rather worse for wear, as though recovering from some horrendous nightmare, usually associated with too much alcoholic input. A bit shaky on his feet he gave a distinctive yawn, and outstretched his aching limbs. Richard however had acquired two bloodshot eyes, and Amariel was injecting a black liquid into his right arm. He did look rather drained and somewhat shaky, but a forced smile to his friend alleviated any concern Jefferson may have upon his well being.

The telepathic voice of Amariel brought both men back to reality, and the warmth of her sensual form soon awakened the life force within both men. 'Come my friends, Borcan awaits. He is to show you the 'Great Star Map', you may return to the library when all has been done, for the spread of the virus upon your Earth has become unstable.' Little was spoken either in telepathic or guttural terms, as Richard and Jefferson pondered deeply on the recent revelations, and the name 'Naasbite' haunted the Lights within them. The corridors and the brisk walk refreshed their metabolism, and the rear view of Amariel's contoured shape assured them there had been no loss of bodily function, whilst undergoing cellular changes somewhere inside their brains. The last corridor elevated to a forty degree angle and was much higher than the rest. The lighting from the normally bright crystal housing was exceptionally subdued some fifty feet onwards, and the Nagosel writing etched deeply into the approaching archway gave some insight into the next port of call. It read 'Here in entirety is the Key to All' Suddenly and without any encouragement from Amariel, both men shouted 'I can read the writings. I can understand the bloody Nagosel writing.' Much laughter accompanied Amariel to Nilrem One, the Scientific and Research Centre. It was perhaps only to be expected thought Amariel, for the release of the 'Gortani' would eventually open many sealed doorways within. Somewhat amused, yet protective, and in some ways grateful to her new found friends, Amariel nevertheless was an honoured Nagosel, few of her race chanced this position to work on Nilrem. But the strange feelings calling her nearer to this earthling Jefferson began to override her sense of duty, and a new fire now trembled at the core of her being. And did not an 'Elder' Verse reveal:

> From Time to Time, with Aeon's past
> The Shores of Space, two souls shall cast
> A Sacred Flame entwined by Two,
> A newborn gate, now comes in view,
> This Flame a Key to open Space,
> And thus a Word, a different place.

Jefferson and Richard were too busy to 'Link' telepathically with Amariel's thoughts, both rather delighted with this newly acquired Gift, which would give them an open pass when returning to the Crystal Library, the wonders of the 'Elders' tapes would now be recognisable. The Universe would indeed be an open book to them.

The approaching Borcan however soon brought them back to the norm. Perhaps it was the subdued light, but Borcan appeared much taller, and his unusually pronounced forehead having gained more of the strange Star marks. Borcan picked up the earthmen's thoughts instantly, and to dispel any worries they may have, he explained the reason for the extra Star marks. 'My friends, firstly I may appear taller to you, because the adjusted light can cause a distortion in vision. It is unfortunate but essential to the Physics about this control centre, the circular corridor about this centre creating an Invisible field necessary to the security of Nilrem. Secondly, the Star marks are operations, each mark an incision to facilitate the entrance and Exit of Crystal Apparatus. I am fifty per cent Nagosel and fifty percent automation, but it matters not.' Richard and Jefferson were quite taken aback by this enclosure, yet had not the Nagosels been truthful in all things, and that this latest revelation was but very minor in the field of knowledge, yet to come. Borcan led the way, a large triangular aperture opening smoothly and totally without sound. The immensity of the centre startled them, the Great Star Map completely covering the roof. In front some ten feet away a number of Nagosel personnel were busily recording information, as the taking out of tapes from one machine and the freeing of the same into a much larger machine would confirm. It was a startling sight, to see so many beings without the organs known as ears. And the circular appendages upon their finger ends also added to the wonderment of the scene.

To the left and right respectively, large screens, not unlike those observed on the star traveller showed images of terrain which could only be from some other side of Space. Sometimes the movement of some space neighbour occupied the entire screen, this sudden confrontation with other worlds sending more than a few chills down the earthly visitors backs. The floor glistened in an ebony sheen, revealing here and there translucent bubbles, which Borcan revealed were born from the rock itself. 'They are very much alive' cautioned Borcan 'And their form embodies powerful chemical formulae. But enough, you are here for less than two mansions of time to gain insight and the Greatest knowledge on the Great Star Map.' Pointing to three opaque ebony seats, Borcan requested the two friends to make themselves comfortable, as Amariel retired to seek refreshments for them all.

Richard liked this chair, he could go to sleep quite easily in its contoured shape. Again the firm but friendly voice of Officer Borcan entered the heads of the two men, reassuring them both his lecture would be as short as was feasible. 'Recline then Richard and Jefferson, the chairs will follow your movements exactly. as we lay back and observe the 'Elders Keys' to Universal travel. The red pulsating sphere close to the centre of the Map is 'Nilrem' and the much larger red pulsating sphere close to the edge of the Map is our planet Geddonia. All other planets are designated with a coloured static sphere which exhibits a pre ordained number, and this number is important to many things, both mystical and magical. You will both receive 'Books' pertaining to the 'living-numbers' and the knowledge therein must be used with great respect and judgement.

There are Seven Rings within each Uni-verse, the 'Spaces' between each 'Uni-verse' are known as the 'Abyssmal-Gardens', they harbour the 'Anti-bodies' and also form the 'Spider-Queen's'

Great Web. It is 'She' whom spins the 'webs of time' and only she can move freely between the Universal-worlds, her fine 'Threads of Time' form the mechanism known as 'MAAT'. The Evil-Shells can be seen glistening within the 'Abyssmal Gardens' They cannot enter the Universal Time continuum which is independent to each Universal System. Yet the Souls of the Dead, of the unjust and the minds of countless Magicians have penetrated their domain, some never to return. At the outer circumference of each 'Universal Web' lies the 'Walls of solid Existence' beyond these walls and before reaching the 'Abyssmal Garden' are the 'Realms of the Shining Ones' these Spiritual lights I shall talk upon later.

So there are Seven rings to each Universe, and each ' Ring' vibrates a different colour or Universal sound. Each ring harbours a number of 'Solar Systems' which in turn mother their relative celestial bodies or planets if you prefer. Each 'Ring' has its own Time-level, which increases in intensification or vibration according to the position within the webbed framework. For example, your earthly planet of Green and Blue Astral light is residing within the 'Ring of three dimensions' the Solar-System called Shunitree. And because it is near to the centre of the Vortex-Gate it's 'Vibrationary Rate' is very high, it's gravitational force strong, and its Time level much accelerated hence your short period of life.

Ring One harbours the region of 'Cyclon' one of the 'Systems' closest to the 'Vortex-Gate' to 'Universe 'B'. Think upon your alphabetical system and the Hebrew equivalent, for therein lies the total Universal webs of Space, which when 'Reflected' produce the Infinite and 'the Body of Truth'. The planets of 'Sion' 'Amegon'' and 'Marattome' are the 'Watchers' of the Tower of 'Elsang', each 'Tower' consisting of 'Two pylons' one of which is the entrance and exit to the Dimensional Realms of the 'Winged-Form of Knowledge.' Your Earthly Magi used an anagram of these forms. Our home planet of Geddonia resides in the System of 'Sirius' and with two other planets of the Trinity guard the 'Tower' known as 'Sehad', the first gateway to the 'Abyss'

Within its dimensional Realms are the waiting 'Forgotten Ones' the Evil egos cast beyond this gate until their release, which now draws near, for their thoughts are free to roam amid the less-intelligent of species, giving great knowledge to those whom are receptive to their malign will. The planets of 'Geddonia' 'Arballam' and 'Shehashe' then are under the influence of the Ring of six dimensions, and as you are aware our lifespan exceeds your own by nearly two 'Aeons'. As explained in the crystal tape in the library; (Thought is predominant in achievement of desire and achievement is the creation of something which was not.) Study then the Rings and the thoughts therein.

Within the system of 'Cyclon' is the planet called 'Porxabrax, it is the home of the 'Lemurian race' they whom frequented your planet after the manipulation of the Primate species by Nilrem. There are thirty two lifeforms within 'the Brotherhood of the Trinity', sometimes known as the 'Brotherhood of the Light'. And between them they are the 'Watchers' of the 'Towers', which are supported by the two pylons of equal currents. For ease of clarification these 'Towers' are designated throughout as 'Pylons' on all our maps. Our ancestors the 'ELS' have allotted certain symbolism to each 'Tower' for recognition of that 'Realm,' within its Gateway. Your Magi on Earth have also allotted Symbolism to a few Towers, however they do not possess the entire system. Feel free my friends to visit the Control centre or indeed any other Nagosel centre to learn or refresh your memory on the Great Star Map, for indeed it is the main 'Key'. From the external circumference of the whole to the centre Vortex, which takes one directly to Universe B there extends numerous 'webbed lines' which permeate through the 'Seven Rings of Time'. And clearly shown by the Blue pulsating Spheres, are the 'Pylons' or 'Gates' to the 'Dimensional realms' or to the 'Anti corridors'. Make a mental note of their number Richard and Jefferson, for their Universal sisters and brothers have an equal number.

The black solid lines which run through the entire Universe, 'The webbed lines' pass through every 'Pylon' and these are the 'Anti-corridors' which Star travellers use for travel. The broken horizontal lines which intersect with the Anti-lines at every Pylon, are the 'Dimensional realms' of which there are many. So the 'Pylons' which support the 'Towers' are both a 'gateway' to the Dimensional realms and the 'Anti-corridor'. Their method of entry lies within their 'Symbolism'. However there is one Gate or Tower that shows no Symbolism for method of entry, and this is the 'Pylon of Sehad', the first Gateway to the Abyss. It is a Sealed Gate, but forever watched, for the 'Elders' have left a warning! The seals will be broken using magical means and this Era draws near!

This Gateway is an anomaly to be found in all Universes, as its length, is fragmented where a number of 'tunnels' open into the Abyssmal Garden. It is so to speak 'The Backdoor' In your books you will see these Zones, the Dimensional and Anti-matter as Great Chasms, with an Infinite height and depth. And in the D/Zones you may find caves or tunnels belonging to the 'Entitys' in that particular zone. This complex, Nilrem, resides within the Dimension of 'Alaxbrasbra' its 'Gateway' or 'Tower' is the Pylon shown on the map as 'Elsang'. The Dimension to the Right of the intersect is that of 'The winged forms of Knowledge'. Their appearance is not alarming and they have assisted your race through periods of its evolution. If standing they exceed eight of your earthling feet. More information can of course be made available at the 'Crystal Library'. To the left of the Intersect is the Dimension of Alaxbrasbra' as already stated. This Entity is a Four Winged Serpent, though rarely seen within the perimeter of our protective shell. It has been known to display its transparent form flying to some forgotten lair, and in each cruel shaped claw carries a mutilated corpse. By Sacred laws we are unable to intervene, the corpse was a sentient form sometimes human, sometimes from a race not unlike ourselves. And the cause of this Soul eating imagery is too much knowledge of the 'Darker Forces' and a feeble strength of mind. Those whom would walk the 'Magi path' take many dangerous steps.

So, at each 'Pylon' there dwells two dimensional realms, that of the 'Left' and that of the 'Right', the haunts for benevolent forms or entitys, and the haunts for 'Malevolent forms' or Entitys. And although much knowledge can be gained by the 'Invocation' or 'Evocation' of both, it is impractical to seek them out by Sigils and Devices, unless you wish to place your light, your 'Soul' in an 'Invitational' mode to Allcomers. Remember, this shell and its two brothers were created by the 'Elders' many Aeons ago, at a time period when all forms of transient being and atomic form was in its primitive mode. Yet, it should be stated, our Elders visited many strange and forbidden places, well before the casting out of their 'Evil egos' into the sealed 'Pylon' of 'Sehad'!'

Before Borcan could continue along these lines a welcoming sight stopped short the Telepathic Lecture. Amariel beckoned all three friends to be seated about the oval table upon which rested half-a-dozen phials and a vessel containing a favourite Geddonian nourishment, the 'Pramasieel' The short but strong legs of Jefferson swung themselves out of the opaque chair, the mention of food any food was music to his ears. Besides which he was eager to down one of the nourishment phials, as unlike human foodstuff there was always an incredible taste, accompanied by the most profound physical stimuli in all areas. Jefferson's psychic ability had until now, remained within the deep waters of the sub-conscious mind. His ability in the past, quite demonstrative and proven, winning much admiration from Rosie Ansai especially in areas concerning the whereabouts of some landed UFO craft. After all, he and Richard knew full well the implications of the Mexican incident back in 1947. Yet, here they both were, in some Dimensional Spacestation, conversing by telepathic means to Alien forms on a very relaxed basis. Jefferson knew Borcan was closing his thoughts on some imminent matter, and either by some advanced sense or intuition knew also, only one of them, he or Richard would be needed. Another helping of the Nagosel 'pramasieel' however, quickly returned his thoughts to 'Amariel'. The bright green eyes from her attentive glare sent their sensual signals into Jefferson's productive channels, and for once in his life he felt the charms of love's fever.

Borcan watched the two earthling friends intensely, and congratulated himself for making the right choice, for how could one give a hundred percent to a task, if such a female dwelled within a loving heart. Yes Richard would go with Borcan to Earth, and Jefferson with Amariel to Geddonia. Besides Jefferson's ability to 'link' physically with the 'Aeonic-flux' would prove useful to some branches of Geddonian Science. The sudden appearance of a smile upon Borcan's lips was rather amusing to Amariel, as the bone caricature of a Nagosel male prevented the muscular rise around the cheekbone, as in a broad smile, and thus only the lips rose upwards and gave all the grace of a Halfmoon in comparative agony. Reaching into the left internal pocket of his uniform jacket, Borcan then produced a peculiar looking object, and without any prompting from the friends now seated, promptly placed the unexpected gift into Richard's grey flap pocket.

A bemused Richard naturally asked Borcan what the hell was going on, his telepathic speech slightly incoherent at this time. Borcan arose from his seat and beckoned the two men to follow, leaving Amariel to dispense with the leftovers and then to prepare the compartments in Alpha block. The two men followed Borcan back to the opaque ebony chairs, and after becoming acquainted with their welcoming comfort, once again observed the Great Star Map.

'Before I continue my friends, I must enlighten you upon a forthcoming matter. Commander Ranubis has asked me to take one of you to the planet Earth to help combat and destroy the Virus which is even now destroying many thousands of your species. But please feel assured my choice has nothing to do with your courage or intelligence. There is less than a full mansion to teach, and before you retire to your compartments in Alpha block, I would ask again for your complete attention.

A star traveller is being made ready for our departure Richard and unfortunately because time is short our craft will materialise within the complex you call Wonderland. Your exit from the craft will, we hope, prevent any aggressive reaction to our uninvited visitation. Be also aware Richard many of your earthly months have now passed, and the removal of your Impulse breathers whilst you sleep will on awakening cause some disorientation and sickness, until we have boarded the star traveller and attired ourselves with vibrational suits. And now for Jefferson, whom I believe has already gained insight into his destination, via his ability to link with the 'Aeonic flux'. Amariel now prepares herself and also your new clothing for a journey to the 'Sirius Star System' to meet the scientists of Geddonia and thence onto the many worlds of the 'Trinity' Three books have been lazer printed for each of you, they are written in our language and relate to the 'Living Numbers' the 'Dimensional Realms' and the 'Great Star Map'. Try not to lose these, for they contain the 'Keys' and 'Sigils' of many strange and sinister 'Denizens'. Such a 'Denizen' or 'Lurker in the Tunnel' resides in the Dimension of 'ZAZBAVOO'.

Seen on the Great Star Map as broken horizontal lines to the left of the Pylon, 'OSHUR'. To the immediate right of this Pylon is the dimensional realm of the 'CHUTULZI' a magical current equal to 93. Perhaps their form is best represented in the guise of your earthly term, a frog, only greatly enlarged, and possessed of knowledge of the 'Spider Queen' and the magical fluid she secretes. To invoke them and converse with them is not easily achieved. Their best medium for Manifestation is 'Osiphiel' that which is in abundance upon your planet. A reference to 'Chutulzi' can be found in the Crystal Library, part of which states:- A Formula is given concerning the 'essences' or 'Kalic-rays' of cylcic-time. The 'Magical current' giving the two numbers of two of these 'Rays'. And that of the same 'figure' equating to the 'Atomic scale of a certain 'Ore'. When the 'Ore' is fused with the two essences a fluid is formed, which according to the 'Chutulzi' has the same attributes to the 'Magical secretion' dispersed by the 'Spider Queen'.

This Revelation of enormous Occult Significance, is itself an intricate web of hidden knowledge 'For She whom spins the Webs of Space, is not of the 'Aeons' making. For when she returns to 'repair a past' she disperses a new awakening'.'

'This brief passage' continued Borcan, 'should enlighten you both to the Infinite powers which we but serve, for indeed this Dimensional-Intelligence is but a 'bubble' in an Ocean of Bubbles. And of course when one pricks a bubble there is a release of something which cannot be replaced. Knowledge is given, but is not always understood, and so such Knowledge becomes 'Free', until used, either for good or bad purposes. So look again at the Great Star Map and see not only the 'Pylon' of 'Oshur' but the other planets within this Ring of 'Seven dimensions'.

Far distant to the planet of 'Megoris' is the 'Imadogon' system, which as you know provides the crystals much needed for Solar Travel and Dimensional Entry. The Imadogon system has been mined for many Aeons, however the removal of crystal from the two planets numbered 69 and 11 does not deplete their 'Body' so to speak. As, peculiar to Seven dimensional physics there is an alarming speed of 'Regeneration' inherent within the Atomic Matrix. 'I see by your faces my friends there is much disbelief, and yet is this not true in a greatly reduced way, but observable in a number of your insect species? Does not your earthworm regenerate itself at a peculiar pace. Does not the water mammal known as Octopus do likewise? To name but a few. However we were talking upon the 'Imadogon system' and I now have little time to deviate. The Crystals formed are born with two important major qualities. One, they accelerate light source beyond the 'Tachyou' level. Two, when introduced into a magnetic flow they generate a gravitational anomaly, what you may liken to a Unified Field. The difference however is their ability to 'interact' with magnetic fields, harnessing phenomenal vibrational frequencies without exploding.

The magnetic ore is also found within this system, it is converted into a large circular housing as observed on the Stella ship you arrived in. And by raising or lowering a Cone shaped crystal into the housing, a 'vibrational flow' is created. The Dimensional space or Destination is achieved by the governed amount of 'Ionised particles' forced through parts in the side of the magnetic housing. A clever network of channels then distribute the achieved 'Field' about the 'outer hull' of the craft. The channels normally extending from midsection floor to open ducts. As recently explained the crystal acts as a 'accelerator' of Light particles beyond the Tachyon level. These Light particles are introduced into the top of the crystal to achieve 'speed' not 'dimension'. They are electrical in fashion but lacking certain polarities.

The hull of our Ships, both Stella and Galactic are made from a highly conductive Ore, which does not react to extremes of Temperature either way, but helps the 'Amplification' of 'Magnetic-fields'. The 'Inner Hull' is protected by a special black ore which can be polished to an incredible degree. Only the vibrational forces coming from the magnetic housing and crystal cause any real danger to a ship's occupants, therefore we all wear 'Dampening suits', their material soaks vibration and then breaks down its field by a system of Intricate circuits moulded into its garment. Again, Richard and Jefferson a more enlarged anatomy of our Ships dynamics and propulsion methods will be given at a later date. I hope this little treatise proved informative?

Next and lastly, we reach the outer circumference of the Great Star Map, here is shown the 'Walls of Solid Existence'. So called because they are between the 'Ring of Creative Regeneration'. The Ring of Seven Dimensions, and most importantly the 'Spheres of Coloured Light'. 'The Shining Ones' 'The Guardians of the Threshold', beyond which as you are aware are the 'Abyssmal Gardens' the abode of the 'Anti-bodies' and an Infernal number of 'Shells', the Evil Cast offs from all forms of life.

A Crystal disc left by our ancestors, gives a very clear definition of the External view of a Universe. The disc is written 'Alphomegratomix' and portrays the perception of a 'Vast tree' shimmering in wondrous colours within the enclosure of a transparent 'Bell'. The roots of the tree having a green lustre, pierce the base of its mothering threshold at numerous points, and like living serpents sway and undulate in the Abysmal-Swamp surrounding them. A Vortex of blue intensity links the base of each Universal Bell with the top of another. Inside, the 'tree branches' reveal their secret worlds of 'Dimensional tunnels' and endless 'Chasms'. There is no top to the tree, only what can be considered as the Utmost level of permeating branches. The great blue Vortex within its central trunk continues upward through the Abyssmal gateway and on into the next ascending Bell. The 'Pylons' are formed at each 'Knot' of the tree, yet not all are connected to the webbed formation. Herein lies the secretways of the Anti-bodies, for the remaining unconnected pylons are 'Fed' by the roots of the tree. The 'Kalic essences' the 'Rays of Cyclic time' flow from the celestial bodies which grow as part of the tree, all other planets and their systems float about the tree. It is indeed the 'Tree of Knowledge', but there are many types of Tree. And they 'mature' on each 'Ascension' cultivating further knowledge from the Infinite 'Abyssmal Garden'. The 'Abyss' holds the Anti-worlds my friends, and again only 'She', the 'Spider Queen' can cross her domain at will. That there may be further 'Queens' in the 'Scales of Ascension' is a possibility to be accepted. Though it is considered by most, such 'Creators' do not tread each others webs.

The threshold then covers the entirety of the 'Bell' and acts as a 'Bridge' between the 'Anti-worlds' and the 'Created Atomic and Sub-atomic Worlds of Spiritual reflection and Concealed knowledge. A 'Uni-verse' is alive in sound, a 'Cosmic-overture' which exhibits its tone in shimmering colours, and as such, each Bell should be perceived as One Instrument, in the 'Orchestral Body of the Great Living Spirit, you call 'God'. So Jefferson and Richard behold the Vastness of Space, and open your hearts to the Infinite journeys a soul may undertake before reaching the 'Highest Ascension', the true Will of God. Collect a 'Leaf' from each 'Tree' and make thyself a 'Coat of many colours' and thus shall all be revealed.'

The sudden withdrawal of Borcan's voice confirmed the ending of this first of many lectures. Jefferson and Richard now much accustomed to the comfort of the chairs, felt little motivation to arise on to their feet. The Great Star Map clearly engrossed all Mystical and Magical Teachings, and both men wondered if this awakening on Time and Space would be beneficial or destructive to their primitive earthly minds? Borcan intervened, 'Please do not ask your questions at this time, for the future holds many such answers for you both. See Amariel awaits, you must follow her to Alpha block and rest, I must talk to Commander Renubis and shall await you both at the Stella port in half a mansion. The tall lean Nagosel walked briskly towards Amariel, some telepathic exchange took place and then he was gone.

Amariel beckoned the two friends to accompany her, the tight uniform about her form alive with sensual provocation. She smiled as Richard and Jefferson tried to conceal their thoughts of desire. 'Come you must rest and take of more nourishment, your new uniforms await you. And I can now explain upon the item Borcan placed in your pocket Richard, for its use will be better understood upon your own planet.' They followed her down the now recognisable corridors. Nilrem seemed far from Alien now, more a secret home amongst the stars. A vast storehouse of Cosmic knowledge and frightening vision.

The triangular-aperture slid silently open. A soft orange hue permeated the room. Between the two beds, a green translucent table, confidently supported by one centre pillar displayed two phials of Nagosel nourishment. Within these phials a movement was apparent, and on closer inspection the thread like worms thrashed violently in their blood coloured fluid. 'There's bloody thousands of them' thought Richard 'what the hell are they and what will they do for me?' Jefferson also acknowledged his disgust, and turning to Amariel begged an explanation. 'Please do not be afraid of this nourishment, we call these 'Entors'. They feed upon the bodies toxins and when full they pass through your system as does all unwanted matter. The coloured liquid is 'alphae' a chemically produced stimulant which slows down the production of white cells and allows the 'Entors' to feed, otherwise your natural defence-system would destroy them. It is a precautionary measure, before entering a different timescale, any small bacteria you may have inhaled whilst here, would have rapidly grown in a faster time scale such as Earth's. But these Entors will cleanse your system. I have already participated, the taste is not too disagreeable, rather bitter and sticky. But before you drink your phials, please replace your grey uniforms with these blue garments, you will find them skin tight, but also virus free, no virus can penetrate them. And the gloves and masks are to be used when first entering a new Time zone. Your wrist-breathers will be removed whilst you are asleep Richard. Jefferson remains, as he and myself will be going to my planet, Geddonia, where the Time level remains the same as this climatised shell.' Richard now using telepathic speech as though second nature, asked upon the purpose of the rectangular box, Borcan had inserted into his pocket? Jefferson listened to the thoughts of both of his friends, whilst at the same time finding difficulty in removing his grey uniform trousers. As there was no undergarments beneath any Nagosel clothing, then Jefferson took great lengths to hide his embarrassment of one rather proud male organ. Its rise, so to speak, greatly attributed to his thoughts on Amariel's bodily presence. However, Amariel appeared oblivious to Jefferson's nudity, being too involved in telepathic jargon with Richard. The odd phrase Jefferson did pick out, alluded to some forcefield, which would both protect the wearer of the Box and at the same time cause an effect of Invisibility. The phrase: 'Ignore these beings when Invisible' however was not fully understood, perhaps it referred to some unseen spiritual-forms which assisted Mankind by Invisible workings? Or worse, these beings were in fact remnants of the trapped Anti-bodies, left behind by their Master 'Naasbite'? All these thoughts raced through Jefferson's mind, as he attired himself with the blue uniform, which to his surprise bore the emblem of Nilrem. 'The Square within the Circle' and the bird motif seen throughout the complex. The bird was not common to him, though the dark raven upon Earth showed strange similarity.

Sitting cross-legged upon one of the beds, he reached for a phial, and although the brain said 'leave well alone' he knew the potion would have to be consumed now rather than later. His large fingers wrapped around its transparency, and the horror inside caused a clammy sweat within the palms of his hands. Looking deep into its depths the minute worms did little to inspire him to drink. Raising the tube to his lips he opened his mouth, and tipped the mass down his throat. 'Tastes like coffee' he exclaimed aloud 'but is in comparison to swallowing raw eggs, and may take some keeping down. What I really need is a stiff brandy to wash the remains clear,' he further remarked, but knew such Earthly pleasures would not be available for some time. Perhaps never, if Amariel gets her own way, oh dear, how awful. And with that he lay his head upon the contoured section of the bed and fell into a deep sleep.

WONDERLAND RECEIVES UNEXPECTED GUESTS FROM TIME

Rather impaired and not at all with it, Richard was only too pleased by this formal conveyance. His frame swung over the right hand shoulder of Borcan, like a sack of potatoes. The removal of the two wrist-breathers had caused a temporary paralysis in arms and legs, but Borcan assured him once inside the craft, the vibrational distortion would put his metabolism back on line. There would be no goodbyes for him and Jefferson, they would both meet at a later date. Richard watched as his partner and Amariel boarded the Star Traveller next to their own. Jefferson glanced at his friend and gestured good luck with a thumb's up, but Richard could do nothing in return, even a smile seemed impossible. Borcan opened the internal hatch by touching the blue crystal, the subdued green light bathed the optic-nerves of Richard and slowly his taut features took on some resemblance of normality. Borcan rested him down against a control panel, the ebony black floor camouflaging his blue trousers. The audible humming, as experienced on the first flight now eagerly infested Richard's ears, he was, as Borcan had postulated returning to sensibility, though his arms and legs ached passionately.

He watched as Borcan operated the ship's propulsion unit, the subdued green glow began to change colour and the humming began to get unbearable. It was clear to Richard that telepathic communication was a no go when the 'Crystal' was in operation, obviously the 'Vibrational frequencies' scrambled any kind of waves, as for a brief period he had tried to communicate with Borcan but to no avail. The red glow and the secondary shaking now catapulted Richard into full physical awareness. Borcan just smiled, and waved Richard into the adjoining compartment, apparently wanting Richard to observe the workings of the Crystal close up. Through the triangular aperture the red glow now took on an alarming sight, instead of density of colour, an unaccountable number of red streams issued forth from the top of the hull and thence down and seemingly disappearing into the dark blackness of the floor. Blue, brown, red and violet rings swam about the magnetic housing. Then ascended and vanished into the dark roof. The 'Crystal' some eight feet in height, glowed with a hypnotic green luminosity. At its tip, tiny sparks were received by some dome shaped container, which was wonderfully alive, not unlike the essence of a cloud. Richard could almost make out the outline of a face within the crystal, but he contributed this apparition to the display now assembled before him. He turned and tried walking back through the aperture towards Borcan, but a sense of fear gripped him, the magnetism brought into play within the room began to pull him back towards the 'Crystal' and shout as he may, Borcan would not hear him or receive any telepathic waves. Would he disappear he conjected or would his atoms disperse amongst the avenues of spacetime forever? He tried hard to move forward, but was immediately drawn back again. He began to give up hope when the tide of fate stepped in, the red stream permeated no more and the grip upon him gave way.

A violet light now immersed the inside of the ship, and the blue uniform appeared to merge in with this violet intruder. Richard thought scientifically and came to the conclusion, the vibratory colour of violet had also been temporarily matched by the uniform. Hence the term 'Vibration suits'. Borcan carried on as normal monitoring his control panel, as though nothing untoward had occurred. Richard acted accordingly and sat down midsection between the two compartments, at least here he could observe the entirety of operations. For sometime the violet glow stayed with them, and in its wake a haunting darkness befell all but the Crystal which remained luminous and almost benign. Richard felt an affinity with its presence, and again perceived a caricature, a face of a beast or some forgotten God. Some distant memory 'Linked' t his visual manifestation with a painting of the 'Earth God Pan' as portrayed in one of Jefferson's 'Old Grimoires' on magical rites. Was this an omen of sorts, thought Richard, or was this actually an appearance of the God Pan? Somehow communicative by Crystal vibrations and entry into Time and Space corridors? There could be no telepathic link no thought transference whilst the craft was in motion, yet a significant 'Contact' had been established between the two forms. It was, without doubt, the movement of the 'Eyes' which convinced

Richard this was no hallucination, slanted in an upward elevation, the eye socket moved with a strange dexterity. The vibrant green pupils also of irregular shape, instilled no fear or malevolence when directly looked upon, but rather gave the observer a feeling of Supreme Knowledge. And then, an Insight, a Revelation, Yes of course, this 'Pan' is in truth an 'Elder'.

A 'forgotten one' existing in a dimensional space close to the system known as 'Shunitree'. Richard now understood the power of 'Gortani', once triggered off, so to speak, its energy flow within such a form as his own, 'Awakened' the latent powers which on Earth are attributed to a rare breed of 'Mystics'. All the other 'Occult sciences' being a fragmentation of a giant jigsaw. Therefore this 'Gortani' or 'Serpent-Flame' accelerated the process of learning by its seemingly simple method of activation. That being the mating between oneself with the Nagosel female. These thoughts and many others would cause the eventual Transformation in Richard, which the Nagosel's call: The coming of Immortality, 'The Wereformaxis'.

As the image of Pan dissolved in the changing colours of the Crystal, the steady rise of its structure denoted a reduction in 'particle flow'. The expected red glow now illuminated the entirety of the craft, and in accordance with its presence Richard again felt the vibrational peculiarities with this colour. Though not as bad as previous shakes, it nonetheless was an uncomfortable part of an otherwise smooth trip. He watched again as the crystal rose further out from the magnetic housing, small electrical particles bombarding its outer-structure at every point. Seemingly coming from nowhere, they would suddenly materialise and begin bouncing against the inner walls and black floor of the compartment. Some particles bouncing off Richard's Vibrational suit never reached the Crystal, but instead disappeared as though drained of their energy source. As the green glow intensified the particles dispersed, and the colourful light patterns emerged within the crystal's body. Blues, reds, yellows an endless spectrum of twirling wonderment giving much enjoyment to the eyes of the beholder. However, as in all things, there was little time for such wonders. The sharp inner voice of Borcan confirmed they had reached their destination, namely Earth. 'Come Richard, before we introduce ourselves, I would show you some controls.'

Richard enthusiastic as ever for learning such mysteries, quickly regained his feet and removed the mask, which was admittedly causing a degree of discomfort. A fairly wet brow suggested to Borcan his friend was experiencing a slight vibrational burn, and perhaps Richard's suit would have to be readjusted on their return to Nilrem? But such minor observations were to be put aside until completion of the mission, if such a completion was of course possible?

Richard stood to the left of Borcan, the tall Nagosel had not removed his mask, and he guessed this had something to do with the time level on Earth. Yet telepathy was at least back to order. He watched as Borcan pointed to the screen directly in front of them, and mesmerised the switches used to illuminate the screen and switch it off. Also Borcan instructed him on the correct procedure to operate the crystal propulsion unit. The sequence of blue red green to initiate drive and green, red, blue to close down. He further pointed out the symbolism on the main control panel. Saying that in time Richard and Jefferson would be proficient to 'visit' all 32 programmed destinations. Richard observed the coloured liquid had stopped at the level of the Symbol for Earth. Which in Nagosel science was a 'Image of the Egyptian God 'Anubis' in union with the female species, and encircled by three intertwined serpents'!

'My goodness' exclaimed Richard in guttural form, 'Whatever next?' Borcan smiled, or at least gave that impression. 'It says much, does it not Richard? The three serpents represent your three dimensional world and the 'interwined body, spirit and mind of Man'. The God form in union with your female kind, relates to your birth and death cycle. Each of the thirty two Symbols you now see, can be found in the book of the Great Star Map. There a full explanation is given on each meaning.' Borcan moved back to the main controls and after pushing down the crystal switch donating an eye, the screen provided the external vision of their new place of residence.

Wonderland remained intact, however there was a number of new faces which Richard found both disturbing and interesting. Borcan showed Richard a series of numbers beside the switch displaying the eye, and explained the magnification powers of the screen by utilising those numbers. 'Now magnify whom you wish Richard, but please inform me telepathically whom these humans are, if possible.' A small group of Specials, obviously armed, were positioned around the craft. By turning a rotating control the entirety of the space about them could be viewed. And slowly the screen advanced upon three figures. The centre figure towered above the other two, in his mouth a fat cigar, and although obviously aged since their last meeting, the now battered square cut face of Rosie Ansai now rolled into view. His steely eyes resolute, as blue as ever and his formidable chin a ledge to be proud of. Beside him and to the right a burly bearded man. Not tall but aggressive looking, and by his medals an important officer in the Military field. His balding head and dead eyes gave him away as Colonel Andy Peterson, 'A bloody mercenary' thought Richard, never have liked him. Borcan watched and took note of Richard's thoughts, but little understood any threat from such a being.

Richard continued, to the left of Major Ansai, stood a diminutive female. I guess she could be rather attractive if she discarded those ruddy spectacles, probably late thirties, but enticing red hair flowing neatly to the nape of her neck. But whom she is I have no idea? Borcan switched off the screen and moved towards the exit door, beckoning Richard to follow, but reminding him to be first out, as a way of recognition. But before entering the Timelock Borcan quickly passed Richard a 'Key' explaining its sister 'Key' was a security panel which housed three 'lazer books', those which were promised whilst under lecture. One dimensional, one living numbers and one of the Great Star Map. Using these books when practical would be most enlightening to him. Yet it would be a great mistake to let others see them, for their reproduction would open man's soul to the direst agencies of space. Both friends then entered the Timelock, a small hatchway used for Time level decontamination, and dispersal of magnetic fields. 'You were born here my friend, so you will soon adjust, yet I must wear my mask and suit until 24hrs of your earth cycle has elapsed. and then with the assistance of your earth scientists have fitted two impulse breathers. Now prepare.'

The crackling of static electricity greeted them both as the external doorway opened. The first words Richard heard in guttural terms was 'prepare to open fire'. Major Ansai tapped the side holster, his trigger action was as good now as it ever was. Though he wondered if bullets were an affective weapon against such unexpected guests? The UFO, if that was the correct term for the Alien Craft, had 'materialised' without any of the usual phenomena associated with Extra Terrestrial visitation. Only the build up of static-charge within the vicinity it now occupied, had given any indication of a break in time. A few of the Wonderland personnel experiencing nausea and hallucinatory visions. Corridor 26 housed the secret experimental zones. And here, close to the two largest rooms in the complex, lay the craft from some other world. Rosie judged its height to be some nine feet, as the top of the craft just cleared the corridor roof. And the width some fifteen feet. There being no markings visible, but an audible humming somewhere near midcentre, most apparent, and at times unnerving. From a distance of ten feet the outer skin shined with a density which appeared Infinite. Like a mercurial colour where one could pass his hand into, being neither solid nor fluid in form. Rosie's conscious thoughts suddenly broken by the harsh voice of Colonel Andy Peterson, 'Look there Rosie, something is coming out.' All eyes now fell upon the blue uniformed figure walking cautiously down the Alien ramp. Behind him another form, much taller and wearing a mask. Both uniforms clearly showing a design or motif, which to all observers was unintelligble. The figure without the mask then stopped and without any prompting spoke directly to Rosie Ansai, 'Could do with a bloody drink Major. Hey Rosie, it's me Sir, Richard's your lost special.' The steel blue eyes of Ansai widened and the granite jaw dropped, as his senses acquainted themselves with this shock.

'Do you know this fellow?' remarked Peterson.

'Put the guns away men' shouted Rosie, 'Whatever the hell is going on here, it certainly ain't aggressive.' A smile developed quite broadly across Ansai's face, he didn't know whether to laugh or cry. 'Richard you have a lot of explaining to do, though, I doubt the answers would be within my comprehension, and where's that bloody Jefferson, and don't look at Miss Foster when I'm talking to

80

you man?' Richard, using his newly acquired telepathic skills, assured Borcan they would now both be in safe hands, though obviously there would be many questions asked within the next few earthly hours. Borcan agreed, however he thought it best not to enter into any telepathic speech until Richard's' friends had grasped the reality of the situation.

The tall Nagosel frightened the young Miss Foster, not at least because of the lack of ears. The mask too, giving a sinister undefined attack upon her emotions, the figure of this Alien form towering over all personnel present. The long arms and the misshapen fingers on each glove doing little for her composure. She listened, as Richard described his trip to a real wonderland, which far surpassed any scientific aspirations that she and her colleagues could have imagined. It was hard to accept this 'Special' had been temporarily lost for nearly a year, and yet in his own words he Richard, had apparently been aware of a loss of only a few days. The time levels being mentioned not at all in accordance with modern day physics. But there could be little doubt about the Authenticity of the Alien or indeed the craft, which to everybody's discontent gave no signs of diminishing the audible humming. As she pondered upon the dreadful noise a 'Voice' entered her head and told her not to worry as this would soon stop. And by the caricature of the Alien's face now staring into her own, it became only too clear, he was telepathic. And if that were so he must also know she was afraid of him. A gentle tap upon her shoulder brought Miss Foster back to a sense of reality. Colonel Peterson may have had a body like a tank, but on some occasions his gentler nature manifested itself. 'Come Miss Foster, we are about to be shown a sample of 'Nagosel science'. And in saying that the heavy ex mercenary led the small party down the 26th corridor towards the underground tube.

'Only room for four on a transporter' barked the Colonel, his mouth clearly visible under the dense forestry of his imposing black beard. 'Major you take the first one with this Borcan fellow, and Richard, and I will accompany Miss Foster on the next. Meanwhile I will share a cigarette with Miss Foster, and try to come to a decision on relocating that damned craft.' Reaching into his camouflaged jacket, Colonel Peterson pulled out a distinctive packet of Russian blacks. 'Give you a cough Annabel but a bloody good smoke' chuckled Candy. Three or four minutes passed before the first transporter arrived, Richard and Borcan filled the back two seats whilst Rosie occupied the front. 'Corridor 18 please' said Rosie, his voice rather less audible than usual. But perhaps this was due to the fact, corridor 18, room 15 was the late Professor Marinetts domain. And rather prone to outbursts as the old man was, Rosie had become rather attached to the Professor's eccentricities, and besides, he would miss his drinking company at the bar.

Borcan listened intensely to the thoughts of this strange human, for outwardly he, this Major would demonstrate a strength of command, yet within his light and the core of his being he was secretive and lacked the warmth of his female counterpart. Such is the downfall of many a human whom lacks the expressive flow of Love, and whom chases the veiled phantasm of Negativity, which haunts the inner planes of this earthly world. These thoughts of Nagosel fashion would be shut off to Richard's telepathic ability, for sometimes it is wise to conceal truths from eager and intuitive minds. Richard's mind however was focused on a more vulnerable person, he was worried about Miss Foster, her companion in the transporter had expressed thoughts of lust and evil inclinations toward her, totally unaware of Richard's ability to read minds. Colonel Peterson would have to be watched for his overbearing mannerisms could break down her defences. And besides Richard never trusted the man, his rise to power within Wonderland had seemed highly suspicious, and his mercenary background proved testament to a hidden destructive nature.

The transporter came to a halt, corridor 18 at last revealed itself. A number of rooms were immediately recognisable to Richard, Rifle-requisition and Robotic-studies had been a constant source of amusement to him, as previous visits had led to more than a casual encounter with the female staff in charge of them. Nobody knows what goes on behind closed doors, thought Richard, temporarily forgetting his friend Borcan was keen to listen to any thoughts that may spring to mind. The normal rotation of rooms started with room one on the right and in a horseshoe fashion ended with room 19 or 20 on the left. A few of the high security rooms required a passkey to gain entrance, and research-ops was one of them. Rosie Ansai inserted a plastic card into a panel to the left of the door, he then typed out a pre-recorded security code on the alphabetical-typeface. A click was heard and the door swung inwardly, revealing a well stocked laboratory and an inner glass walled area purposely built for Virus containment. The door closed magnetically behind them, and Rosie ushered the two companions forward along a aisle towards the containment area.

'Come Borcan and see for yourself the affects of this plague, though I warn you it is not a pretty sight. This was a female we think, she was found outside the aerodrome yesterday afternoon, and I should perhaps bring your attention to the fact, the body now has wings.' Richard walked behind Borcan on either side of him the bisected anatomy of some poor human wretch, lay quiet and still, lifeless matter submerged in some embalming fluid, covered in hideous scales. Tall glass tanks were now home to strange decapitated heads, large webbed hands and thick unsightly torsos. A chill moved swiftly down Richard's back, he wondered what sight he was about to behold, and yet his inquisitive human nature urged him on. The harsh reality of the plague however, still took its toll upon his visionary organs.

'Good God' cried Richard, 'It's terrifying we have to destroy it, we have to wipe out the bloody virus Ansai.' A shaken Richard composed himself, and with some inner strength looked again, slowly recording every detail of the hideous form behind the glass wall. 'The head of the Beast or thing was clearly abnormal, being twice the size of a human cranium, and with the extra faculty of a pig like snout. The eyes portrayed no light whatsoever, there being no pupils and no colour variation, just a dense blackness, reminding one of pools of ink. The teeth being similar to that of a jackal, they displayed a lack of concern for the living. Two three inch long stems had replaced the ears, spiralling out of their respective sockets. The torso was entirely covered with brown scales, the arms and legs also formed in the same pattern. At the end of the 'webbed hands' sharp Talons protruded, curling as though in the grip of some unseen prey. The feet also webbed, had grown two extra members, there now being seven appendages or toes, each equipped with similar Talons.

Richard judged the height of the Beast to be seven feet, its total weight probably exceeding some thirty stone. Behind each shoulder and in direct line to the waist either side, were wings now obviously closed, but one could assume their actual wingspan would be more than enough to propel their attached body off the ground. These black feathered members however, were not attached in any fashion to the arms, and would therefore be completely controlled by back movements in some unknown way. The face seemed bloated with green glutinous bubbles, the jaw had dropped or perhaps broken, revealing not a tongue, but a system of minute tubes, which formed part of the throat cavity and ran from somewhere within the form outward to either side of the jaw. Richard pondered upon their purpose, but was given some insight by the telepathic Borcan, whom for sometime had been reading Richard and Ansai's thoughts. 'These tubes are feeders Richard, they suck the blood from the host after the sharp teeth of the Beast have torn upon the flesh. And if you look closely at the upturned right hand, there is a similar system of tubes on the underside of each appendage or finger.

And here again the Talons would be instrumental in breaking away the flesh. Such a predator would quickly empty any bodily form, which would also include earthly animals. It would be interesting to capture one such as this, to find a blood grouping which would prove harmful to its functioning.'

'Alive?' responded Richard 'Rather dangerous Borcan, particularly when they can fly. Most of the cases I have seen floating in glass jars about this room, appear to have been blasted by grenades or split apart by heavy rounds of ammunition. To propose to capture one alive for experimental study may prove too difficult. I suggest you use your telepathic speech on Major Ansai, Borcan, he may be better influenced than the Colonel.'

But before such a request could be made the operations door had opened and the burley Colonel Peterson and Miss Foster now made their entrance. 'Where have you been Candy?' asked a not too bemused Ansai. 'Been around the circle for a spin no doubt.'

'Well Rosie, quite simply, Miss Foster here was taken short and had to pay a visit to the Ladies, and so we then had to await a further transporter. Anyway I've seen that glorified mess before, both complete and in fragmentation. This special friend of yours and this Alien, Borcan, if that's his name, time they did some explaining and what about that box of tricks you have there Richard, let's see what it can do boy.'

Borcan beckoned Richard over to a corner of the room, some twenty feet away from the other three observers. Then by telepathic communication asked Richard to depress the yellow and red buttons on the box simultaneously. This Richard did, and immediately a green glow bathed the entirety of Richard's body. Borcan then assured Richard that whatever happens he was well protected. 'Ask this aggressive fellow to shoot at you until his weaponry is empty.'

Richard looked at the reddened face of Peterson and asked him to empty his automatic into him. Richard admittedly rather worried at the outcome. Candy raised his powerful pistol at Richard and fired, the confined area of the ops-room doing little to silence the six explosive bangs of the Colonel's favourite firearm. Candy, still holding his magnum at arm's length, was visibly shaken by the result. Richard stood motionless, the green glow still intact, but around the room six large holes confirmed an impact.

'Bloody marvellous' shouted Rosie, though the ricochet from one of the bullets had smashed one of the tall tanks, and its spillage left an unsatisfactory fragrance in the air.

'I'm satisfied with that test' said Candy, 'but what about heavier armoury?'

Borcan explained to Richard that nothing upon this earth would penetrate this screening, the force about him being impervious to matter, and that the field could be further strengthened by a simple adjustment.

Now Borcan asked Richard to depress the two yellow buttons and he prepared for a new reality. This further test thought Borcan would convince these earthly people of his scientific skills. Richard pushed down the two buttons and awaited the outcome. The room lights began to dim, his friend Rosie and Miss Foster faded into a sea of bright whiteness, the ops-room had disappeared, there was no Borcan and no other human form. Slowly the eyes became accustomed to their new environment, yet he dare not walk for fear of falling or getting lost forever. Then he saw them! swimming quite effortlessly through the white space. There were hundreds of them, naked full breasted women, their waist ending with a long plume of smoke. Long nails and flowing hair added to the visionary splendour. The faces were aged and yet possessed an enduring beauty, their eyes were of ebony black and their depth was infinite. The mouths too when opened revealed this same depth of blackness, but a blackness which shined brighter than any star. They observed him for a while, their transparent form illuminated by the green shadowy mist which formed them. And then as suddenly as they had appeared, they then disappeared. The whiteness remained, his senses swam in a sea of tranquillity, it was very hard to regain any conscious perception. He dared to turn around but there was nothing behind him, no sound, nothing, perhaps he was dead? The Nagosel box glowed red in this white space, his reasoning asked him to return, to depress the two yellow buttons, but no this was too good, let's stay a while.

Eventually without any conscious effort on Richard's part, another astral embodiment presented itself. A large blubbery worm, glistening with that slime so reminiscent of the walls in dark subterranean caverns. The eyes were of a triangular nature, and the redness of them pierced the still whiteness of the void. A circular gaping hole lacking any means to devour its intended prey did little to relax the malevolence of its vision. The head now fast approaching Richard seemed inquisitive, as its oval shape swayed to and forth, studying Richard as man would study an insect. The thing stopped short at an arm's length from the now frozen being. The stench of death penetrated deep into Richard's soul, he had tasted such vileness only once before. At the home of his late uncle Barnabas, a reformed drunkard and professed 'Occultist' whose wish it was to be ceremonially embalmed as in the way of Egyptian Priests. Richard, in his early twenties, had expressed a wish to assist the embalmer, to gain insight into the chemical formulae used and its action upon a dead corpse. The entirety of the operation Richard recorded on video. And now this filthy smell had reacted badly upon his memory. For it had been Richard's task to wrap the sticky bandages around his uncle's form. The unearthly face moved closer to Richard, the triangular eyes now so close they resembled two blazing red spheres. But deep in their intensity, deep in their unknown Astral sublimity could be sensed a message, a garbled speech. Richard concentrated, his fear subsided, for if the thing had meant him harm, it would surely not waste any time in devouring such a morsel as himself. A sharp pain was felt in the back of the head, and then an explosion, a release of something, a coolness of either blood or water gushed across the top of his head. A new awareness had emerged, transforming the garbled speech into a recognisable pattern. Thus was Richard able to translate!

'My name is Tasaramee, to call me forth from this Realm,
the number of my name should be written on Virgin
parchment in the way of a Sigil.'
'And my name written in 'Magical form' using nine
squares.'
'In darkness call me, but when your moon is fullest
bright, then shalt thou adore me, as we move in
Matter to unite.'
'My incense is of sulphur and myrrh, and fumes of
rotting flesh.'
'Call me and I shall show you the treasures beneath
thy Earth.'
'For I am both Worm and Gate, Fear and Hate,
Study then the worms of your Earth, for all things
have reflection in Time and Space.'

'Now return to your Illusory world Oh Spiritual Man, for it is my task in this Realm to swallow the remnants of things, not conducive to its physics. And my creative hunger knows no bounds.'

The worm spoke no more, the burning red eyes moved away, the gaping hole upon the face of the thing closed, and very slowly turning its head, the gigantic worm disappeared into the depths of the void. Again stillness, no sound, no more images only the white emptiness. If it were not for the glow of the box, harnessed to his uniform trousers, his mind may have been lost forever. An index finger depressed the two yellow buttons on the box, it was time to return to the norm, but what was the norm? And in which reality would he find Truth? Gradually the whiteness faded and in its wake black negative pictures replaced the empty space. The dimensional shape of a cube formed about him, the walls, floor and ceiling rapidly changing from a molecular matrix, which closely resembled that of a 'bee hive' into the earthly plane of dense matter. It was hard to recognise any objects for what they were, the lack of colour seemed to deprive them of substance.

Matter began to clothe itself into the recognisable shape of the human form. Fascinated Richard watched his friends emerge into the atomic planes by the manifestation of bone, the skeletal framework and then flesh. The abundance of electrical fields around the cerebral matrix and again through the body as a whole, enlightened Richard upon the 'Unionisation' of Mankind with his planetary body. Soon the Illusory world of man would present itself, but he Richard had gained an insight into the hidden planes of existence. A smiling Rosie Ansai uttered the first welcoming words 'Good God my boy, I thought you would never return, must be some thirty minutes since you disappeared, why even Candy here was getting concerned.' Although now fully materialised, the protective field was still around Richard, and he was finding it difficult to concentrate on the combinations he must use on the box controls to remove this field. He thought hard upon what Amariel had said and with a little unsurety upon the outcome, pressed down a single red button. Immediately in doing so the protective field dissipated, he was now back in this world, he felt 'earthed' again he had a purpose.

THE DESTRUCTIVE ELEMENT

Richard put the nauseating smell down to the recently extinguished forcefield, and yet it bore some resemblance to a chemical used in the embalming process. Neither Ansai's large cigar or Peterson's black Russian could match this lingering stench 'What's up Richard?' barked Candy Peterson. 'Can't stand the odour sunshine, you should bloody well try inhaling the aftermath of their blasted torso, after a grenade or two their guts ain't too good either.'

Rosie however cut short Candy's report, as he observed Miss Foster was looking rather queasy. 'Richard my boy, Candy's firearm richoched a bullet or two into one of these filthy tanks, but don't worry the mess has been dealt with. I think we have all seen enough for one afternoon and suggest a visit to the eating hall, time this Borcan fellow tried some decent grub.'

'I agree' said Miss Foster, 'I'm feeling rather empty inside, and find it hard to have a clear head on an empty stomach.'

'Guess that's settled it then,' said Candy, stomping his cigarette end out underfoot. 'Give the bloody cleaner something to do.'

His broad frame led the four figures out of the ops-room, his thick fingers finding it difficult to engage the correct sequence for sealing the magnetic door. 'See you all in corridor 5, room 8 in about ten minutes then.' An unoccupied toilet grabbed Candy's attention, the old black Russians never gave him constipation.

'At least we can all grab the same transporter now, and get a break from the barking dog,' growled Ansai, clearly unamused by Candy's recent performance of Ops-floor ashing. The transporter, some eight feet in length open-topped and propelled by magnetic rails, usually gave comfortable sitting positions for all, but the largest human species. However the tall Borcan found it very exacting to place his legs in a relaxed familiarity with the imposing seats in front. Beside him sat Miss Foster, whom in her own thoughts gave way to the relaxed composure she had shown in the face of this strange Alien. Richard blurted out 'Miss Foster, I think before we establish ourselves within the framework of the restaurant, a few important facts may be readily announced. Both myself and my friend Borcan here possess the ability to read minds, and although Borcan cannot speak gutturally he can however enter your thoughts, and make a voice visible. I am sure he was awaiting the proper occasion to make this known amongst you, as I would suspect his sudden intervention into your usually closed minds may have been a little shocking?'

'So why the mask Richard?' said Ansai, his head turned slightly towards the seat now occupied by Borcan. A gentle voice began to drift into Ansai's head, it began to talk of many things, it was of course Borcan's, as he explained to both Annabel and Ansai simultaneously the telepathic ability of the Nagosel race, and the purpose of retaining the mask for another 22hrs of earthly time.'

Ansai interrupted 'As far as security is known, our Alien friend wears this mask because of burns to his face, however this is a high security establishment and nobody asks any questions unless asked to do so.'

The talk stopped as the transporter pulled up at corridor 5. Ansai again was reminded upon the attractive quality of Annabel's legs, as the split in her skirt did little to hide the bare flesh at the top of her stockings. He was not alone in this area of reconnaissance, for Richard rarely missed such sights.

As they walked into the eating hall, the tall Alien seemed rather perturbed about the Earthly nourishment. Casting his thoughts to Richard he enquired upon the bowl of coloured liquid. A telepathic response assured Borcan that 'Soup' was of goodness and possessed no worm like form as would be found in Nagosel nourishment. Richard pointed to a bowl of lentils and a tall glass of cold orange juice, suggesting his friend might try these? The next courses were perhaps unsuited to a Nagosel diet because of their bulk, so perhaps two bowls of soup may for now be practical. Richard feeling rather peckish and greedy for solid foodstuff, helped himself to a double portion of steak pie and a similar plate of chips. 'Bloody lovely' exclaimed Richard, as he made his way over to an empty table. Ansai grabbed fish and chips whilst a reluctant Annabel plumed for the Madras Curry, and a steaming hot tea to accompany the hot subtle flavour. Little was said as the four companions refreshed their thirst and hunger. The absence of Colonel Peterson was apparently unnoticed, or indeed appreciated. Most of the restaurant's tables were empty, only a few gave any indication of the mixture of personnel in Wonderland. The air was filled with an abundance of sweet smelling tobacco, most preferring to smoke a pipe than cigarettes. The eating hall was representative of most public areas, having little decor about the walls, veneered wood tiling making up for otherwise concrete floors, and the ever present security cameras rotating in their own distinctive metallic globes. Ventilators hidden behind artificial fauna provided the circulativn air from above ground, whilst concealed underfloor heating gave an almost habitual summer feeling. Annabel Foster reached deep into her Lab apron and produced a packet of Gaulois blue, a French cigarette of which she was fond. Her student days were spent near one of the many vine producing regions of France, and this particular brand reminded her of the passionate acquaintance of ones wild adolescence. Her long red hair had been tied neatly at the nape of her neck, and she blushed as she drew hard upon the cigarette. Rosie's attentiveness towards her was becoming more apparent. Yet, he was kind of dishy in a funny sort of way, and he was definitely a gentleman. A date would have to be arranged, she had kept the poor man waiting long enough.

Rosie averted his eyes for a while, it could be seen as rude to stare so intensely at such a young lady, and besides, his manly emotions were becoming increasingly harder to hide. He therefore drew immediate attention to the ongoing crisis. Richard would accompany him to his office, for further update on this dimensional space station. And Borcan could go with Miss Foster to the experimental lab in corridor 26. There perhaps he and she may find a solution to prevent the plague spreading further? Then at 2100hrs they would all meet again here and prepare a plan of action for tomorrow. A message would be left for Colonel Peterson to join us here in the eating hall or early in the morning in Ops- research.

'Fine with me' said Richard as he raised himself up from the table. 'Take good care of my friend Borcan for me Miss Foster, and be careful of your thoughts.'

'I shall see you both later' said Annabel, 'and perhaps we can sample a couple of nightcaps before retiring, the bar in corridor

3 is the best in Wonderland.' The slim physicist then gave an unexpected wink to Rosie, raising both eyebrows as she did so, it was time to be wild again she thought, time to love.

'You're in there Major' said Richard, giving a sarcastic wink to Rosie. 'She is very pretty, but there's a certain 'Sophiel' I would like to introduce to you one day, whom I think would also give rise to some feelings in the old fishing tackle.'

'You never change Richard my boy, do you, still the cheeky special from some ten years ago? Come on let's hear about your escapade on the other side of space, and more importantly what has become of that other schoolboy Jefferson?'

Colonel Andy Peterson watched impatiently as two leading physicists tried vainlessly to open the craft's outer door. 'Must of locked the damn thing with a magic spell,' barked Candy. 'Can't you try a laser or acetylene torch for goodness sake? There must be some bloody way to open it.'

The non bemused physicians shook their heads, restating to the red faced Colonel, that such measures would not be wise at this moment in time. The hull of the craft appeared penetrable and alive at the same time, and without conforming to the density as in earthly physics, it would be extremely difficult to ascertain the 'Kind of Key' which would unlock its entrance mode. 'What the hell do we pay people for?' he again barked, his frustration showing signs of disorder. 'Alright, alright, gentlemen, thank you for your efforts. It would seem we must wait until morning, for our Alien neighbour to enlighten us on Dimensional science. Good day gentlemen, shall we say ten o'clock sharp.' Candy's abrupt nature was at the best of times rude and uncalled for, but it did get results. He was not a man to play around with words. Because of the nature of the craft and because of this particular section in Wonderland, smoking was now out of the question.

He noted the time was 20.30hrs, he had been notified of the meeting between Major Ansai and the others at 2100hrs. 'They can manage without me for today, he thought, besides I need a fag and a strong drink, this Alien had better come up with some answers tomorrow, or. He cut short, his mood was irritable and standing next to this craft didn't help the situation. Before departing however, he left strict instructions with two armed Specials to allow no person entry to this corridor until his return in some 12hrs time. On the way to the Communal Bar on corridor three, which from corridor twenty six would take sometime, his thoughts regressed to other Alien encounters. And in particular the possession of a minute craft which now awaited further probing, it too had found its home housed in zebra room, in corridor twenty six.

There had been a number of minute craft on that day, they had been hovering about the ancient monument near Salisbury, 'Stonehenge' had always proven fruitful. At around midnight an Intelligence officer had rang Candy, informing him of Extraterrestrial movement near the monument, and as far as could be ascertained, the 'Objects' had 'materialised' within the Circle. Candy ordered an immediate 'Clampdown' on communication and further a 'Staged' accident some miles up the roadway to prevent the public eye interfering. Such things being normal practice on these occasions, a special acting crew were fully mobile and well rehearsed. Not far from Stonehenge a camouflaged unit filmed the sequence of events, and on direct orders from Colonel Peterson prepared to obtain one of these Craft.

Using a 'magnetic web pulsator' a ring of magnetised particles would be quickly dispersed into the perimeter in which the Alien craft were hovering. It was an Invention of Professor Marinetts, conceived he said from experimental studies with other Alien artefacts. Indeed, Wonderland housed numerous other worldly objects, as well as frozen bodies. The sequence of events that followed were unexplainable in scientific terms as all but one craft 'Entered' or appeared to be absorbed into the surrounding-stones, creating a portal or starway. Which in turn created a Luminosity throughout the accommodating stones, and gave forth a beam of light which ascended far into the heavens. A single craft caught in the Magnetic web lost control and smashed into a horizontal stone slab occupying dead centre of the circle. All then went quiet and the special unit nearby quickly recovered the fallen Alien craft. Although its dimensional shape proved awkward to carry, only a small truck was used to convey it to Wonderland. Some four feet in size, and to all intents and purposes representing a miniature pyramid. The object however weighed in at seventy stones. Obviously the hull was composed of an unknown ore whose substance or atomic density was higher than any known metals on earth.

Candy's thoughts were engrossed in this scenario so much that he did not hear the transporter pilot shouting out corridor 3. A gentle tap on the big man's shoulder however, awoke him from this line of thought. 'No need to shout man' said Candy, again on a short fuse. The thick heavy legs swung out of the low slung seat, the impression left behind from a mighty backside clearly indicating the man's proportions, which gave a certain amount of amusement to the transporter-pilot. Room three housed the communal bar, here at least one could relax in relative comfort and drown the thoughts of recent events. Drown being the operative word in the case of Candy, for in Wonderland all alcoholic beverages were duty free. After purchasing a bottle of Jamiesons whisky, and acquiring a freshly filled jug of water, he quickly found an empty table which had the added advantage of well padded couch like seating, where presumably the big man would if needs be, fall asleep. Setting his wristwatch alarm for six am he conjectured he would have a good three hours in the morning to wash, change and enjoy a hearty breakfast before the meeting with Rosie and the others. But now it was time to wind down and get bloody drunk. Candy was not one to curl up in front of a warm fire and talk nonsensical crap to a woman, whom in his eyes, needed a good bedding or a shoulder to cry on. A lot of blood had been spilled by his hand, a mercenary career had seen to that. And besides many a young thing had been privileged to sample his manhood. At fifty two Candy had experienced more than most, and with his Rank money was never a problem, so why shouldn't he fancy a young attractive woman like Miss Foster? An empty tumbler broke this wave of thought, and with an urgent passion Candy broke the seal of the bottle, unscrewed its cap and watched intently as the yellow liquid filled to the brim of the glass tumbler. A steady hand poured a heavy mixture down his dry throat, that and a black-Russian eased his frustrations. Soon the bar would be packed with thirst egos, some rather like himself, unable to relax on one bottle, merry and out of it on two, and clinically dead on three. The night would be a long one, but at the end of it he would sleep well.

Removing his jacket he placed an unopened pack of black-Russians onto the table, an expensive cigarette lighter providing companionship. The world was a bloody illusion alright, Aliens, Saboteurs, Double-agents, fuck the lot of them, at least drink could be relied upon to be consistent and at times controllable. He scratched at his overgrown beard, all the while observing the young female agents, their curvaceous bodies blending in with the terrifying effects of too much drink and strong tobacco. At last relaxed, Candy gave a wave to a fellow drinker 'Get over here' he barked, 'Get pissed, don't be an old fart all of your life.' Normally such a response would have deserved a reprimand, but the Chief knew the big man well.

'A large bottle of Red Label barman, one glass and one of those Cuban cigars, put it all on my bill thank you.' The Chief carried the bottle over to Candy's table, his overweight frame testing a bar chair to its capacity. Unlike Candy he was unfit, his fifty years looking more like seventy. No physical prowess just fat, and far to excessive in his eating habits to have longevity. However, he could take his drink, and he was not a womaniser, he was good at his job and admired respect. The Chief rarely talked to the lower ranks, but this plague had relaxed his attitude somewhat, what was once closed doors, he had now opened. Security was important, but certain areas in Wonderland had now been made accessible as ultimately he knew all secrets had their 'Keys' and these 'Keys' were not immune to Infiltration by persistent minds. Even the tube which now housed the Havana cigar trigged memories of 'UFOs'. The long cigar shape a proven source of sightings from the early fifties. Only himself and Candy had seen the occupants retrieved from the crashed UFO in the Russian forest some twenty years ago. Their resemblance to humans was uncanny. And their planetary origin a top secret. Now, this 'special' Richard, had brought to light even more confirmation of Dimensional capability, in terms of sentient worlds who exist on the 'Shores of Time and Space', rather than participating as beings in Space time and its known 'Planes of Existence'. This 'Borcan fellow' would perhaps have the final answers to the Great Mystery, or some 'Keys' to the beginning of life? Whatever the outcome, the human race would welcome any solution to eradicating this hideous plague. And if the answer was forthcoming from another world then so be it.

Candy had been muttering some nonsense about the craft in corridor 26, but the Chief paid little attention. This was a time to relax, to forget work and its pressures, to live in the material world for a while, or else become insane with the 'Supernatural' and the timeless worlds beyond this. 'Pour me a good measure Candy, you old fool, and let's get plastered. It's well worth the headache in the morning.' The bar clock showed 2330hrs, the forty or so tables were now filled with a variety of spirits and small beers. A Juke box in one corner of the complex played sounds of Reggae and Rock, whilst a tiny dance floor provided a release for youthful expression. Outside, above in the inner cities a War had begun. Flying mutations, spawned from the plague fed tenaciously upon the mutilated victims, quivering hosts completely drained of blood, awaiting extinction or transformation into unspeakable forms. The forces had taken great losses, small arms were useless against the flying beasts. Many whom had escaped the Vampirish ghouls, had taken to the underground stations, whilst others sought sanctuary amongst the steel ships of the Naval forces. Few human souls were safe, in some populations 'Clouds' of Evil forms had been recorded in the night skies. A military curfew now prevailed in almost every major city, anyone seen between the hours of midnight and seven in the morning would be put to the 'Fire', which involved the use of flame throwers and flares. Such extreme measures eradicating the chances of additional mutation. All those found to have contracted the plague were also 'Put to the fire'.

The flames never went out, the night skies heralding the flames of hell. Special masks were issued to all those considered safe, though their factory production was slow, and distribution of masks between cities was dangerous, and extremely unsafe. The American Government had put forward a notion to 'Napalm' the worst areas, but a NATO Decision prevented such implementation as many thousands of unaffected innocents would be caught in the holocaust. Time was running out, both for the scientific fraternity and the major governments of the world. The virus mutations now had a name, they were called 'Mondemon' short for monstrous demons. Wonderland for the present remained safe, because of its underground advantage and special air filtration, all personnel were free from contracting any virus through airborne spores or chemical bacteria. However the continued use of these filters would eventually deplete stocks. Therefore it was crucial to all concerned to find an antidote or 'destructive element' which would eradicate the plague forever. On 3rd March 2015 a Special's black helicopter landed at the hanger concealing the Ministry's Wonderland. Three Specials wearing appropriate masks, and one further person, dressed entirely in black apparel, made their way into the empty hanger. Below ground in corridor 5 room 8 a small entourage of important people had gathered. It was 0845am the only missing person was a Colonel Andy Peterson, 'Candy' for short. The eating hall was out of bounds until midday, however there was adequate machines throughout Wonderland providing hot food, and drinks for just such occasions. 'Please be seated everyone, our guests will be arriving any moment now.' The Chief nursing a sore head had received an urgent communication at 0200hrs 3rd March, he had just retired to bed after consuming heavy amounts of scotch with his friend Colonel Andy Peterson. A call on the internal phone had alerted him of an urgent visit from the Pentagon. Seated to the rear of the hall were Richard, Borcan and Miss Foster. Behind the command desks were Rosie Ansai and the Chief, an empty chair was presumably waiting for the larger than life Colonel Peterson.

The sound of thunderous boots bombarding their way along the outside corridor prompted the Chief to elevate his large frame. A quick glance at his watch indicated the punctuality of his American guests, 0900am exactly. The double doors of the eating hall swung open, the barking voice of one Andy Peterson breaking the silence of the occasion. 'This way gentlemen, I imagine all important parties are now present.'

The American Specials remained outside, obviously as a preventative measure against intrusion, their black uniforms bearing the word 'Acets' just above the right shoulder of their jackets. Both wore dark glasses and both carried a sidearm, their outward appearance reminded Candy of his mercenary days. Such men were not to be messed with.

The Chief shook hands with the American Lieutenant, his rank in 'Acets' taking priority over any other associated branches, such as the CIA, FBI and OSS. The Lieutenant was rather young to hold such an important position, but his background knowledge and hands on experience with Extra-terrestrial-phenomena accelerated his promotional prospects. A little over thirty years old his clean cut image seemed out of place in such a service. However James Borncastle could be a formidable opponent, as Candy well knew. Five years in the Navy-Seals had earned him a reputation as an executioner-par-excellence. Skilled in Martial Arts and fluent in ten languages, he had his uses. However, the young Lieutenant neither smoked nor participated in the odd drink, which to Candy seemed rather strange. The smartly dressed young man had caught the attention of Miss Foster, his well groomed hair, blue eyes and rugged physique appealed to her womanly ways. The caricature of his manly face being sleighted only by the deep scar etched into his right cheek. The cut of his black suit expensive and except for the silver tie pin there was no other signs of military authority upon him.

Now at last he began to speak! 'Please remain relaxed everyone, it is not my aim to disrupt daily proceedings. My name is James Borncastle, and for those not acquainted with the word 'Acets' it simply stands for Active-communication-with Extra-terrestrial-source'. Myself and other officers are sometimes referred to as the 'MIBS' or 'Men in Black' And it is my aim here today to co-ordinate a Task-force which includes the Russians the French, the Chinese and Canadian establishments. Everything possible has been done to try to remove this plague of Beasts, however the following should enlarge upon this issue.

A general pattern has been interpreted across these countries and your own, the 'Mondemon' preferring to mass in their hundreds within forest areas. Perhaps this is because of the food or blood available from the inhabitants of such places. Large forested areas in China and Canada have been systematically burned, in an effort to eradicate as many as possible, however because of their flying capabilities the ' Mondemon' find solace elsewhere. And this 'elsewhere' unfortunately is the inner cities. The Mondemon fly in mass hordes and from a distance appear as dark clouds. We are deploying all defence tactics available though as yet Nuclear capability is not seen as a answer. Chemical suits are fine in armoured vehicles, however ground troops are vulnerable if attacked, the talons on these mutants are razor sharp. As no doubt Colonel Peterson is aware, grenades appear to be the only effective ground weapon. Large nets to capture our quarry have been deployed in the air and on ground, however they are either torn open by talons or ripped apart by sheer strength. Therefore I feel the only option open to us is the 'Live capture' of a Mondemon. Our Alien visitor is not the only form whom seeks to assist us. Other outside forces are willing to help, but the presence of many UFOs in the skies would not help our predicament. The people of our Earth are already hysterical with the plague, and further confusement by Extra-terrestrial phenomena may even assist the Mondemon. Remember, this virus was brought to our world from the outside, and thus such a virus may also be harmful to other forms. I would like to spend a short time with the Alien, two hours perhaps if of course this is acceptable by himself and the Chief? I know enough of Alien visitors to realise they will tell me only that which is useful at the time. So young lady and those gentleman present, I finish my little discourse and shall leave the plan of action entirely upon yourselves.'

The Lieutenant then called for a short coffee break before the Chief's briefing. Miss Foster volunteered to dispense the coffee or tea from the canteen area, hoping as she would to get acquainted with the good looking Lieutenant. Rosie would not be alarmed by this, for the young American would certainly be returning to America later on today. Besides she had convinced Rosie of her fondness for him, though marriage would be out of the question. Candy had seated himself beside the Chief, a stale smell of tobacco permeated his nostrils and drew his attention to two half smoked cigars, momentarily at rest in the oval shaped ashtray directly in front of him. He assumed quite rightly, that the large cigar was of the Havana leaf and belonged to the Chief, and the much smaller tightly wound leaf to be the cigar much loved by Ansai. He had cured his hangover by drinking a hair of the dog! a blend only common to himself, two raw eggs a splash of brandy and two spoonfuls of honey. Although concentrating on the matter at hand, his thoughts rarely left the 'Ship' which was still blocking corridor 26. There was much to do, but little time to do it in. He would have a quiet word or whatever was needed, to convey the urgency of this craft blockade to the Alien Borcan, though he felt Richard may be needed to get the message across. It was a rarity to work alongside this 'Acets' branch, perhaps there was more to the crisis than here revealed, never did trust the Americans thought Candy, might just be making use of us and then throw us all to the crocodiles? Time alone would tell, so let's be nice to the young Lieutenant.

Richard returned to his table with a second coffee and a glass of chilled orange for Borcan, he had made time to chat quickly with Rosie Ansai whilst at the canteen counter, relating his thoughts on the crisis and at the same time taking an eyeful of Miss Foster's superb legs. Consciously he wanted her, sub-consciously he wanted 'Sophiel' he 'felt' her thoughts were with him. The coffee tasted bitter, although drowned with milk, were they brown sugar sachets he had used? Oh dear there was the distinct possibility he had emptied the pepper-sachets by mistake, temporarily blinded no doubt by black fishnet stockings. Alas one earlier coffee would suffice, anyway too much caffeine he thought. Borcan hurriedly finished the coloured drink, it was not to his liking, he preferred that which humans called soup. This young human named 'James' knew little of the Universal-matrix, his mind was not for enlightening, yet he was gaining some insight to 'Dimensional-zones'. Human life had been extinguished by him many times, his spiritual growth now followed the wrong pathway. Still, Borcan would communicate with the young officer, revealing little of the Nagosel race and even less about the Great Star Map. The face mask would also be removed today with the help of the female Foster, she had understood the importance of the impulse breathers. The fitting would cause no problem, as two scars on each of Borcan's wrists provided the necessary alignment for the probed entry.

The oval shaped timelock now showed 11.00am thus indicating perhaps an hour's talk from the Chief and Ansai, and thence onwards to the Ops research room to fit the impulse breathers? The young lieutenant passed a number of papers to the Chief, and after a brief whisper in the big man's ear, turned his attention to Borcan. Glancing at his wristwatch the lieutenant then made his way to Borcan's table. 'Miss Foster, Richard, I hope we may meet again in the next two or three weeks, indeed, as soon as we catch a Mondemon'. Borcan observed the scar on the lieutenant's face, it was a deep penetration, more a zigzag cut than a straight incision, telling Borcan that such an infliction was undoubtedly due to torture. The lieutenant said nothing to Borcan, being aware of Borcan's telepathic ability, a thought transference was all that was needed. His message passed he then turned and made an exit through the double doors, his waiting Specials outside accompanying him down the long corridor to the transporter rail.

Richard had also received the thoughts from the lieutenant, and turning to Borcan remarked, 'I read his thoughts my friend, though at times, even now you close your mind and it is impossible to grasp certain waves. If you would like me to assist at this interview, then I shall of course be there. Though I sense you have more than enough confidence to deal with this matter.' Borcan thanked Richard, the hour with Borncastle would rapidly pass, and at three o'clock he would meet Miss Foster at the Laboratory to remove his mask and fit the impulse-breathers. And then a dissection of the Beast would be in order, the Mondemon's circulatory and biological functions perhaps giving a Key to their destruction? For even Miss Foster's expertise may have overlooked a significant factor.

A sharp tap on Borcan's shoulder by Richard broke Borcan's thought, the Chief was about to speak. His large frame now seated, as his legs were now showing signs of an unsupportive measure, pain came with age. The thick eyebrows rose before he spoke, his larger than life mouth reminding Annabel of a bulldog, the rounded face the dark eyes and the offensive teeth. She chuckled to herself, though no one else was aware of her thoughts. Borcan's telepathic ability was rather strained at a distance of thirty feet, and much concentration was needed. 'Ladies and Gentlemen, now the 'Acet's branch has removed itself, a little on their function maybe forthcoming. As you are now aware, Acets are in direct communication with a number of alien sources, some good, some bad. There are bases upon our planet, and obviously it is in everybody's interest to eradicate this plague, and its hosts with the utmost expediency. Therefore I propose to start a plan of action tonight. Richard and Borcan appear to have protective devices which will keep them free from harm, and as such these two will be significant in capturing a Mondemon. The Colonel will provide a measure of ground cover, and he shall have the extra backing of a unit of Flame throwers. At midnight tonight two armoured personnel carriers will take this task force to the Exmoor forest where we hope to disturb an unknown quantity of these beasts. We have managed to procure form the Acets branch a 'Titanium web', it is fired by the separate arm launchers and its approx covering area is thirty feet. We only have one such web, so it is imperative we use it on a non flying beast, that is to say a wing must be removed without causing major damage to the rest of the body.

A third personnel carrier will follow some distance behind the other two, the vehicle will be the command link to HQ, and shall be under orders from Major Ansai. Its weaponry is advanced to Laser level and shall be engaged if needed. Miss Foster and myself shall prepare an area of containment, which hopefully will hold and subdue a captured Mondemon. I again cannot over express the importance of removing a wing from the chosen beast, a prepared section of Major Ansai's carrier should prevent the captive from escape, and although uncivilised as it may sound, a few live animals are provided in Ansai's carrier for the beasts barbaric acts.'

Maps of Exmoor and the surrounding areas will be provided, and you must all wear protective uniform and masks. You will all carry a remote link to Ansai's carrier, if the link is broken then unfortunately Major Ansai will assume you are dead. It is only a suggestion, but perhaps Richard and Borcan can fire the web, when within range. Also such situations as these are better planned 'hands-on' than pre thought. So I wish you all success, and hope to be buying you each a drink on your return. Please be at the Hanger entrance at 2340 sharp, time is of the essence.' The briefing finished, the Chief pulled from his breast pocket a large Havana cigar, the air filling with a mixture of hand rolled leaf and machined tobacco, Candy's black-Russians, a little insignificant next to the Chief's big brother.

'Well that was quick' said Annabel, again showing no restrain in revealing much of her sensuality as she rose from her chair. As the three companions removed themselves from the table, the unmistakable barking voice of Candy assured both Richard and Borcan that they would get little time to rest over the following hours. 'See here gentlemen I would be grateful if you could both accompany me to corridor 26, there is a little matter of a blockage in that vicinity, and I just wondered if our Alien friend could illuminate our physicists on the craft's structure? Indeed would it be possible to relocate your craft in an area less intrusive, say the inside of the hanger?'

Richard stared into the dead eyes of Candy, completely void of any life, they contained a darkness without clarity. Smug bastard, thought Richard, he has authority, and as we have to work with him tonight, we may as well pander to his wishes, 'OK Colonel, lead the way, but remember our Alien friend has an interview with Lieutenant Borncastle at 1400hrs, and you wouldn't want him to miss that would you?'

Candy looked Richard up and down and after shaking his head in a sarcastic manner replied, 'No I wouldn't my boy.'

Everyone now left the eating hall, there being little conversation between any of the team, as they all awaited transport to their respective rooms. Corridor 26 remained under armed surveillance, the Nagosel craft as intact as ever. Seated on a bench some five metres away from the craft were the two physicists Candy had so kindly asked to meet at 10am. It was now fifteen minutes past midday, and obviously the two men were not amused with the lack of punctuality. 'Look here, Colonel' the smaller of the two men unable to restrain his anger, 'We do have other priorities in this complex and two hours is money down the drain.' Candy in his usual blunt fashion gave little respect to the issue and barked 'Gentlemen you are damn well paid in this establishment, and if sitting on your butts is too much trouble then perhaps you should work alongside me, as it is highly likely those butts would then become part of a glutinous mass after our Beasts had ripped you apart.' Candy then asked the two armed guards to go somewhere and grab a bite to eat.

The humming from the craft had ceased, but its presence in corridor 26 seemed unreal, it was half in this dimension and half in another. The strangest thing appeared to be the lack of Density, the mercurial colour alive, and to all intents and purposes shifting like a slow moving sand. There was no supporting legs and besides the apparent doorway, no markings whatsoever. A strange voice suddenly drifted into Candy's thoughts, neither harsh nor sweet but quite understandable. It was of course Borcan's 'Would you wish to see inside my friend, and of course your two scientists? For I doubt either would understand the craft's workings in such a short time? No need to speak, just reply with your thoughts, and I shall receive.'

Borcan then made his way to the triangular doorway. Borcan's hand alone, was the 'Key' to open the hatchway, touching the Blue Crystal the interior 'Timelock' revealed the craft's inner door. Candy and the two scientists then followed Borcan into the interior. Richard utilised the bench seat, he had knowledge of a star traveller, and there would be little point to a further inside inspection. Across from his seat was room 13, here was the 'Zenith mapping', all manner of satellite and defence aerial technology would here be watched and kept under a 24hr surveillance. Any 'unknown' entering 'International Airspace' would at once be detected, and by this means UFOs were also trackable. Richard had watched many a UFO splash down into the waters about the British coastline, but these 'Objects' were not of Extra-Terrestrial origins. He had yet to visit the secretive 'Seabed' Research Base, known to some Wonderland personnel as simply 'Deep Waters'. Jefferson had been given the opportunity once, mainly because of his psychic abilities, there being much undiscovered territory down there, and one or two 'odd artefacts'. However Jefferson had politely declined, a foreboding, an inner crawling fear which Jefferson described as Malignant Desolation, lie waiting in caverns beneath the seabed rock. He felt such an 'abomination' had been sealed there by 'Space Gods' and although not the Beast of Genesis, twas far worse.

Richard postulated upon the 'Crystal tapes' he and Jefferson had 'Experienced' whilst on Nilrem. If such an Evil mass were below the seabed floor then it could hardly be a remnant of 'Naasbite', nor a product from the unions of Anti-bodies with Earth's elementals. Perhaps the answer would be found in one of the three books provided by Borcan, it was a possibility. He looked at his watch, twenty minutes had passed and the corridor remained silent. He never had liked this corridor, it housed not only 'Mummies' but a freezer full of Alien bodies. Oh, he had seen some, but they were Angelic beings in comparison to those ghastly Mondemons. In the interest of science it was 'ethical' to quickly freeze the 'Alien bodies' as our earthly physics would have decomposed their cells rather alarmingly, as the recent post-mortem on the Nagosel-runaways quickly proved.

Room 3, Zombie Cells was rather aptly named. There could be no doubt that these six different bodies were once part of the 'Brotherhood of Light' as portrayed by the Nagosels. It was like a giant jigsaw puzzle which only now began piecing itself together for Richard. Wonderland had debris from a number of crashed saucers and a number of minute 'intact craft' which had been captured at different periods, around the 'Stonehenge monument'. Itself being a 'landing structure' for ancient 'mother-ships' hence its power source within the stones. If only these UFO-Buffs and 'Druids' knew the real truth thought Richard, and as for 'Merlin' well Nilrem had put him wise to that ancient figure. The 'Acets' Branch however appeared to be in the dark when it came to historical legends, and indeed upon the Universal-Matric. Richard was beginning to understand the wise words of Borcan. 'To release such knowledge, would open man's soul to the direst agencies of space', and yet had 'Merlin' left behind three of these dangerous books in some hidden forgotten place? For as his psychic friend Jefferson had rightly said 'There are some of us whose dreams are the 'Visions of Truth' and the sensitive has seen these hidden places.'

Still, all good thoughts have to come to an end, for Candy Peterson's voice would indeed wake up the dead. There being little time to linger in subconscious territory whilst he was within earshot. 'Richard my boy, seems we have to put up with this damned craft a little while longer. 'Our Alien friend has a convincing way with words, I have seen all I need, I am a Military man not a HG Wells enthusiast. For now the Traveller shall remain, with a guard. Only yourself and this Borcan have access, I shall now grab some sleep to prepare for tonight's scenario.'

Borcan sealed the craft's door again, his telepathic voice assuring Richard that many of the Universal secrets remained hidden, though the earthly scientists had gained deeper insight into Time travel and its dimensional matrix. He, Borcan had persuaded the Colonel that relocation of the traveller above ground would not be a good idea. There might be a risk of virus contamination and he would not wish to take this plague back to Nilrem. Borcan then accompanied his friend to the transporter rail, explaining little knowledge would be released when conversing with the American Borncastle. But by reading the Lieutenant's mind, much would be gained. And a few questions concerning other 'Outside forces' would perhaps indicate their origins and purpose for visiting Earth. Clearly Nilrem knew of no such visitors, at least not from the 32 lifeforms of the 'Trinity'. Therefore Richard my friend, we can only assume such visitors are from another Universe, the question being which one? Richard had little time to answer, the emergence of a transporter from the tunnel network temporarily halting his telepathic awareness. Borcan clumsily obtained a seat, he did not like this mode of travel, clearly the designers of such a conveyance had not planned for large feet, nor his long limbs which earthlings called legs. He noticed too, that the earthly torso which housed the main organs, was considerably larger and longer than a Nagosel's, but this could possibly be explained by the difference in Timescale?

'Corridor 2 gentlemen' shouted the driver, or 'pilot' as he was called in Wonderland. 'I believe the new gentlemen wished to get off here?' Borcan just nodded, it was not wise to reveal telepathic abilities to everyone. Richard understood and looking at his newly acquired wristwatch pointed to three o'clock. Borcan again nodded, indicating to Richard by a thumbs up. He would see him at that time. Richard had earlier expressed a wish to watch the removal of the face-mask by Annabel Foster, as a precautionary measure against Borcan not adjusting to Earth's timescale. Getting out of the transporter appeared to be easier than getting in, thought Borcan. A puzzlement which he decided he would analyze later. He watched as Richard disappeared into the tunnel and on to corridor 18, room 15. The Nagosel shoes made no noise whatsoever on the complex floor, they neither gave off vibration nor received it. Being formed from a similar synthetic to the one used on the floor inside a Time traveller, they would never wear out either. The long sudden strides soon brought Borcan to room 18, there were no American specials awaiting his approach, which gave the immediate impression to Borcan, that he was just a bit too early for this arranged meeting.

DARK RITUALS LONG FORGOTTEN

Borcan could perceive no thoughts emanating from inside the room and considered it wise to enter and wait. The door handle turned evenly and without much effort at all, swung inwardly to reveal the briefing area. A chalkless blackboard, some three feet in diameter occupied a central position to the rear of the room, overshadowing this and hugging tightly to the full length of the right hand wall, a large containment of books. A 'miniature library' neatly stacked on various shelving and the whole protected from humidity by sliding glass partitions. Titles ranged from 'Himalayan Secrets' to 'Seabed Monoliths'.

A Title in gold lettering seemed misplaced amongst its companions. 'The Grimoire of the Gate of Azain', a powerful source of active-sigils and Sentient-symbols, supporting books such as 'True-astronomy and the Stars' and various works on human psychology. Borcan was curious, and there was no apparent sign of Borncastle as yet, so why not take a look. The protective glass partition slid easily along the track, and unlike most library shelves, this row of assorted literature was rather loosely stacked. He was careful not to dislodge any of the other books as he lifted the volume from its place of rest. The leaves were of a rusty colour and their composition was of metal rather than paper or its substitutes. Where did mankind obtain such a book thought Borcan? Further study showed signs of a link between the 'Els' his own Ancestors, and numerous Denizens which he knew inhabited tunnels within this Universal tree. But an alarming number of Denizens or 'Haunters of the Deep' he personally had never been aware of. There must be a Repository of space books somewhere upon this planet thought Borcan, but where, and whom brought them down from the stars? Someone had obtained information from the Crystal Library, but how would they have conveyed such secrets to earth without a star traveller? But wait there was still yet a further book, though not embossed in gold, its Title also held a fascination, and perhaps the answer. Replacing the Book on the Dark Gateway, and sliding back the glass partition Borcan just managed to reach the top shelf, his height enabling him to do so. This partition appeared heavier than the last, but finally slid across its track. The reach stretched his long arms, but his efforts were rewarded as the book fell away from its stacking. The heavy black book contained some three hundred and sixty pages, each treatise eloquently written in forty pages, there being nine chapters in all. Written on the inside cover of the book in bold red lettering were the words:

'This book is the haunt of darkness, let those whom read it immerse themselves in conscious terror!'

Then followed a list of chapters, of which it was said by the author were 'Dimensional keys' in Anacryptic form. And therein each treatise of each chapter, the 'Forbidden speech' to call forth other worlds and their dark inhabitants. The title of the book being 'Mirrors of Darkness' and the professed Author no other than 'Merlin' himself. A smile came to the lips of the Nagosel, truly his Elder Nilrem had used well his time spent on earth. But his smile was also an indication that very few earthlings would be within grasp of de-coding the 'power-words' and 'Sigils'. Indeed, few earthlings would view such speech with a 'third eye'. But those whom were mystical would find the main 'Key' within the title/ Merlin had lived for 1200yrs on earth, returning to his home planet on the year of the great spider. His magic mirror had enabled his long life, and still hidden within a cave stands a time-generator'.

With no sign of the Lieutenant, Borcan acquired a chair adjacent to the blackboard. Facing the chair toward the briefing room door and settling into a comfortable prose, he turned the old yet intact leaves to the chapter entitled *'Oometcinus'*. The figure of this chapter always reminding Borcan of two intertwined serpents. The writing had faded in certain places, yet was distinctive to the trained eye, the treatise talked upon the 'Two creative fires', the *'Omegra'* 'The Outside Master Existing as God in Radiant Atoms'. And the *'Allfhar'* 'The Ancient Lords Life Force His Ascending Reality'. The chapter began, 'All is a particle born from the mass, all is born from the mass. The vibrating 'particles' of a positive and negative nature are it's 'Life'. No thing is known and yet nothing is unknown. I am all that is, and all that is is me. The mind is the quicksilver of space, not being bound by physical laws, that is, not being clothed in matter. The mind freely travels spacetime, collecting knowledge and returning to 'Reform'. Much of this 'knowledge' is *rarely* obtained by the 'Incarnate-Brain' as the levels of Vibrationary-consciousness are subdued by Man's preoccupation with 'Material Forces' 'Tis sleep that reveals such secrets, for only then is the 'Illusory-world' shut off from man, and his 'Vibratory-consciousness' increased. Magicians use 'Rituals', Occultists use power words, and Mystics their Meditation. All useful to increase Vibratory levels and true awareness of other worlds. Words are Vibration and therefore Creative, being more so with 'Desire', the true will. In this treatise are such words of power, let thy 'desire' be positive if thou would use them. A negative approach is the way of madness and the 'Shells'. (Qlipoth).

'Vibration' has two forms, that of 'Positive' *Attraction* and that of 'Negative'. *Attraction,* choose them wisely. The flame within your Form, and within many others, vibrates with the two creative fires, the *'Allfhar'* (the positive) and the *'Omegra'* (the negative). By intensifying their Vibration, by the stated means or by the 'Power-Words' spoken aloud, or intone, many doors 'will be opened'. *Such Doors never to be closed.* Once contact has been made it remains. Be not afraid at this point however, for even now things stir. Tis the Sublimety of Words that is Magic! Knowest then that the *Soul* (The Substance Of Universal Light) is a 'Flame' of wondrous colour, gaining its 'Virtues', its lifeforce by the 'Channelling of Rays'. Rays which can be obtained from other life forms. Rays which bombard all Universes, and Rays brought down from the Constellation of Stars at the Time of your Birth or Incarnation.

Emotion such as Anger, or Hatred, can make this 'Flame-volatile', and the consequences can be fatal and damaging to your earthly form, by ways of 'Overheating' and 'Higher vibrationary levels, *Too quickly obtained.'* Earthly passions of a 'Sexual Nature' also channel rays from one flame to another. 'Tis the Mastery of Sex Magic' which channels forth 'Space Teachings' to the 'Adepts'. The 'Kalic-rays' which inhibit womankind each lunar month possess the necessary Vibrations to 'Attract' 'Outside Forces'.)Such secretions contain much power). To create, to 'achieve one's will', one must either use the Fire of *'Allfhar'* or the Fire of *'Omegra'*. *Nothing* will be achieved by using both for the same results. A Ritual for both is hereby written, if the Words of Power are found, then repeat them to chant, standing within thy 'Circle'. And by wearing an 'Amulet' about the neck with either the word *'Allfhar'* or *Omegra'* written, and the accompanying numerological values, much will be 'Intensified'.

THE RITUAL FOR ALLFHAR

To heighten consciousness to its highest level and to open doors to the beyond.

Prepare thee a 'Circle' whose diameter is exactly nine feet. Draw then within this Circle, a second, whose diameter is exactly six feet. The Illustration at B gives adequate information.

    The boundary between both Circle edges shall be written as the 'Abyssmal Consciousness'. To each magnetic point shall be drawn the 'Sigils' as shown. three to each corner. And the words written in black between them. If you are also to use 'Power-words' then additionally write these also between the 'Sigils' but in 'red'. *'You must stand naked, or clothed only in pure silk'* the colour of Saffron. Between your feet, a 'Goat's skull' with this 'Sigil' across its cranium.

      'Sigil' to be inserted from manuscript -(page 185)

    An additional 'Sigil' also the same is to be painted between thine eyebrows. The time of the Rite must be three minutes to midnight, preferably on a stormy winter's night. The only light provided must be four candles of black colour, each positioned just outside the outer circles, and close to the magnetic points as shown.

    Write then and only then, *'Your three main desires'* upon either a 'virgin parchment' (Papyrus) or a Metal amulet. Previously engraved with the name of the Creative fire and its figurative value (an orgasmic-Incantation upon these Amulets 'Three days' before the rite would give the Rite much 'Potency') Then say the following:

> I call upon thee Almighty Spirit and Guardian
> of All planetary forms. To protect this form
> this night, from these darker angels, whose light is
> not of your making.'

'I seek only the pathway to knowledge and its
understanding. I seek not to destroy or cause ill of
being to those beings whom share my Karmic-
Life.'

Then reading from the virgin parchment which lay in front of you,
(to be written in red ink) turn first to the North Pole or Gate and say:
'I call forth the Great Guardian of the Abyss, by the name 'Shugal
Choronzon'. I call thee. You are the Key to the first Gate of Mind
and Matter. Open thy Gate oh Beast! Then chant the name 'Allfhar
nine times only, before repeating the phrase. I call Forth and so on.

Move next to the South-pole or Gate and read aloud. 'I call forth
'Samael', the Great One of old, whose task it is to show the hidden
places of Knowledge. By the name 'Samael' I call Thee. You are the
Key to the second gate 'Desire and Understanding'. Open thy Gate
Oh Demon!' Then chant slowly 'Allfhar' nine times only, before
repeating the phrase: 'I Call Forth and so on.

Move next to the East pole or Gate, being careful not to move the
'Goat-skull' at all costs. And staying within the internal-circle. Now
say 'I call forth 'Lillith' She whom guardeth the third Gate of
pleasure and understanding. By the name 'Lillith' I call Thee. You
are the third Key to the Secrets of Love. Open thy Gate Oh Whore.
Then chant as before the Name of the creative fire and repeat the
phrase, I Call Forth until completion. Finally, turn to the West pole
or Gate and say: 'I call thee Forth 'Tanith' Serpent of Astral Light,
the Dragon of the Deep. By the name 'Tanith' I Call Thee. You are
the Key to the fourth Gate of occult teachings and Symbols. Open
Thy Gate oh Great Serpent (Again chant as before, and repeat as
then indicated.)

A useful indication of this Rite succeeding is the sudden
extinguishing of each candle after each Call. A Tempest, a great
storm will present itself, ignore this and any other 'Visitors'. Ask
your questions in a firm voice, do not quiver or they will use this
weakness against you. They can be frightening spectres but they will
not cross the Circle and the 'Skull' is your strongest Ally. Your
Amulet too will keep you from harm, but 'Beware' any tiredness,

there must be no break in your assertiveness. After receiving knowledge from these beings, ask them to depart in the following manner:

'I Give thanks to All of Thee
For this Knowledge and opened doorway
I now give thee Licence to depart,
Close thy Gates and ways of Entrance.
In the Name of the Great Guardian
Whose Light forever Shineth Brightly
I ask Thee to depart.

Remain in the Circle for a good length of time, touch not the 'Skull' until the hour of the cock crow, for it is now a storage for much Occult Power. The room must not be used again for three days, for there is a great danger of Cerebral Stagnation, the room now filled with unwanted Vibratory influences. Leave the Circle intact, but remove the 'Skull' at the appointed time and cover it with a piece of unused Dark cloth. Guard it well, for it is now a source of 'Contact' and 'must not perish'. The increasing power will soon become obvious.

THE RITUAL FOR OMEGRA

To initiate Contact with all manner of 'Denizens' and 'Dimensional Beings' and to open Doorways of the Mind and 'Bridge' the crossing between Matter and Spiritual Awareness. This Rite once begun must be finished. Ignore all Supernatural-disturbance.

Prepare then a Circle, its diameter nine feet exactly. Then draw a 'Pentagram' within an inner-circle, its diameter eight feet exactly. Ensure the five points of the Pentagram do not break the first inner-boundary. Refer to Illustration 'A' Using the 'Sigils' as shown, (To be drawn in red) Carefully ensure they are in the exact positions as shown, with the 'Sigils' touching both Circle circumference.

Next write the 'Power words' between each 'Sigil' do this in blue ink. Spread a fine layer of sand around the outer circle, six inches across. Prepare four silver or copper goblets or vessels.

1.   Fill the Northern goblet with an equal mixture of blood, urine and wine, adding three ounces of sulphur before mixing. (The blood and urine are to be extracted from thyself).

2.   Fill the Southern goblet with Seaweed, a dead frog or toad and stagnant water, collected from a remote lake or pond.

3.   Fill the Eastern goblet with Frankincense, Cedarwood, four feathers and the head of a bird, preferably a Raven.

4.   Fill the Western goblet with Earth, an acorn and rotten flesh.

These preparations are necessary to 'make contact', yet there is no Sacrificial aspect to either Rite. The light in the room will be provided by three candles of a red wax, and these must be positioned nine feet away from the edge of the sand. And in direct line with the Apex point of the Pentagram. (Which every good occultist knows, should be facing the Northern Gateway).
Stand the candles in a horizontal line, with three inches between each, see Illustration 'A'.

Again as in the 'Allfhar' Rite, the Adept, the 'Enquirer' must be either naked or clothed in pure silk the colour of 'violet'. Between your feet a 'Dagger' with the 'Inscriptions' as shown in the Illustration. It is to be used for the 'Banishment of the Forces' and the 'Opening' of the four Gates as written. An amulet must be worn preferably made nine days before this Rite, better with a full moon t night. Engrave the word 'Omegra' and the 'Sigil' and its 'number' (Numerological value). Also add your three Desires at this time, unlike that of the Rite of 'Allfhar'. Add also to this Amulet the word 'Abrahadabra' the 'Sigil' and its number. Now you are ready, *'Lock all doors into thy house, Thou must not at any point be disturbed. For fear of madness.*

THE RITE OF OPENING EACH GATE (OMEGRA)

The dagger is more potent if made from 'Bone', however any 'Pure' metal can be just as effective. (Ensure the dagger has been wrapped in dark silk, and untouched until this Rite, the Inscriptions being

engraved fifteen days exactly before this Rite, unlike the Amulet) (The opening of the Northern Gate) Be aware of things to Come,
                              - ignore them.
Take thy dagger in thy right hand (always this hand) and point it towards the Northern Gate (It is assumed everything is in preparation as diagrammed, and the Candles lit). Now saying loudly the following, stab at the air with thy dagger (A pointed thrust not a raising of the arm as if to kill).

I call thee, and I invoke thee Oh Master (Shaitan) see thy symbols upon my worldly sphere, engraved the Names that men do fear.'

I Call thee 'Eurynome, Prince of Death, Come fast ride on this Wizard's breath.

I call thee 'Zett' to make the three, the 'Key' to reincarnate thee. (Await the cold, then begin) 'Oh Tempest that does fire from hell, unbind these locks that served thee well. The Gate, the stronghold from the North release the powers to Come Forth. Let the Gate be opened, in the name of 'Omegra' and 'Argemo', Break the Mirror of this Light (Repeat the entirety, three times, always stabbing at the air). Thou shall know of 'Their Arrival' they are 'Fearsome' but be not afraid. Turn then if you must to the South Gate.

(The opening of the South Gate). The Emergence of the 'Deep Ones'. 'Take thy dagger in thy right hand and point it towards the South Gate. Now saying loudly the following, stab at the air with thy dagger (As one draws blood forth from piercing a body, a similar reaction occurs within the Astral sphere, be firm with your intention in mind) Say

> 'I call thee and I invoke thee 'Aowoss' the Elder of that which was gone before but is now.
> I call thee 'Lham' the 'Iggneytorr' of the current that unites.
> I call thee 'Chulltoo' Oh Sleeper of the Deep, Tis in Man's mind thy Tentacles do creep.
> (The candles may extinguish, and a dense darkness prevail).

Thence begin:

> 'The Leapers in the Dark abound, in waters here and
> underground.
> Great Giants of Time from distant past, I call thee Forth to
> live at last.
> Let 'Megramo' 'Argom' 'Omegra' speak, from this
> Wizard's mouth to seek.
> Material Form upon this sphere, I chant this name thence
> you appear.
> 'Armegrom' 'Morggemra' (Chant this name 11 times if
> all remains still, repeat entirety).'**

A Doorway may appear in your room, be not afraid, such things are
to be expected. *But do not leave thy circle or perish the soul.*
(Continue if thou must to the next Gate).

(The opening of the Eastern Gate) The Gate of Wisdom.
'Take thy dagger in thy right hand and point it towards the Eastern
Gate. Now saying loudly the following, stab at the air with thy
dagger.

'I Call thee, and I Invoke thee, Oh 'Isis' thy current sweeps
thy beauty from afar, I call thee by thy Sigils. Here you are!

'I Call thee, 'Osireis' to be reborn, I Call thee here, In thy
New Form.

'For' here are the sands of your 'Offspring Zett.' Come face
to face lest you forget!

'I call thee 'Horus' to make the three, thy Father, thy
Mother, here they be.
(The sands of the outer circle may swirl, 'The breath of Horus' upon
the 'Desert of Zett')
Then say thus:

> 'With the Eye of Ra the Sun God, does the body of
> 'Osireis' Slain now Rise.
> Let his 'KAA' walk upon this Earthly plane, let his light
> shine once again.
> 'With the wings that give Her beauty flight, I call forth the
> current of Isis' this night. Open thy eyes Oh Raven, and see
> thy Destiny.

Let the Four Feathers aid her flight.
Oh thou, the Brother of Zett, whom fought upon the Desert Sands.
Come Forth with the Power of this Dagger,
I hold within my Hands.
Come Forth Oh Horus, splendour of the Night.

Then chant thus, Atem, Setem, Katem, Atem, Setem, Katem, Thou will know when to stop!
(Continue to the Western Gate if thou must, all Gates can be used in the Ritual Or singularly for different reasons of Knowledge).

(The Opening Of The Western Gate) Tis a Gate to Great Power.
'Take thy Dagger in thy right hand, never thy left, unless Madnees be thy friend, and point it towards the Western Gate. Now saying loudly the following, stab at the air with thy dagger
        'I Call thee forth and invoke thee 'Negamphormis' from the Mists of Time. I call thee to this Earthly sphere through this ancient rhyme.

> 'Space Undone, Time Begun,
> I Ne-gam-phormis-en.
> 'Space Begun, Time Undone,
> Negamphormis is Risen.

Repeat, soon the vibrations will be felt.

'I call thee Forth 'Zommsfaron' thy Name once Secret Hidden,
Now come thee Beast, come to my bidding.
I have a task for thee to 'spell', ye whom issues from the Jaws of Hell.
I call thee 'Zommsfaron' with thy 'Sigil' brought to 'Light'
I manifest thee by this dagger, I thrust into the night.'

Now cast this 'Spell' into the 'Darkest Hour' As I call thee 'Sabetasomec' from the Darkest Tower.
'That which rides on Blackest breath, comes from time not from death.
This circle is the wheel that turns, and not the fire from which one burns.
Enter by the 'Key's now shown, the Sigils that you call your own.'

Borcan turned over another rusty coloured leaf, a small paragraph on The Banishment of The Dark Angels, finished the Treatise on Omegra. His face mask was now becoming intolerable, he was perspiring a little too much, yet he dare not risk the removal of the Mask until the Impulse-breathers had been put in place.

A glance at the clock showed the time at 14.30. If Borncastle was to show his face he would have to be quick. Though this 'Grimoire' begged Borcan's attention he would nevertheless have to study the deeper meaning at a more convenient time. 'Nilrem' the Mirrored Merlin had cast little doubt unto the authenticity of this 'Higher-Magic'. Borcan was perhaps duly worried upon whose hands the Black Book had fallen into? The Black Brotherhood and their Shadow forms would be drawn to some of the Rituals. But also, thought Borcan, those Elementals that sought union with 'Naasbites-Legions' were still functioning upon this sphere. And would be eager to please these earthly Magicians, doing so with every intention to manifest their Dark malevolence into the worlds of matter.

Though Borcan and his race bore no external-hearing organs, the visionary organs were highly sensitive to light variations. And the sudden shadow now cast upon the room light alerted him to the presence of Borncastle. The Lieutenant's thoughts displayed no apologetic symmetry, he was late, but had been delayed by news of an Alien craft found intact beneath the sands of the Gobi desert. Thermal imagery had alerted a low flying helicopter of its mass. This was an impressive find for the Acets Branch, as the long cigar shaped craft appeared untouched. Indeed it may even be intact as far as the propulsion unit was concerned. Borcan had read these thoughts, the young Lieutenant's mind being easily accessible.

He returned an answer to the Lieutenant in a polite but firm manner. As always never wishing to frighten a form by quick thought-transference, his voice though somewhat distorted because of the urgent need to wear impulse-breathers, entered the young Borncastle's head at a slower scale than most. 'My friend I shall say this much upon your find. It is a 'needle ship' a scout craft used by a Reptilian race many aeons ago. There was a time when such a race were happy upon your earthly sphere. Twas they whom filled your waters with an abundance of life forms, they came from the planet 'Vrom'. However, another Evil form descended amongst them, and for a while all Star craft and Time generators upon your planet began to lose power. You will find decayed remains of the craft's occupants, there will be no clues as to their build or Bio-chemistry. But you will see tapes and coloured glass which will be useful for your earthly sciences.'

'The Great City of Krasshid has sunken deep beneath your waters, yet two of the four towers which housed the Crystal generators of Time remain active.' Borncastle instantly turned his mind to the Bermuda Triangle. The pieces were now closing in, and he wished he had turned up earlier for this appointment. He would have gained further insight. Looking at the strange masked Alien he thought upon a question, for truly such means of conversation was fast and left one's mouth for more efficient tasks to undertake. 'Have you heard of the Lemurians?' he enquired. Borcan seemed surprised at this question, he stood up, closed the black book of spells and returned it to its original position on the library shelf. Glancing only once at the Lieutenant, he observed the time on the briefing room wall, '14.45 only fifteen earthly minutes remained, strange he should talk upon the Lemurians, thought Borcan. The Lieutenant watched the tall Alien regain his seat, had he by asking this question hit upon another Universal Key? Obviously the Alien was somewhat unnerved by the Implication, Borcan's voice broke the silent waves of thought in Borncastle's mind, it was a weird constructed sound, there was no comparison, just like a ghostly voice reaching out from the depths of some other world.

Borcan continued 'My Lieutenant friend, I know you have much knowledge of other worlds, yet why ask upon the Lemurians, have you conversed with them perhaps?'

Borncastle laughed, and for a while forgot the telepathic conversation, his human voice saying 'You must be joking my Alien friend. It is just that the Acets Branch possess a 'Crystal Tablet' which was given to them by a Tibetan Monk some years ago, and its Inscriptions are indecipherable. The Tibetans claim the LMS or 'Lemus' were once living in an area of mountain peaks close to their Kingdom. In fact there are many records in their manuscripts of the

'Golden ships' seen frequenting the 'Himalayas.' They believe Shamballah is a real City, a City of Light, a Godly Abode. Yet it is hidden by a 'constructed' landscape, an illusory vision, to keep away the eyes of Man.' It was then that Borncastle realised his mistake, the Alien Borcan had no ears, he would have to repeat the damn thing again. 'No wait my earthly friend, I Borcan can read your earthly speech through your thought waves, and I find your lively explanation interesting. No let me say first, the Inscriptions you cannot decipher are not Inscriptions. They are indeed 'Areas' of the mountain range of which you speak. The 'Tablet' is a Map Borncastle, and a clue is the shape of the City you call 'Llhasa'. I can reveal no more, except part of the Crystal is denser than the rest, this is the Area of Illusion my friend.'

The Lieutenant was now on a high, and was about to ask further questions when again the firm voice of Borcan interrupted his thoughts, 'I am sorry Lieutenant, perhaps another time, it is now 1500hrs and I do have an urgent appointment with Miss Foster.' And without further explanation Borcan rose to his feet and strode quickly across the room, out of the briefing room door, and down the corridor towards the Transporter tube. As he waited for the next tube a smile graced his otherwise sombre looking countenance. Perhaps now these earthlings would treat their outside guests with respect and attend such meetings with some sort of punctuality.

THE MEETING IN THE WOODS

Annabel Foster had prepared the instruments needed to fit the Nagosel Impulse-breathers. It would be a straight forward operation, the scars from previous attachments of this device remained as alignments for the insertion of the Two needle like probes. The device was very light, but rather well sealed, as to stop the more inquisitive of eyes from determining its function. Of course, as an inquisitive scientist herself, she had examined the Alien object, with all the latest apparatus at her disposal. But to no avail. The internal spectroscope had revealed only the slightest clue to the object's construction, but the apparent lack of channels or wiring within puzzled Miss Foster. Perhaps Borcan would comment on the workings? The minute microscopic tubes or probes may function as blood ports, which were pumped independently by some strange means. Annabel concluded they assisted the heart in circulation, the bellow type aperture on the top of the breather somehow analyzing the external air levels, and compensating by increasing or reducing heart-pressure and oxygenation to the blood vessels. Or maybe, she postulated, the external bellows on each Impulse-breather was sensitive to the air-pressures put upon it, and acted like a miniature lung? She looked at her watch, ten minutes past three, unusual for Borcan to be late.

But as is common with all of her male admirers Richard had been more than punctual, and had kindly agreed to wait outside the Ops-door for the arrival of Borcan. After all the Security Pass Key was available only to a chosen few, and unfortunately Borcan was not one of them. She lit a cigarette as she waited, the rich flavour of the Galois-blue satisfied her craving. A strong animal current dominated her sexual nature, and although many men had satisfied her abandonment when aroused, she had yet to find a match for her voracious lust and appetite for lovemaking. This was ultimately why marriage was out of the question. A preoccupation with 'positions' appeared more attractive than motherhood. Children to Annabel were best heard but not seen. Women were now liberated, far more than men. And anyway, she was well aware of her womanly attributes, mankind needed her. Before contemplating further along these lines, however, her thoughts on the niceties of life were broken by the entrance of Richard and Borcan. 'Just finish this ciggy' blurted Annabel 'then we will remove that wicked mask from Borcan's face so he can breathe again, and I can look upon his true facial features.' Richard ushered his friend over to a prepared chair. A couple of surgical masks and a flask containing Iodine appeared to be all that was needed to fit the Breathers. Borcan looked at Richard and telepathically asked him for a glass of 'Osiphiel' temporarily forgetting he was on earth, and here it was named water, as he felt overheated and somewhat disorientated. He felt the earthly time was ageing him too quickly. It was time to act. Whilst Richard obtained a glass of water from the purified tanks, Annabel guided her delicate hands into a pair of surgical gloves. A mask would not be necessary but she felt any fluid loss from Borcan could contaminate her skin. Borcan thanked Richard for the 'Osiphiel' and then instructed Annabel to remove the mask with a pair of cutters, as the mask had bonded too tightly to his face. Annabel found a pair of scissors from the surgical tray and proceeded to slowly snip down the back of the mask to avoid any cuts to his facial area. As she cut, Borcan's hands began to shake, his vision became impaired and violet colours filled the laboratory.

A sharp pain began to manifest at the back of his head slowly gaining intensity. At last the mask was removed, Annabel wasted little time on fitting the impulse-breathers. She worked swiftly under Richard's watchful eyes, the fluid loss from Borcan's wrists barely visible. There, they were fitted, all they could do now was wait. 'A cup of coffee Miss Foster?' enquired Richard, 'whilst we leave our friend to adjust to his breathers?'

'Good idea' replied Annabel, removing and then discarding the slightly stained surgical gloves. She glanced back at Borcan, and for the first time she saw the 'strange smile' Richard had often joked about. Indeed as Richard had said, it did appear to resemble a half moon in comparative agony. She laughed aloud and with an unapproachable passion kissed her Alien friend on the cheek. Half an hour elapsed before Borcan decided to regain his feet. Holding onto a nearby table he pulled himself to an almost erect position, a slight dizziness occurred but he felt he had overcome the worst of the transference. He left little doubt in Richard's mind about the state of his wellbeing! 'Two glasses of water please Richard and try to keep the bubbles down!' Richard replied telepathically, that he was only too pleased to get his friend a drink, it proved Borcan was on the way to recovery. Soon the three colleagues in science began the filthy but important task of bisecting the Beast, housed in the containment area. It was now 4.30pm giving Borcan little time to find a destructive element they might use against the Mondemon. A decision was made to close down experimentations on the Beast's tissue at 8pm giving time for a few hours sleep or a hot meal before tonight's planned visit to the woods. Borcan decided on three hours rest, 8pm - 11pm but impressed upon Richard the need for him to awaken Borcan at 11pm, as he Borcan had no doubt the fitting of the impulse-breathers would deepen any sleeping state. Annabel on the other hand would return to the Ops-Lab about midnight, and she and the Chief would prepare an area of Confinement for the captured Mondemon. A task easier said than done.

The transportation of the beast from the hanger entrance to the Ops-Lab would need careful planning, but that was why the Chief was the Chief. Let him accept that responsibility. There would of course be the option of the control centre which was positioned in the centre of all corridors, and hence one of the emergency lifts could be utilised for conveyance of the Beast, instead of using a transporter.

'Oh hell,' thought Annabel, let him, the Chief sort it out. Wonderland remained a 24hr Security Complex, shift patterns guaranteed constant staffing of the more important areas. Trained professional soldiers manned all Exits and Entry points, equipped with rather more than the usual lethal weapons. A large number of rooms in corridor 19 housed the 'Specials', the MOD's finest hand-picked by Colonel Andy Peterson, enlisted at an early age, and retired with a comfortable pension at fifty years. A security check on all of Wonderland's personnel, including Colonel Peterson and the Chief was considered an 'Initiative not to be forgotten', by the Defence Ministry. To eliminate any unwanted surveillance by Foreign Agents or Inquisitive Groups, a civilian police car operated by 'Specials' would monitor the surrounding area within 10 sq. miles. All supplies were generally delivered once a month, usually by ambulance, as it was known locally, the airfield was used as a training ground for some of the Emergency Services. And to keep up the pretence it sometimes was. However because of the plague and its destructive offshoots, a military presence around the area was considered normal, leaving Wonderland perfectly hidden beneath its airfield watchdog.

Across the world the Mondemon fever had reached a critical level. Wherever it was possible, groups of ordinary people built large protective fires around their homes, most of the tropical islands were considered dead territory as the trade winds had carried Mondemon deep into their habitat. Increasingly, large amounts of people were flown to 'Safe areas' in the more mountainous regions. The lack of forests and community dwellings preventing the Mondemon from establishing any residence there. Instead the Military and foreign engineers had built emergency underground shelters. Crudely fashioned out of hundreds of goods containers, taken from dockyards or heavy goods units. Underground tube stations or any tunnel networks now came under Military command and were provided with emergency Air filters to prevent the spread of the plague. For those of mankind whom were unlucky to gain entrance to these improvised shelters, there was little left except death by fire or transformation. A number of local citizens would join the Military, though their chance of survival were slim, as more and more plague mutants transformed into the flying Beasts, ensuring more airborne attacks on those not yet succumbed to the plague spores.

At night in the major areas of Infestation, howls of hideous rapture saturated the heart with unclean thoughts. In the forest, in the thickly wooded hills that skirt the larger towns, dark inhuman shapes crept in sinister fashion amongst the rocks and broken passages that lead into some dark subterranean world. They fed on their own kind, like some cannibalistic nightmare, one felt sorry for some of these transformed wretches. Night flying Mondemon was rarely seen, it was their time of rest, to indulge their appetite, to slowly drain the blood fluids from their hosts. There was a kind of intelligence there, though there appeared to be no leaders amongst them. In daylight they would take to the air, amassing in their hundreds, dark assassins winging their way back to the places of conquest, to find new hosts and battle for a new Mondemon world. Exmoor, though heavily populated by Mondemon, retained a considerable number of plant species, though some genetic-transformation had taken place. Those of the poisonous variety, such as deadly nightshade and Vervain now growing in abundance. Therefore, masks and chemically sealed suits were essential when visiting such areas. The productive plague spores and rotting flesh contributing to a highly toxic and virulent atmosphere. The plague however could only be contracted by the close proximity to a plague victim or transforming mutant. The 'Spores' being released into the air at every new transformation of the host's body. Like microscopic thistles the airborne spores then enter a virgin form by either the breathing channels or the naked skin itself

Hence the 'Monster Demon' was considered evil in two ways. If the spores didn't transform you, then the Mondemon, the 'Monster Demon' would tear away your flesh and consume large parts of the internal organs and completely drain the living essence of life, the spiritual blood. The rains had stopped and the wet filthy roads glistened with the recent droppings of a beast. Green translucent patches of slime, containing undigested pieces of bone and gristle. The light of the moon illuminating the scene and casting any conscious doubts of illusory horror into the reality of conscious terror. As darkness veiled the little villages with its subtle curtain of malevolent intrusion, tiny fires began to spring up far and wide. Sleep amongst the living became an unwanted nature, fear was predominant and death appeared to be the only real method of escape. Inside the three armoured personnel carriers, last minute checks were being made. Sergeant Matthews shaking his head at the newly installed partition in his vehicle. The area converted behind the new partition now housed a number of live animals. A dog and two cats lay still, their eyes rapidly moving in an uncertain rhythm as though searching for something which to them was an Harbinger of Death. The personnel entrance door now becoming the trapdoor of containment, once the Mondemon was safely inside the carrier. The extra reinforced shell would prevent the beast from bashing its way out or into the driver's compartment, but Matthews had little doubt about the animal's future.

He was a trained weapons specialist, the Laser gun would prove its efficiency in Mondemon decapitation, he was sure of that. At least until an affective capture had been initiated. Sporting a well groomed moustache and a cliffhanger chin, his huge powerful shoulders and thick muscular neck, left no doubt to his prowess in the combined art of Judo wrestling. Fifteen years as a 'Special' had placed him in the Columbian jungles, the sensitive watchtowers of Tibet and the undersea base known as 'Deep Waters'. He had Ansai's respect, he was all Military, marriage had never presented itself and children he could do without. In fact the only female he ever really loved had deserted him for another. Life had been good so far, that is before this bloody plague. Anyhow, what's the use of worrying he thought, die if you worry, die if you don't. A last adjustment to the Laser guidance system and a quick glance at the fuel gauge and oil pressure, assured him of a trouble free run to the forest and back. At least in the way of engine mechanics. Looking at his wristwatch and feeling rather dry-mouthed, the idea of a quickie sandwich and a steaming black coffee decided his next steps. Inside the hanger, above ground a small marquee had been provided for tonight's participators. Beside himself there would be three others. Four Sergeants in all, and a jolly good bunch too. Security had been tightened above ground, two heavily armed patrols guarded the carriers, and ever watchful for the presence of Mondemon, though at night no attack would be considered unusual. The time was 22.30 pm. The Major and his entourage would not be surfacing from below until at least 23.30 pm, so Matthews and colleagues settled around a portable gas fire, playing with an old set of cards belonging to Sergeant Cork, an ex royal marine. 'Pretty strong stuff eh?' said Cork, pointing directly at the first overturned card.

'Not my sort of Gal at all,' replied Matthews. 'A bit too big on top and as for her legs, well I guess I've seen thicker cricket stumps.' Both men referring to the explicit poses on the adult playing cards purchased by Cork,. whom as a young marine, loved spending leave in the more seedier of areas. Saigon at that time

126

providing endless girlie bars and massage parlours for the pleasure seeking soldier. Turner and 'Bronx' as he was affectionately known, said very little, more content playing their hands between sips of black coffee and the rolling of emergency cigarettes for their respective tobacco tins. Both were 'Mature Specials' the juniors looking up to them for advice and sometimes assistance when things got out of hand. Bronx was a muscular macho type, whereas Turner was renowned for his 'Jekyll and Hyde' type character. The former being a 'Karate' expert, and the latter having ten years service in the Special Fraud Squad.

All four men had set their wristwatches on 'Alarm mode' ensuring that at 23.30hrs they would be ready for the arrival of the Major and Colonel Peterson. Each would drive his own carrier. Matthews taking Major Ansai and four combat soldiers, Cork taking Colonel Peterson, four combat soldiers and a further unit of flame throwers. Bronx would carry Borcan and Richard, whilst Turner, a handyman where bombs were concerned, would accompany the latter two as far as possible into the Beasts lair. A special cache of grenades had been prepared for him, acting at first like an incendiary bomb, a heat sensitive trigger would then explode a lethal cocktail of Titanium fragments, and Cyanide pellets. His secondary defence consisted of a rapid fire sub machine gun, especially modified for the Specials, allowing the quick attachment of an armour piercing barrel and larger shell cartridges. Borcan and Richard being only protected by their Alien boxes, the need in limitations in weapons for these two because of the weight of the Arm launchers. Holding some fifteen feet of webbing each, once in position for capture, the two webs would be linked together and then fired as one. An additional fitting to Matthews carrier would prove invaluable, some fifty feet of steel-cable wound tightly around a motorised drum, would be released like a 'Harpoon' and targeted at the Titanium webbing enclosing the Mondemon. The plan being, to rewind the attached cable and drag the captured Mondemon up and into the prepared containment area. Such was the quick brief, given by Major Ansai some hours earlier. There had been no questions from either of the four sergeants, for they had all experienced the flying beasts at close quarters and fear was even now a more predominant word.

Major Ansai was their Father, their Teacher, his command unshakeable. They knew he would not ask them to go into Hells-arena, if there was some alternative to the forthcoming eventuality. A loss of fifty percent of tonight's task force had been estimated, and such a figure would no doubt include the four card players.

Still, they had a 'Motto' Bronx and the others, and it was quite simply this, 'I fear not the Unknown, Only the obtaining of it'. It was a motto the Specials held in high regard, the emblem of their particular branch bearing: '*A mythical beast devouring the tree of knowledge*'. For it was said, We all taste of Good and Evil, but we know little of what we digest? As was the usual undertaking before battle commenced, Matthews produced a flask from inside his jacket pocket, and quite properly bid each of his friends to participate in a sip or two. Rum was the order of the day, it was all Matthews liked to drink. ' 'Black Jamaica' me old chums, warms the cockles of the heart and burns like hell.' He smiled, but not too intensely, as he was aware humour was now a quality best left to the comedians in life, around the corner could be death. He looked at his wristwatch, it showed 23.20, he motioned to play a quick game of cards, his friends agreed' Pontoon' blurted Bronx. 'Ain't played that one for ages.' The cards were dealt, and they managed to squeeze in eight plays. Turner winning the last round with a Black Ace of Spades, and a Black Queen of Spades. The sound of four wristwatches and the Internal lift surfacing, awakening them all to the darkness that lay ahead. The rather abrupt voice of Colonel Peterson stood them to attention, he was disliked by the Combat units, and at times irritated the Specials with his *I'm the Boss* attitude, never being a diplomatic fellow, even at the craziest of parties. However he had seen the raw evils of life and his years as a mercenary more than educated the man in the field of strategy and thus he had to be deserved of some respect. Oh Bronx had hit him on numerous occasions, but Candy as his friends called him could be a raging bull and retaliate without compassion. Bronx learned his lesson the hard way, but considered Candy less of a man than his card playing companions. 'Gentlemen, Or should I say 'Hardmen?' the big man boomed. 'I believe the good Major has enlightened you upon the task ahead of us. I am sure I can rely on your full support. Each man will be issued with a 'Remote phone', basically to alert the Major of your impending deaths. I have no immediate plan at the moment, however a hands on situation, as you know, will cause some spontaneous genius to issue from me at the vital time. So let's start those damn motors and go kick shit, as our American allies so quaintly put it. Richard has a bag of phones, so grab one and move.'

The little task force moved off silently into the night, the newly fitted engines complimenting the latest in soundproof engineering. Ansai's carrier keeping a marginal distance behind the other two, was more vulnerable to attack as the speed and manoeuvrability of the vehicle was much reduced, due to the added weight of the steel cable drum and the additional Laser. 'All lights on low beam Major and perhaps just as well Sir, considering the bloody mess littering the roads.' Matthews voice echoed through the living machine but played little upon the ears of the combat crew. They sat like zombies, unmoved, calculating and shut off from the real world. All wore the chemical suits sealed at the wrist and neck by means of a bonding spray. Gloves and face mask would be attached when entering a contagious zone or indeed when under attack from Mondemon. Ansai felt their apprehension, understood their fear, but at the end of the day they were all soldiers, and as such prepared to lay down their life for brother man. Ansai checked the condition of the livestock, a slight condensation showed on the glass window. Poor things, the condemned were breathing rather heavily. Ansai then regained his seat and switched on the radio transmitter. 'Calling Blue Dog One, calling Blue Dog One, Over.' His message received loud and clear by Blue Dog One. A reply was quickly administered 'Hello Blue Dog Three, this is Blue Dog One, Over. Just twenty minutes from houseparty, repeat just twenty minutes from houseparty.'

'Relay to Blue Dog Two, Over.'

'Roger Blue Dog One, good luck.' Ansai then relayed a message to Bronx 'Calling Blue Dog Two, calling Blue Dog Two, Over.' A sharp crackling proceeded the recognisable voice of Richard. 'Hello, Blue Dog Two here, is there a problem, Over?'

'No problem Blue Dog Two, but prepare for houseparty, Over.'

'Thanks Blue Dog Three, fitting rest of suit, mobile on exit, Over.'

'Roger, Blue Dog Two, Roger and out.'

The village fires some miles distant, lit up the surrounding countryside. Matthews counted maybe six or seven good burners, glowing in the darkness like a runway to oblivion. He would have to turn off soon, down a little unused farmtrack, which would eventually lead into the heart of the forest. Bronx and Cork would have already turned onto this trail, switching off their headlights and relying heavily on the moonlight, and glow from Mondemon slime, dripping amidst the woods about them. Exmoor Forest, once a haunting ground for gypsies and magical covens now lay open its arms to a more abominable following. A thin mist hung low in the forbidden trees, the filthy remnants of a feast and numerous plague-infested organisms let rise to a poisonous vapour. In whose cloud the Elementals of the air would form, and cast their unclean thoughts into the hearts of men.

'Stop here Sergeant,' the familiar bark of Colonel Peterson's voice left one in no doubt whom was in charge. 'Right pull off the damn road, and then switch off any existing lights.' Cork did as commanded, avoiding the steep embankment to his right by a few feet. 'I have a plan gentlemen, but make no mistake, it's bloody dangerous and those whom survive this can get bloody drunk on my expense, if and when they return to base. On masks and gloves, you too Cork, and switch on the remote phones.' When all were properly attired the Colonel pushed hard against the door lever, causing the two restraining bolts to rise, and thus releasing the mechanism holding back the heavy reinforced tailgate. Cork followed out after the last of the flame throwers. He had witnessed a degree of destruction against the Mondemon, with these weapons, but such victories were shortlived, the flying Mondemon ripping the gas containers from the backs of soldiers and leaving them engulfed in flames. Their agility in the air and speed of flight was awesome, an attack by hundreds of these beasts was usually in their favour. To capture one tonight, and alive, would be some miracle. Everything relied on Richard and that Alien to pull it off, though what the little boxes were for he could only wonder.

An abrupt voice through his earphone startled his line of thoughts. 'Cork, Sergeant, can you hear me?'

'Yes Sir, sorry Sir, I was jut about to close the tailgate.'

'Then do it, and listen. Blue Dog Two will soon be on the scene, and I want you Cork to stay put and tell them to wait for my signal for a capture. I and my colleagues shall create a defensive position along the perimeter of this embankment, giving covering fire on Borcan and Richard's return. I shall position a flame thrower every fifty feet, with an additional grenade launcher for back up. Thereby giving a ground defensive area of two hundred feet. I'm now going, tell Richard to move when I radio 'Redlight' and lastly tell Bronx to get off the bloody road, so Blue Dog Three has a clear runway to harpoon the Beast, and then tear arse out of there, got it?'

'Yes Sir, Colonel Sir.' Cork watched the disappearance of his Colonel, a bastard at the best of times, but when in the field, a bloody good soldier, a Mercenary in fact. The time was approaching 0130hrs and the lights from Bronx's carrier now made themselves visible. Cork looked nervously at the sky, there was no sign of them. Hopefully they were resting, it was doubtful they suffered with a bad gut from over eating, but one could wish. The distance to the outer edge of the forest was, in Cork's view, about quarter of a mile. Unfortunately it looked like the three men in Bronx's carrier would have to walk this.

A CAPTURE AND A LOSS

Blue Dog Two came to a halt, the red flag waving in the wind preventing further movement. The top hatch of Blue Dog Two pushed forcefully upwards by a large muscular Bronx. He was followed out by Richard and Borcan, Turner making some last minute adjustments on his special grenades. 'Sorry to stop you buddy, but you know the Colonel, seems he wants your carrier out of the road. Part of the plan. And unless Blue Dog Three wants to give you a lift Richard, you're walking in there.' Cork quickly explained Candy's plan. It seemed ambitions but all agreed it might just work.

'OK let's go for it' said Richard, 'but remember I doubt either of us or Sergeant Turner will be able to remove one of the wings. So please tell your Sergeant Matthews to steam in there on my word. If he is as good as I've heard with weaponry, he should be able to decapitate a wing when the bloody monster is being winched in, and that word for steaming in will be 'Harpoon'. Borcan assures me we will both be protected by the 'Boxes' around our waists, but if the Beast manages to move within the webbing, we will both be dragged with him. Good luck,' and with that Blue Dog Two moved out.

'Well, seems we are out of the action for a while buddy' Bronx clearly getting some irritation from his mask as he spoke, his large hand scratching his face quite briskly. 'Damn beard growth, should of shaved closer, always itching in these bloody things. Guess I had better start her up and move her off the road, then you and me can prepare a little welcome of our own for those Beasties.' Bronx said no more. Sergeant Cork knew exactly what Bronx had in mind. Both carriers were fully armed, a 'Mini-gun' using armourlite shells was positioned on the front and rear of each vehicle. Both weapons being remote controlled from inside. A short range missile launcher, capable of surface to air targeting gave additional support, each of the six missiles having a range of three miles. Ansai had however ordered both men to use weaponry sparingly, as on the return to base there would be no support for the carriers, either from the air or any other means. Therefore keep something in reserve he had said. Cork, now seated back into his driving chair, observed the rest of Blue Dog

Two as they cautiously manoeuvred their way along the old farm road. Through his field binoculars he could just make out another movement on the outer edge of the forest. It was a Mondemon and it appeared to be looking at Blue Dog Two. Shit, where was Ansai?'

'Has he seen us Richard?' asked Turner ducking into some undergrowth for cover.

'No I think he was looking at the glow from a village fire, some miles to the left of us. If he had seen us I'm sure the others would have been alerted, but he just seems intent, maybe mesmerised by the colour. Let's move in a bit further, it's my feeling if we can fire this webbing at two Mondemons or even three, we have a better chance of catching one. Let's face it we have only one shot.'

'OK Richard, we will play it your way. But let me create a diversion first, that way their attention will be drawn towards me, then you go grab one.' Richard gave the thumbs up, it might even the odds. The trio then kept close to the trees, avoiding any further glances from the Mondemon. Nothing more being said as they covered another hundred yards, then the noises of evil revelry became distinct. They were nearing a small encampment, some fifty or so Mondemons appeared to be ravaging at a large indefinite host.

It was hard to see clearly and one's mind worked overtime in the semi-darkness. There was little doubt about their insatiability for blood, as streams of the life giving essence was eagerly lapped and sucked upon, by their monstrous mouths. That which wasn't taken immediately by mouth, was ripped apart by merciless talons and the inner organs thrown to one side, perhaps for a later meal. It was a hideous sight, and if it were not for the need of a mask, Richard would have gladly thrown up. Borcan using his telepathic power, suggested Richard concentrate on a group of the beasts whom appeared to be sleeping off their meal, some ten yards to the right of the eating party. Richard turned to Turner, who immediately raised his right hand showing five fingers. Now that's a fair game thought Richard, five against three. He nodded to Turner and in doing so relayed a short message 'Wait until we get the 'Redlight' don't forget the Colonel's plan/' Turner waved in acknowledgement then cautiously moved away through the bush, to find himself a position someways behind the group of Beasts.

All was ready, 'Now what about these protective boxes?' Richard asked Borcan, his telepathy now as good as any Nagosel's.

'Remember our little experiment in the Ops-Lab Richard? All one has to do is press upon the red and yellow buttons simultaneously and immediately you will be bathed with a 'green glow'. And to disengage the protective energy, again press upon the red and yellow buttons simultaneously. We shall be able to fire the webbing and be protected at the same time.'

Richard nodded to Borcan, sometimes body movement was just as effective as telepathy. Turning his back on the gory spectacle, Richard raised his field binoculars and looked down the farm road towards Bronx's carrier.

'Ah' he faintly blurted, Blue Dog Three at last. Switching his remote to relay position, he quietly signalled the Major. 'Hello, Blue Dog Three, Over.' Again some intermittent crackling then 'Hello Blue Dog Two, nice to hear from you, received message. Awaiting your call sign to move, over.'

'Blue Dog Three, prepare to move fast, awaiting Blue Dug One's signal. Keep to road once moved, once inside forest look for grenade fire on right, over.'

'Loud and clear, Blue Dog Two, awaiting your call sign to move, over and out.' Keeping his eyes trained on Ansai's carrier, Richard could just see a figure scrambling out of the top hatchway and taking a position behind the 'harpoon gun', he could only guess it was Matthews. Richard's heartbeat informed him his adrenaline count had risen, this was it, all now awaited the Colonel's signal, 'Redlight'.' He looked at Borcan, he seemed calm and unattached from the reality of the situation. 'I read your mind I'm ready' said Borcan. 'When you wish to release the webbing, say 'Gortani' my friend.' Little more was passed between them. Richard tugged hard at a drawrope on his arm launcher, and three feet of webbing loosened itself from the main bundle. Borcan did likewise and attached the two webs together by three circular links. Neither dare switch on the Alien boxes until the time for capture, as a sudden glow of green energy would startle and alert the Mondemon to their position. The Colonel must of seen Blue Dog Two entering the woods, and now also be aware of Ansai's position, so what was the problem? Time, bloody time, why do we always observe our watches when we get restless? thought Richard. A mind so full of many things, Annabel, gorgeous Annabel. Matthews with the harpoon, and his friend Borcan, what if he could not find an antidote to this plague, what then? Oh yeah, and I bet buddy Jefferson was having a swell of a time with Amariel. He gazed at the thickening mist now lowering its dimensional layer to just below his knees, when, 'Redlight Redlight Redlight. Go Borcan, go, hit those buttons, it's party time.' As the two friends ran towards the group of five beasts, a blast from one of Turner's special grenades lit up the sky. Another and yet another exploding indiscriminately around the eating party. Turner's bombs were good, those bastards won't forget this night. The ploy was good, the eating party drawn to Turner's gunfire and dirty grenades. The five awakening beasts not used to surprises seemed startled for a length of time. 'Gortani Gortani' Gortani' his telepathic voice rendering loudly within Borcan's senses. They both fired, their aim was not misjudged. Three Mondemon had risen together and looked towards them, their wings had movement, they began to spread, but one became entangled in the Titanium web thrashing violently within its noose, its talons tried desperately to tear the powerful cables.

'My God' cried Richard, my arm, my arm, harpoon, harpoon, harpoon' he cried. Flying Mondemon were now everywhere, swoops upon their attackers proving unsuccessful, sharp deadly talons initiating sparks against the green glow.

'Stay still Richard' a voice said, 'we are safe, stay still.' A sudden burst of machine gun fire cut a number of Mondemons in two, Turner now using the armour piercing attachment. But he was getting heavily outnumbered, where the hell was Rosie? The trapped beast began to rise, his wings limited to any flight movement, he tried desperately to walk, and in doing so forced his two captors to do likewise.

Richard hardly got the word 'Harpoon' out of his breath, when a heart rendering scream echoed in ghastly form about the forest. It, the Beast had been hit, the bloody Harpoon had embedded its arrowed shaft into the Beast's right leg member. It was time to disengage the webbing from the arm launchers, the calvary were here. Still protected by their boxes, Borcan and Richard ran for their lives to the beloved carrier. Behind them an injured Turner, bleeding badly making a similar pace. The two mini guns now giving a good measure of covering fire. 'Say nowt' said Matthews 'just get inside, I've started winching in the bastard. I'll join you in a sec after lending a hand to Turner.'

'The buttons, Richard, the buttons, red and yellow, together, red and yellow.' Richard did as he heard Borcan's voice like an Angel in his head. They had done it, they had bloody well done it. Richard and Borcan dropped quickly through the hatchway, outside the heavy fire from Candy's defences reminding them they were not out of the woods yet. Ansai a rock under such precarious situations, steadily picked up the radio phone and spoke 'Blue Dog One, calling, Blue Dog One, Over. Blue Dog One, calling Blue Dog One, Over.'

A weak, rather subdued voice responded 'Hello Blue Dog Three, Over. Heavy losses, self injured, some fifty feet from main carrier position, Over.'

Rosie replied 'Colonel, sending in four combat, repeat sending in four combat, request hold your position.'

'Roger Blue Dog Three, hurry, running short of ammo.' Ansai turned to the driver, 'stop this thing soldier, Matthews can take over, get out the hatchway and you three follow. I want the Colonel back here, got it?'

The carrier pulled to a sudden halt, alerting Matthews to some inside problem. 'Matthews get down here man, and get that laser in action. Richard you try your hand at that mini gun, but try not to hit our side, OK.' Richard had been trained in all weaponry, but he actually hated this remote system. Reminds me of a game in an Amusement Arcade he thought, but there was little time for thought with Ansai about.

'Leave the winch running Matthews, and I will drop the tailgate at the given moment,' commanded Ansai, swiftly moving to the rear of the carrier. 'When you can clip one of those wings off, or at least damage it badly do so Sergeant. Matthews aligned the laser at the moving target on scope. A simple touch of a button, put on line a graph of the Titanium webbing. Enlarging the frame he then picked out the two wings on the rear of the Beast. Whilst on the right of the screen, a picture box illuminated the decreasing target distance, 16ft, 15ft, 14ft, 13ft, turning the computer target stick, a line of fire was projected. 'Now you bastard, try that for size.'

'Seems he didn't feel a thing,' shouted the Major, his voice a little distorted behind the mask. But I've now dropped the tailgate and can make out a dismembered wing.'

The winch ground to a stop. Through a hole in the roof above the containment area, the steel cable had successfully pulled the monster up and into the carrier. Ansai pulled another lever and hydraulic arms raised the heavy tailgate back to its closed position. 'Leave it in the webbing, it's not a pretty sight, it's gorging at the dog already, and either the cats have jumped out or fell victim to its heavy weight, I can't see them?'

Ansai turned away from the observation window, he felt drained, emotionally drained. He was sweating and had only now noticed the dark patch of blood on his Sergeant's arm. 'Matthews, you're hurt, boy, and I am afraid that also means infected.'

Matthews rose slowly from the laser-command control, and made his way to the driving console. In doing so he looked hard into the Major's face. 'Turner's bought it Sir, brave man, not a pretty sight that, clean off his shoulders Sir, clean off.'

Turner spoke no more. Ansai knew what he meant, and after tapping the Sergeant's shoulder he sat down once again in front of the radio phone. 'Hello Blue Dog One, calling Blue Dog One, over. Hello Blue Dog One, Over.' He waited a few minutes and then 'Hello Blue Dog One here, sorry for delay. Taking Colonel onboard, over, taking Colonel onboard.' Ansai took in a number of deep breaths before responding. He felt he was getting a bit too old for this job. 'Hello Blue Dog One, good news, wait for our passing, then follow as support, copy?'

'Copy Blue Dog Three, Roger and out.'

'OK Sergeant, leg's get the hell out of here, you Richard, continue to waste those guns, Bronx and Cork are giving splendid covering fire at the moment. They will follow us out as rear defence, keep the missiles intact they may be useful, later.' Borcan meanwhile had placed himself in front of the observation window, being fascinated by the Beast's eyes. Perhaps the Beast too was a little interested in Borcan's eyes. 'Still, with no colour' even when alive,' thought Borcan. Such blackness like a pool of ink, endless, flowing, not a static mass. It's pig-like snout, was as Richard remarked, revolting, but alive all t he same. Borcan's eyes followed the contour of the beast's upper torso down to its two leg members. The flood of its internal life essence had subsided. The wound was open, but nothing flowed. His eyes continuing to the floor, he saw the remains of the cats. This beast didn't like bones, although the body was sucked dry there remained a very tight skin around a twisted carcass. The dog had been torn open, its upper portion pulled apart. There was little to see, any internal organs obviously used as an aid to nourishment. Two empty cavities were where the eyes should have been, but at least the poor thing retained its tongue. The patches of internal fluid splashed about by the Beast, were of a green slimy colour, clinging to the walls of the containment area, not dripping down as would most terrestrial blood he had seen. The laser had cut part of the Titanium webbing, allowing the Beast to move one arm freely, and with this arm he now began to try battering down the outer door and observation window. Borcan retreated a little, he had come this far, it would be foolish to be ripped apart or contract the plague now. He decided it best to sit down for the rest of the journey, and let this Major Ansai take over for a while.

Matthews drove as fast as he dare, this farmtrack was patchy in places, and he could not afford to slip off down some water dyke at this particular moment. Fine if on manoeuvres, great fun, but with such a distinguished guest on board, whom might provide an antidote. No not today. Clearing a couple of bends, of Mondemon was allowed however. The Monsters just stood there, maybe three or four in line, trying to stop the carrier or perhaps divert it somewhere? Just run the bastards over, they deserve that, thought Matthews. There's one for Turner and there's another for me. The view from the driving window was rather limited, however, if you pulled yourself up close to the windscreen, you could just see the caterpillar track running nicely over a Mondemon's head. Time for full headlights, wipers on, wash their filthy blood away. The road narrowed for about a mile, then at last the jolly old carriageway ahead. 'On the main belt Major, foot down all the way Sir.' Ansai turned his head, he then looked at Richard whom by now had finished firing. Richard sat next to Borcan, his head bowed forward, he was probably nodding off, but unfortunately he didn't have time for that. Richard, Richard' shouted Ansai, forgetting he was still wearing the mask and back on line with the mobile mouthpiece. Richard woke startled, nearly toppling out of his personnel seating. 'Oh sorry Sir, did I drop off?'

'Richard there will be time for a vacation later, if we are lucky, but for now please keep alert. Check that thing in the back there and then watch the guidance system on the Missile-radar for any Mondemon attack.'

'Yes Sir.'

Ansai switched on the radio transmitter, it was time to get a message to Wonderland. Disconnecting his remote line he then plugged into the Transmitter. 'Blue Dog Three, calling Dormouse, Rabbit in tunnel, over. Blue Dog Three calling Dormouse, Rabbit in tunnel, over.'

'Hello Blue Dog Three message received, Over. Any problems Over. Blue Dog One has injured member, like Candy. Blue Dog Three is following OK. Blue Dog One has injured member, likes Candy, Over. Correct Dormouse, estimate party back at 0400hrs check. Blue Dog Three see you at 0400hrs. Candy doctors on ready. Over, Roger and out.'

Ansai readjusted the frequency level and continued 'Blue Dog One, calling, Blue Dog One, Over. Blue Dog One calling Blue Dog One Over.'

'Hello, this is Blue Dog One Over. Blue Dog One, how is injured Over?'

'Blue Dog Three, Blue Dog Three, injured sleeping but infected, over.'

Ansai responded 'Quarantine alert, Blue Dog One, do your best. Dormouse advised, Over.'

'Thanks Blue Dog Three, will inform injured if he wakes Over Roger and Out.'

Last call before home arrival thought Ansai, as he tuned the frequency level round once again 'Calling Blue Dog Two, Calling Blue Dog Two, Calling Blue Dog Two, come in Blue Dog Two.'

'Hello Blue Dog Three, Hello Blue Dog Three, Over.'

'Blue Dog Two, you are OK Over?'

'Negative, I repeat Negative, Blue Dog Three.'

'What is your situation Blue Dog Two Over?'

'Fuel leak, repeat fuel leak Over.'

'Can you keep up Blue Dog Two, Over?'

'Negative Blue Dog Three, Have to initiate plan 'D' Over.'

'Blue Dog Two are you alone Over?'

'Blue Dog Three one combat with me, fuel leak danger, have to initiate plan 'D' Over.'

'Okay Blue Dog Two, understand, will send out searchers ASA|P, good luck.' Ansai removed the transmitter connecting lead, and plugged back onto mobile. 'Richard, Sergeant listen, Blue Dog Two has to initiate plan 'D' There is nothing we can do until our return to base, and then I shall organise a search party, but as you know I cannot authorise a search until late tonight. It is the only period when the Mondemon are subdued, so to speak. However, as you are aware through training, Bronx will be more than equipped to look after himself, and further there is a combat with him.'

Matthews said nothing but he didn't like it. Turner was gone, he didn't want to lose another. Maybe the Major would let him volunteer in the search, it's the least he could do. He looked at his watch, it showed 0330hrs. That meant about 30 minutes back to base. If Bronx had broken down recently then he couldn't be far away. On foot he could manage an easy 5mls an hour, but the risk was the damn mask. It had been tested up to a constant use of 4hrs.

Unless he carried a number of spares on his carrier, he was walking a tightrope. Ansai knew the face mask only lasts a period of four hours, what the hell was he thinking of, sending a search party tonight, some 17hrs away? Shit, he would have to risk a court martial and go back to Bronx after refuelling this carrier. Plan 'D' would attract hundreds of Mondemon, especially early in the morning. Detonation of a carrier was not a quiet spectacle. If the fuel tank had ruptured it wasn't worth salvaging anyway. No good crying over spilt milk at the moment thought Matthews. I'll sort something out back at Wonderland. Bronx was a survivor. Matthews turned his full concentration back on the road, they would have to pass through a number of villages, one of them his own. Good old Smithincott, his parents used to drive him down to the old station every morning to catch the early train to Exeter. It seemed as big as London in those days, he would be met by his mother's friend and taken to school, whilst his father and mother made their own way too their respective jobs. They would all return on the 5pm train back to Tiverton junction. The weekends were free, Matthews and his father spending memorable days biking to the Blackdown Hills. Mother having less physical pursuits to break the long weekends, she began weaving rugs, which although took some considerable time to complete, proved an extra money spinner. This extra money being stashed away to provide for the Christmas festivities. Yes, those were the good old days, he missed them badly, they had both died in a horrific car crash, just before his fortieth birthday. Fate had a lot to answer for. He consoled himself with the thought of a very large double rum, and a number of cigarettes would ease his frame of mind. The fuel gauge showed quarter full, three quarters of a tank in the space of some 90mls round trip wasn't all that good, though maybe the extra weight from the newly fitted containment wall and the fifty feet of reinforced steel cable could have something to do with it? Whatever the newly fitted engine bad proved its worth, extremely silent and it must be said, a lot faster than the old version. Plan 'D' was a defence measure, to protect Military secrets. To stop outsiders prying into the latest technology and indeed engines which these carriers possessed. The Ministry were good at explaining away sudden explosions, it was their job, though the loss of civilian casualties didn't come in to it. They were all under surveillance, A to watch B, B to watch C, and so on. No wonder the country was bogged down with paperwork. Sometimes Matthews had wished he had picked the Specials' Arrow-unit', Alien Recovery, and Research into other worlds, at least Richard and Jefferson had experienced 'Other-worlds'. There was too much 'Uniformity' in this world, too much 'belief' in what the papers and politicians say. And too much greed for materialistic values. Too late now, to join the 'Arrow' he was only five years off retirement. A tattered old windsock now came into view, the orange colouring had seen its best days years ago. It indicated a strong wind though, as it blew with some gusto in a south-easterly fashion. 'Nearly there Sir, I can see movement outside the hanger, could be the Chief and Miss Foster, not many legs about like those.'

'Thank you Sergeant, If I require a commentary on Miss Foster's vital statistics I will ask for it, until then kindly keep your mind on the matters at hand.'

'Yes Sir, sorry Sir, just not used to such sights so early in the morning Sir.'

Ansai gave a sarcastic grin, he inwardly agreed with his Sergeant, but such observations were best left for off duty hours, even though the sight of skin tight chemical suits left little to the imagination.

The Chief, Miss Foster and three medics stood waiting outside the hanger. 'Right pull up here Sergeant, and take a breather, as I go outside and find out what's to be done with our captive?' Ansai climbed down the outside of the carrier. Miss Foster's rear butt was clearly in view, as she now faced the hanger entrance pointing to a makeshift tent, which was an addition to the small marquee erected for the drivers earlier that night. Sensing his approach by observing the eye movements on the Chief's face, Annabel turned back around to face Ansai. The Chief was first to speak! 'Phone on Rosie?'

'Yes Chief, got the Beast you wanted but lost a good man. The Colonel's in the following carrier, he is under quarantine, but as yet I don't know the extent of the injuries.'

'Right Rosie, this is the next step. Me and Miss Foster here have arranged for a portable box to be constructed, to safely transport the Mondemon from the hanger, and down to the Ops-lab. The seats being removed from a transporter to accommodate the box and its capture. The box will be hermetically sealed to prevent any escape of the virus, and thence unsealed once placed inside the Containment area, which has been additionally strengthened in your absence. Getting the Mondemon from the rear of your carrier into the box, however, will be your problem. Have you any questions for the Major Miss Foster?'

Annabel had in mind many questions to ask the Major, but they were not all relevant to this operation . . . .However, she did wish to know whom had been killed, as she had felt some inner stirrings for Richard, though to what relevance these feelings referred to, she wasn't quite sure. So she condensed her words a little. 'Major Ansai, just how many men have been killed capturing this Beast?'

Ansai was pleased someone was taking an interest in his men. And responded 'I fear we may have lost a unit of flame throwers, as the usual scenario is, gas-tanks are ripped apart by the flying beasts and then explode about the men's backs. Some further combat soldiers maybe four, and my Sergeant Turner, whom unfortunately suffered a nasty decapitation. And lastly, though not dead Sergeant Bronx and a combat will have to make it back on feet, unless I can quickly recruit a searchparty for their rescue?'

On the mention of those last words, the Chief began to shake his head from side to side. 'No Ansai, I am sorry, but any type of rescue is out of the question for the moment. Sergeant Bronx and the combat will have to rely on their own ingenuity to get back.

Ansai was not amused 'I see Sir, well with all due respect Sir, I would like to discuss the matter later, in your office.'

'Oh as you wish, Major, but for now let's concentrate on the task ahead of us shall we?'

Rosie was about to let off more steam, but the appearance of Blue Dog One diffused the situation. The brakes squealed a little, but the carrier's body appeared unharmed. The tailgate dropped slowly on its hydraulic ramps, and Sergeant Cork and a combat carried the Colonel to the awaiting medics. Still unconscious but bleeding heavily from a slashed right arm and deep wound in his side, the medics took him inside a makeshift theatre inside the hangar. 'Guess you all know what this means' said the Chief? 'He is well infected and if our Alien friend Borcan cannot find a quick recovery antidote to the contamination he now has, then we must shoot him before he begins to change.'

Ansai walked over to his carrier, climbed up to the hatchway and before lowering himself inside looked directly at Miss Foster, and said over the mobile mouthpiece: 'Get that damned containment area ready Miss Foster, and I will get this Beast down to you, one way or another.'

A NIGHTMARE JOURNEY HOME

The time showed 0400am giving Bronx and young Curtis approx ten minutes, to salvage any equipment which would assist them on their walk back to base. Beneath the now redundant carrier a steady flow of fuel expanded the necessity to get the hell out of there. Bronx had implemented procedure 'D' on the computer, and the detonation of his beloved carrier would be over within the next few minutes. Shoving a handful of weapon cartridges down the external flap of his chemical suit, he then swung a combat survival kit over his shoulders 'get your mask on young Curtis, we have four replacement masks and a spare suit, so we should make it.' The young Combat was ready, he pulled on another pair of gloves and sprayed on the bonding agent. The damn stuff had stung on the first application, and the area of skin between the sleeve of the suit and the glove now proved very sore. A second application to his neck area didn't seem quite as bad, as he now hurriedly pulled down the face mask onto the bonding agent. 'Three minutes Curtis, come on boy.' Bronx pushed upward against the heavy circular-hatch, his right arm controlling its descent onto the roof. With a trigger happy finger positioned on his SMG, he cautiously peered out of the opened canopy.

    The Mondemon had gone, perhaps to the villages ahead of them, though they had left their mark upon the carrier. The rear mini gun had been ripped from its placement and as was common to their tenacious acts of destruction, a number of broken talons had broken off from their owners and now lay embedded in the carriers shell. God they were trying to rip the bloody carrier apart, thought Bronx, which sent more than a shiver down his well proportioned back. Wasting no further time on ceremonies, he scrambled down to the caterpillar enclosement and jumped from there. He ran some fifty yards before stopping short to check on the young combat. Curtis, heavily laden with weapons wasn't far behind. 'Move it soldier, move it, in a minute the damn thing will blow. Jump down this blasted dyke boy, and kiss your arse goodbye, know what I mean boy?' The masks and the attached remote earphones did little to soften the tremendous thunderclap seconds later. The debris blown across the dyke, as though carried on gale force winds. The carrier now lay still, black and twisted its life extinguished and a million pounds of defence money consumed within minutes. The roads would now be unsafe, they would stand out too easily, rather take to the fields and the undergrowth for cover. Bronx raised his head, he gave a wink to young Curtis and said: 'Follow close, we'll leave the main road and follow the river Exe into Tiverton, using the fields on the other side of the bank for cover. Hopefully, once in Tiverton we can latch onto the old canal and follow it before crossing the railtrack to Appledore. Keep your remote on and your bloody eyes peeled.'

The village of Stoneleigh lay a couple of miles to the right behind them, it possessed a few inhabitants and the fields about it showed Mother Nature at her worst.

The burning carrier now attracted unwanted attention, and from the forest glades hundreds of inquisitive Mondemon took to the skies. Bronx moved off in a slow but determined fashion, stopping every fifty yards to observe the route ahead and watch closely the movement of the Mondemon. Their direction unfortunately appeared to be in line with Tiverton. 'That's right, follow us you bastards,' thought Bronx, brushing yet another branch aside, the overgrown foliage giving both men a measure of cover. Bronx kept eye contact with the river, looking for a suitable place to cross. The water was flowing steadily, small rocks and tall reeds forming their own communes along the rusty banks. Daylight had arrived and with its wake further testimony to the plague flooded the senses. Dead animal carcasses 'moved' with Military precision, as the filthy maggots within, consumed the remains of an earthly life. Bloated fish, water rats and snakes, all moving, unconditionally with the rapid ingenuity of man's worst insect, the soon to be transformed 'Fly'. 'Well the bloody plague wouldn't kill these parasites. Evil looks after its own' thought Bronx. A broken tree branch pointed the way across the river, stuck as it were against the sunken boulders. 'Seems shallow here young Curtis, let's give it a try.' Bronx put down his SMG on the edge of the bank and lowered himself into the water. It was deep, but not too deep to cause concern. He wasn't about to test the mask's waterproof ability. Having gained a good foothold he reached back to the bank and retrieved his SMG. 'Right soldier, follow me.' The big man made his way across to the other bank without much effort. His large army boots crushing any resistance under foot. Curtis felt he was sinking somewhat into the riverbed, his survival bag was heavy and his tiny feet didn't cover the same ground area as that of Bronx's size thirteens.

'Hurry up man, what's keeping you?' shouted an impatient Bronx. Not realising as he did so, the ear battering effect of the remote on poor Curtis' ears. Curtis was not amused, and once back on dry land he would give a similar roar to Borcan. It began to rain however and this dampened both men's enthusiasm for a slanging match. Footwork proved difficult along this stretch of the river, small carpeted areas of mushroom and toadstool growth giving rise to thick thorn bushes and decaying trees, the ground felt spongy underfoot and hindered the walking pace of both men for some miles. Observing the skies, Bronx noticed three dark clouds had gathered above the town of Tiverton. They were of the menacing type, not rain clouds not nature's work but the work of evil of 'Vampirish Quality'. 'Are you there young Curtis?' Bronx's voice now strangely muffled, as if in fear of being overheard.

'Yes, I'm reading you loud and clear big boy' replied the young combat, keeping a discreet distance behind Bronx. 'Well look, there's bloody hundreds of them massing above our port of call, we cannot afford to go back and I don't want to use the roadways, these chemical suits gleam in the daylight like a bloody shield, fresh from the Armoury. Best to carry on to the outer perimeter and if it's too risky we'll have to wait for our chance nearer midday. It's a hornet's nest boy but we have little alternative. Can't see the Chief sending out a rescue crew until dark and by then we would have succumbed to the plague. We have until 1600hrs, if and only if the spare masks last up to their tested time. After that, if we happen to cross the path of a plague-mutant or rotting corpse, then the airborne spores will then impregnate us.'

'Cheers Bronx, you certainly know how to instil calm in a person don't you? OK, let's do it, but if there's any route which might escape their baleful eyes I suggest we take it. I don't relish hanging around waiting to be eaten or sucked dry, I have no plans to go to hell just yet.'

'Yeah, yeah,' said Bronx, sounds reasonable, but for the time being open up that bag of tricks you're carrying and give me one of those belts full of grenades. If we have to go, we'll take a few bastards with us.'

The two said little more, Bronx attaching the heavy belt across his shoulder and waist, and Curtis refitting his SMG with an armourlite barrel and larger shell cartridge.

Across the river, a mile or two to the left of the road stood Bolham Manor, its nearby woods housing a substantial number of Beasts. Curtis observed the nearby country lane leading up to the Manor, through his field binoculars he could just make out some movement. It was a car, a large Bentley or its like. Curtis watched as it sped down the lane, he couldn't see if the driver was a man or woman, but whomsoever was behind the wheel certainly had guts. The expensive limousine now roared straight onto the main road, blue smoke pouring from its exhaust, taking a right hand turn the driver, whom Curtis could still not clearly see, gave her full throttle and the metallic blue machine opened up for probably her last time, and thundered down the 8ml road towards Bambton. 'I wish you well you crazy human,' muttered Curtis, forgetting for a moment the open channel to Bronx.

'What's that Curtis?' replied Bronx, 'What's the problem?'

'Nothing Bronx, tell you later, nothing that we could help with.'

The dark clouds had dispersed, and if Bronx was right, Tiverton had provided a new feeding ground for the Mondemon. Curtis had seen the demonic-capabilities of these beasts, he had watched them tear, limb from limb and gorge themselves on the essence of human life. Manchester, Newcastle and Durham had given themselves over to the horrors. At the early stages, he and other combat soldiers fought the Beasts on home ground. Curtis glanced at his wristwatch, the time was now 0530am. Those townsfolk who had been sleeping would now have had a rude awakening. A small force of soldiers were barracked in the town, though their weaponry would be of little use against the beasts. The soldiers main task was to repair communication systems and electrical power stations, which had been attacked by the beasts.

There was some protective shelters, which mainly housed the children and their mothers, the rest of the community would have no option but to fight. There was not enough manpower to provide any instant reactionary force, especially at times such as this. Britain was infested with Mondemon, as was the rest of the world.

In the early days, before they could fly they were stopped dead by the effective use of mortar shells and grenades. But the disadvantage of using such weapons was the spread of the spores, not everybody wore chemical suits, and the common working man became quickly inflicted by the tiny parasitical thistles. Curtis had watched Transformation from a common man into a beast, a filmed presentation of the horror being shown at frequent intervals at Wonderland. He, a combat, was not privy to other experiments and Alien-research carried out in Wonderland, only those on a higher security level gained insight to any of that. Richard and Jefferson of the Specials 'Arrow' unit had indeed broadened their minds. Curtis' father Joshua knew of the strange Alien writings and had seen strange artefacts, not of this earth. But, as close as he was to Major Ansai he knew little of corridor 'Z'. Working in the De-coding section at Wonderland, Joshua had elevated his position as 'Trainee-decoder' to Chief-decoder, and this responsibility suited his talents well. He was of ordinary height, slim well presented, always clean shaven and smartly dressed. He neither smoked nor drunk alcohol and always carried a small bible inside his jacket pocket. Curtis took after his father in build and facial formation, narrow eyes betrayed an unusual hint of mixed colours, bordering on a light green to darkest brown. His nose too was unusually large, reminding one of a boxer who had lost too many fights. Compared to Bronx he was quite small. He was, like his father, very efficient in his chosen job. A combat was there primarily to kill, not be killed, trained to expect authority above all else. Sometimes however, Bronx did push his patience to the limit, but at the end of the day Bronx could be a very dangerous man, and he had seen far more action than most.

A soft squelch of something under Curtis' left boot focused his attention back to the present situation. He kneeled down to take a closer look at the mess beneath his boot. It was in fact the half eaten torso of a child, the head was still attached, but the arms and legs had been torn away. The frail little body was not decomposing, fresh blood had burst from the tiny heart, the organ that gave in to Curtis' boot. He wouldn't be sick or squeamish, he had seen similar cadavers before. Although perhaps not quite so fresh. A Mondemon had probably been taking the sad remains back to some forest for a late feast, but for some unknown reason dropped it in flight. Curtis thought of burial, but where would he bury such remains. No, best to leave it, the bloody maggots were everywhere anyway. Another mile and the real horrors would begin, he had to shut his mind off, treat the scene like a film. The French guillotine never saw so many decapitated heads, as he was about to see.

Hell couldn't be any worse, could it? Bronx had stopped also some twenty yards in front, he too was looking down at something. Curtis didn't want to know what. He removed his field binoculars from the combat bag and after turning the bezel wheel to maximum magnification turned his observations onto a block of derelict houses, behind which ran the old canal. The canal, water level was very low, hopefully the drainholes would provide a necessary escape route. Trouble was, he and Bronx would have to cross a couple of main roads, and go through a shopping precinct to get there. Replacing the lens cover on his binoculars, he then quickly rubbed off the mess from his boot, onto some long grass. As he turned in the direction of Bronx he caught sight of something being thrown into the river. 'What was that Bronx, are you responding big man, what was that, over?' Bronx didn't answer on the remote, instead he just waved the young combat over to where he was standing. Curtis flicked over the safety catch on his SMG, now he was ready for action. 'So what was it Bronx, part of a body?'

'You don't want to know, young Curtis, you don't want to know.' With that Bronx marched off, and whatever it was had disappeared into the murky waters forever. The rain continued to pour, as they made their way further into the town's boundary. The Army barracks now came into view, the makeshift walls taking a heavy battering from around fifty or so Mondemon, their sheer strength gradually demolishing the metal panels. And so providing a means of entry. Bronx and Curtis could do little at this point, to intervene would be suicidal, as more and more Mondemon poured into the gaping hole.

The roof of the barracks now also fell prey to Mondemon, their sheer weight enough to collapse the middle sections of supporting beams. The brave soldiers now leaving their quarters reluctantly, carried away like broken dolls into the night air. Their cries would be long remembered by the Tiverton survivors. 'Can't use grenades in an enclosed space, the poor bastards,' muttered Curtis. 'But I bet they cut a few down before surrendering to the talons. I just hope that Alien Borcan finds a way to eradicate them painfully and quickly. Look there Curtis,' Bronx was pointing to a shopping precinct, a large store now becoming a shooting gallery for some of Tiverton's residents. 'You don't find those sort of guns in your common gun shop, Curtis, those guys must be from a local rifle club, let's hope their ammo doesn't run out too quickly.' It was a diversion Bronx would rather of not had, he knew the Beasts would soon dominate the giant store. But, it gave him and young Curtis a chance to break for the old canal. Hopefully along the way he and Curtis would get the chance to take out a few Beasties their own way. 'Right Curtis let's go, fire at will and make for the main road to the left of the cop shop. I think once we get to the derelict houses, we should be pretty safe, so let's move.' As Bronx had so accurately stated, the two silver suits though protective towards the plague, now acted as allies for the Mondemon. They could be clearly seen darting amongst the more uniformed population, thus a large mass of Mondemon took to the skies in pursuit of the new visitors. Bronx and Curtis had crossed the first main road, guns blaring, they had not turned back to view the skies. A plague mutant suddenly rushed out at both men from a side alleyway, his wings not yet formed. The face was under transformation and the revolting pig like snout had grown disproportionately to the rest of the mutant's facial features. The talons were there, they were dangerous, a single cut to the uniform exposing any prevalent spores, and as this was a transforming mutant, there would be plenty to go around.

Curtis sent a couple of rounds into its face, it exploded instantly, large lumps of filthy gore depositing themselves on both men's uniforms. Two Mondemon landed behind Curtis, they seemed much taller than before, some eight feet or more. Bronx shouted 'Drop boy,' and let off a volley from his sub machine gun, it stunned the beasts for a time, giving Bronx and Curtis time to escape. The beasts gave chase as the two men ran across the second main road and towards the derelict houses. 'Keep going boy, I will stop them short with a few of these,' said Bronx, pulling two grenades from their respective clip. Curtis then disappeared into one of the houses, from the backdoor he could just see the canal. 'Hurry up Bronx, get those bastards.' He heard the explosions and waited, his finger nervously tapping the machine trigger. As he waited he noticed two large clouds encircling the skies above the derelict estate, shit it was them, they must of been following all the while. He ran to the front door, but there was no sign of Bronx, just the bloody aftermath of exploding beasts. There was little time to think, he would have to go for the canal now. His heart pounding he ran as fast as the suit would allow him movement to do so, looking all the time from side to side for Bronx. Where was he? The canal seemed miles away, but in reality it was just a few hundred feet away. He was alone, and would later write:

> 'I threw myself down a drainhole, to hide from their grotesque barbarity, the pursuing clouds now seemed unreal, as they poured down their elemental deluge. I was safe for a space of time, and fear and apprehension forbid me speech. Alone, save the presence of my mind.'

A cold sweat came over him, he collapsed exhausted, his eyes zombie like, watching, waiting for any sign of movement near the entrance to the drainhole. He could of slept, but he dared not, he would wait to see if Bronx would turn up. He looked at his watch, it showed 7am he would rest for a couple of hours, and then move on into the darkness, for he dare not go outside not yet anyway.

Darkness had never given reason for fear, only the presence of something lurking in its unseen depths, haunted the solitude of one's existence. Curtis was thinking, rationalising, seeking the internal spirit, to guide and assist him for a few hours more. Or he would give in here and now, in this prepared grave and let the filthy sewer rats close by, devour him. Unable to stand because of the confined space in the drain, Curtis had little option but to leave most of the weaponry and survival pack behind. Above him were the Mondemon ahead of him who knows what? All reason pointed onwards, onwards down the drain. He removed a small torch from the bag and two more gun cartridges, deciding grenades would not be a good idea in enclosed proximity, and anyway their use would alert the Mondemon. Throwing the SMG across his shoulder he removed the final item from the survival bag, the spare facemask. The removal of one mask to fit another always presented problems, especially when one's skin was already recovering from a previous application. The trick was to completely cover the neck circumference, pertaining to the suit, without spraying too much bonding agent onto the visible skin. When one tore off a face mask the bonding agent broke away completely leaving a dry surface area to recover with spray. Clever stuff this, thought Curtis, but a complete pain in the arse. He threw the old mask aside, hoping with all sincerity that a filthy rat would choke on it. The torchlight beam projected some thirty yards ahead of him, the effluent water still showing a steady stream from the previous downpour. It was a hands and knees job, reminding him of the underwater pipes on the army assault course, only difference being, they were clean and only thirty feet in length.

The town's main sewerage system fed into these larger displacement pipes. Every 100ft, an outlet from the town's pumping station, poured its unwanted waste into these canal fed drains. The plan was to cover about two miles of drain, and then leave the main feeding pipe by way of a canal outlet. Perhaps destiny favoured him after all, as it would have been asking too much to expect poor Bronx to crawl on his hands and knees through this lot, his size alone would of made it impossible. A glance at the wristwatch showed the time at 8.45am, it also displayed when illuminated an accurate compass reading. Which was now showing a strong direction to the northwest. It was decisively cold, the unknown did that to one. The circular pipe wall doing little to alleviating the task ahead, its surface area covered with brown transparent bubbles, which when squashed burst forth a 'witch's brew' of unfathomable substance. A fungi, a hybrid formed from the plague? Call it what you will, it felt revolting, and securing any kind of adhesion with these gloves was unthinkable. Human waste formed tiny dams at intervals, it was an unavoidable obstacle, the trick was not to slip and plunge one's head into its mass. The plague had destroyed 50% of the rat population, those rodents whom remained had developed a third eye, and an immensely long tail. They were inquisitive of him, the torch beam catching them unawares and sending them scurrying off into the murky waters. Two hours is enough for any man thought Curtis, this would test his endurance to the limit. He decided that at approx 10.45 he would look for a way out. By then it would be very doubtful if the Mondemon could see him, as his suit was already covered in a new camouflage. 'Never thought shit would prove so useful,' sniggered Curtis. now unafraid of his voice being overhead, this being one place the Mondemon could not squeeze into.

The grates linking the drainhole and the town's sewerage system glowed eerily in the darkness, the green moss clinging to the bars, throwing out its luminous quality. Perhaps he wasn't up to joining the 'Arrow's unit, best leave other worlds to the likes of Richard and Jefferson. This old Earth had aged him enough, there was only so much time in one's life. Bad news on old Turner's part, lost his fucking head, and the rest no doubt. Must push on, thinking too much, imagination running riot. He crawled onwards for a further 500ft, counting the outlets from the town supply to give him an accurate judgement of the area he had covered so far. Some twenty feet ahead of him the drain appeared to dip, he could see deeper effluence and for the first time a fear now overwhelmed him. Something was moving in a circular fashion amidst the black gunge. There was no tail visible so it wasn't a rat. He had heard tales of huge eels, eels which possessed uncannily sharp teeth, underwater pythons which could crush a man to death. Another manifestation of the plague no doubt. The suit was fine against the microscopic thistles and chemical agents, but if it were torn or punctured by some unknown horror, then he would be open to all the filthy parasitic germs and bacteria going.. Whatever it was, it seemed quite content to circle itself around the much deeper waters. Curtis was crawling in about 6ins of effluent, the new depths ahead of him looked to be at least two feet deeper. Perhaps the drain had cracked at this point and a marginal subsidence had set in. He quickly made a decision to arm his SMG, with every intention to blast the unnameable creature to Hell. It was in the way there could be no other option, a short burst of fire should bring it to the surface he thought. And then if necessary cut the bastard to shreds. It was awkward to move from the crawl position into a seated prose. His arm muscle being at first quite reluctant to allow any new kind of movement. It had locked itself between the powerful shoulder muscles and the forearm. 'Bastard' said Curtis, as it gradually unlocked and delivered an unwanted measure of pain. Now repositioned and literally sitting up to his knees in shit, he flicked the safety catch on the SMG and pointed its barrel towards the movement in the deeper waters. The armourlite attachment had been removed, there was little point in using heavy shells down here. The torch beam illuminated the chamber enough to get in a good shot. Curtis raised the SMG and fired off a round, his trigger finger glued to the mechanism in case of sudden retaliation. There was little change to the murky water, if there was any kind of blood flow, it must of been transparent. Nothing surfaced, the thing had stopped its irritating movement of the waters, everything was still. 'Must of got the fucking thing,' muttered Curtis, his eyes straining to catch any glimpse of life. His forehead now dripping with beads of sweat, he began to lower himself back into a crawling position. Dangerously unaware however, of the build up of three-eyed mutants, suddenly appearing from every conceivable grate and hole, behind and in front of him. With his weapon slung back across his shoulders and his gloved hands submerged once again, he eased one knee forward and then another, until he could move no further. The torchlight beam quivered upon their faces, chunks of glutinous flesh hung down from their ravenous open mouths, their teeth snarling at the unwanted intrusion of light. Curtis froze, he sensed them behind him, dark furry bodies swimming frantically past him. Waves and waves of them negotiating a pathway between his transfixed arms and legs. He could only observe and pray to God, it was his fault anyway. He should of left the damn thing alone, it wasn't doing anyone any harm. Red malevolent eyes and purpose built teeth directed the vision now playing before him. They splashed awkwardly about, some losing their long tails down their brother's greedy throats. It was a free for all, a surgeon would have been proud of such a neat dissection. The scissor-teeth leaving a machined-type bone void of any protective layer. Curtis looked in horror at one of the larger rats, it appeared to have four eyes not three. But on further observation, it was quite obvious the fourth eye was that of the thing, now torn from its maker and disappearing, with some reluctance, down the throat of its predator.

Ugh, a cold chill ran down Curtis' spine, he felt physically sick, but dare not vomit for fear of choking himself. Besides which the removal of his facemask was out of the question. The water level had now drained considerably, and the skeletal form now revealed itself. A vertebrae some six feet in length, crowned with a skull equal to any man's, convinced Curtis of the existence of the eel type horrors. Hell, this wasn't going to be an easy crawl. He watched as a large contingency of rodents moved off down the drain ahead of him, their swollen bellies proving there was a life of sorts after death. They had fed and the remaining rats now looked upon Curtis, their black hair matted and knotted with a mixture of their own blood, and the internal essence provided by their recent Benefactor. Two larger rats, the size of domestic cats, sat preening themselves. At a distance of six feet they were too close for comfort, and much too close to forget. Though not an artist, Curtis would be forever painting them on a conscious level, in this world and the next. The three eyes formed a perfect triangle, they possessed no pupils. bore a crimson colour and could be quite hypnotic. Between the two lower eyes, the start of the snout, some three inches in length and tapering to a sharp point. Not unlike that of a beak of a bird. Two tiny slits, purportedly the nostrils, issued out streams of white mucus or some other fluid attributable to their kind. The teeth consisted of two sets, a front set of long sharp protruding molars and a secondary set with a much shortened version, but this time jagged and closely aligned. The inner teeth being formed for the more stubborn removals of flesh. There was no tongue present, however there was evidence of some sensory awareness to taste, as four dark tentacles could be clearly seen undulating in the throat cavity. The cranium was small, the neck being a little longer than usual, about three inches. The arched back reaching perhaps a foot, whilst the hind legs could be judged to be no longer than four inches. The two King Rats as Curtis now called them, possessed abnormally large stomachs. Stomachs which were even now regurgitating part of the recent meal. But as luck would have it, any fallen undigested pieces didn't go to waste. The smaller subordinate rats lapping up the regurgitated overspill. They seemed happy with this second helping, being easier to digest and much warmer than the first indulgence. Still transfixed by the scene, Curtis began counting the remaining rats. Thoughts of using the SMG had crossed his mind, but his physical body didn't want to share his enthusiasm. Being a trained Combat he was prepared for most situations, but an Army of Germ carrying rodents, capable of lethal bites was not a scenario he had been prepared for. The preening session over, the two King Rats made their move. Curtis couldn't help himself, his own eyes had to follow theirs. He watched as they moved closer, one gliding beneath him in the shallow water, his formidable tail showing tell-tale signs of battles for leadership. It reminded Curtis of Rope, thick strong rope some half inch in diameter. There were numerous punctures to its length, and a noticeable growth of some kind in places. Which resembled tiny tubes or tumours betraying a possible cancerous development. A movement around Curtis' lower right arm, which was still in a crawl position, alerted him to the other King Rat. This was one investigating the suit, the shiny composition obviously appealing to its triad vision. It appeared to be sniffing the attached filth which was easy to collect down here. And then to his horror, Curtis watched as the revolting creature urinated with some force upon the patch of shit he had found particularly conducive to his sense of smell. It then took one last inquisitive look into Curtis' eyes and quickly disappeared down the side of him, taking his army of followers with him.

All was still again, drenched in perspiration, Curtis tried hard to regain his mental faculties, to overcome the immobility he now faced. His arms though excruciating in pain did not want to move, his legs were shaky and his breathing a little too erratic. 'What am I, a bloody Zombie?' he garbled, finding it hard to correlate his speech into recognisable form. It was neither fear nor panic that motivated his next move. It was the greatest of all unseen forces, the need of Mother Nature, but there was to be no toilet facility down here. He would have to relieve himself bladder wise, just couldn't hold it any longer, the other necessity would have to wait. The time now showed 09.30hrs, he could make it, his father would be waiting. Just crawl over this feeding pit, trying not to disturb the resting bones, and I'll be back on track he thought. For some 100yds or more the effluent waters remained at a depth just under two feet, on odd occasions the town's sewerage grates would pour out a further deluge of waste, some of its contents being the unfortunate remains of a Mondemon's feast. The compass still showed a positive bearing to the Northwest, at least he was heading towards home. Broken bottles and household tins proved another hazardous obstacle, a deep cut from any of these would be enough to initiate a death sentence. To his immediate right he came across his first canal fed outlet, there was no grate here but there would certainly be one at the Canal end. These outlets were much smaller, but large enough to squeeze through and make an escape. Feet first thought Curtis, that way I can kick the grating away when I get to it. He crawled past, wanting to progress a mile or so further, there was a new energy inside him a new fever. 'Another twenty grates and I will have covered a further 2000ft' muttered Curtis, 'and then I will make my exit. I reckon it should be the fourth outlet along this drain, they seem to be connected every 500ft.' He was breathing easier, the nausea had gone and the sweating back to a controlled level. Although his knees were now suffering from some kind of friction burn, sending signals along his leg joints, that not all was well.

A dead, heavily bloated rat floated by him, its eye sockets void of any lens, indeed the empty cavities now acted as caves for some parasitical lava. The offspring of a cockroach no doubt, considered Curtis, 'or those filthy maggots'. Further down the drain he went, counting the grates along the way. 'Five, ten, fifteen, nearly there combat, nearly there.' The last five grates, the last five hundred feet proved the worst. The chemical suit now completely covered in an efficient camouflage, made it tricky to keep one's balance. 'Can't get a positive hold anywhere, damn wall o f this drain covered in as much shit as me,' he muttered. His main concern was the visor attached to the face mask, if that should get tarnished with the filth he would have problems. He stopped and rested for a while, taking a few minutes to rub some filth of his watch, he could barely see the time as 10.25. At least he was on target, his face mask would be safe to use for at least another good two hours, by which time he should be consoling his inner self with a good meal and drink in Wonderland. The Alien Borcan was never far from his thoughts, could such an earthly visitor find a destructive antibody to this plague? and eradicate these Monsters for ever. Curtis had been taught about a God by his father Joshua. He had told him of a 'great being' existent in all of space, the 'Father of All' and the ever present manifestation of Love in all of Mankind. Truth and Justice being the perfectly balanced scales of his might. Though he never went to church, Curtis did believe in his Father's words. And indeed it was a foolish man or woman whom believed in a 'Devil' and yet denied a 'God'. Curtis held in his heart a place for such a God, and now more than ever he called upon him to disperse the evil now confronting Man. If there were 'Angels' in Heaven, then maybe they would lend an ear to Borcan's task? Time to move young Combat, that's what Bronx would have said. Curtis quickly checked the clip holding the torch, took in a deep breath and moved onwards.

THE HAPPY REUNION

A blood stained chemical suit lay in a heap, some yards away from the upturned 'Bentley'. The car's blue metallic finish now beyond any panel beaters expertise. The driver, a woman in her late thirties lay slumped across the steering wheel, a branch from the battered oak tree piercing her chest and continuing out of her back cavity. She had saved Bronx and now she had saved herself. The full transformation could not take place, the body was dead, only the face betrayed the hideousness of it all. Bronx was cut, and even though the wounds were not life threatening, the entrance of the plague spores would be. It wasn't the Mondemon that caused the crash, it was the change taking place within her, the olive type complexion greying, the manicured nails elongating then curling into indescribable talons. The eyes once a beautiful dark brown, so complimentary to her long wavy brown hair, now looked like pits of the damned. The transformed sockets now a malignant shining blackness even in death. Bronx had removed his chemical suit, what use was it now? The force of the crash had sent him through the windscreen, the facemask minimising what may have been serious facial disfigurement. Plastered with broken glass and torn by numerous branches, it was now redundant. There was no gun, no ammo, nothing. The combat survival bag had been ripped off his back by a Mondemon.

Sitting on the edge of the road, shaken and oozing blood from a makeshift bandage on his right leg, Bronx reviewed the recent events leading up to his present situation. It was a hazy remembrance, his head still sore from the collision with the windscreen, and then the ground. He was outside the derelict houses, that's right, about to blow the two chasing Mondemon to Hell. But what then? Oh yes, he had pulled one grenade pin and thrown the grenade in their direction, when a yank on his survival bag from behind knocked him backwards onto the ground. The grenade exploded and that's when the shit hit the fan. Still on his back he watched the Mondemon who had been behind him take a chunk of shrapnel between the eyes. The damned thing was none too happy, but the unexpected intervention gave Bronx the few minutes he'd needed to regain his feet. By now though, many more beasts had landed preventing him from following Curtis into the derelict houses, there was no option but to head back into town. They were all around him, coming down from the skies in droves. He ran, emptying his machine gun into their unsightly bodies. The first main road came into view, it was a dual carriageway and it was beginning to pile up with abandoned cars and bodies. He had lost his combat bag and with it the spare face mask and the armourlite barrel. Feeling into his left pocket flap he pulled out the last cartridge of shells for his SMG. Time was running out, he couldn't maintain a burst of fire in every direction, they would fly down and grab him in a moment, and he would experience the same fate as the poor bastards taken from the town's barracks. Across the other roadway he could just make out the large superstore, it was on fire, the local gun club had lost its war. At least his life was not in vain, he had diverted the Beasts away from young Curtis, he prayed to God the lad would make it back to base. Then inevitably his gun dried up, he turned around and just stood there, what was the use? Three of the Beasts crossed the dual carriageway, their terrible mouths exposing the torture to come. No, he couldn't, not this way. Bronx released the stud fastening on his combat knife, the seven inch blade shone spectacularly in the morning light.

He raised it to throat level and prepared to release himself from this world, when like an angel in the moment of darkness, he heard a woman's voice, screaming at him. 'Here, for God's sake here man.' Bronx dropped the knife and turned, a blue metallic Limousine had stopped just a hair's breath away. A good looking woman was waving to him, it was a chance, by thunder a chance. Running as fast as his legs knew how, and convinced he was dreaming, he at last reached the car. 'Quick jump in, they are closing in on you.' Bronx dived into the rear seat, keeping his head down as the beautiful machine roared off into salvation. They turned off at the roundabout onto the A373 towards Halberton, the Mondemon giving chase for a mile or so. And then easing off the accelerator slightly she introduced herself. Bronx had switched off his remote and could just barely hear her words, he asked if she might pull over so he could acquire the passenger seat? They were outside Tiverton now, she felt a little safer, so just before entering Halberton she brought the car to a stop. 'Quick then, hurry up.' Bronx swung open the heavy rear door, and after assuring himself the Mondemon were not following, gained the passenger seat beside her. She moved the automatic box from neutral into forward mode and pushed hard down onto the accelerator. The engine coughed and spluttered a little, but soon proved it wasn't quite ready for the knackers yard. Bronx removed his remote and unplugged his earphones, he liked the look and nerve of this woman, and needed to know whom she was? He was about to risk taking off his facemask so that he could talk to the lady without distorting his speech, when she suddenly remarked 'I am Joan, Joan Herne. My family history goes back three centuries ago, back to the days of smuggling and the wreckers off the Cornish coast. I am wealthy but don't mix with the social elite. I'm not a Daddy's girl, more a tomboy. Afraid though, that I may have caught the damn plague. Ran out of food and drink in the cellar, been hiding there for two weeks. A friend had it purpose built, bit of a wino really. Unfortunately they got him before he made it to the car. I went mad behind the wheel for a while, taking whatever roadway crossed my path. Eventually I came down a country lane and turned off onto the road that takes you into Bampton. That's where I was heading earlier, but unfortunately had to turn back to Tiverton 'cause of fallen trees across the road. Guess I don't know where the hell I'm going to now, unless you have any suggestions?' Bronx had plenty of suggestions, but the more obvious for the moment would be Wonderland. What the hell, she had saved his bacon, why couldn't she go there with him? Besides it was her limousine. He looked at the speedo, it was clocking sixty, and her driving now seemed to be more erratic. Ahead of them was a fork, showing a signpost to Tiverton junction station. If she didn't break in a moment or two it would be impossible to negotiate the next bend. But he need not of worried, the big car cruised around the tight turn with very little effort. 'Phew that was close,' he blurted, his right foot pushing down hard into a non existent brake pedal. 'Look Miss Herne, Joan, I think we can slow down a little.' She seemed oblivious to his voice, maintaining a speed of seventy plus miles an hour, intent it would seem to really put the old car through its paces.

Bronx attempted to tap her shoulder, to gain attention, she was going too fast this time, much too fast.

He never did touch her shoulder, but in those few seconds before the collision with the tree, he had seen a metamorphosis he was not likely to forget. The acceleration from a once beautiful woman into a 'Vampirish ghoul' had been completed in seconds. The last thing Bronx remembered before being catapulted through the windscreen, was the searing pain at the top of his right leg, and the removal of her sharp talons from the torn skin. There could be little doubt that he too now, had the plague within him . . . An aching head now brought him back to his senses, the blurred vision had almost disappeared and further examination of the top of his skull convinced him that he had cut it deeply, but not fractured it. Recounting his earlier experience in Tiverton and now this one, he was convinced a third mishap must be on the cards. Getting to his feet proved easy, but there was a substantial thumping inside his head causing some disorientation. He imagined, or at least perceived, a new landscape, interwoven and co-existent with the earthly plane. Everywhere he looked, vast skyscraper buildings rose from the ground and disappeared beyond the clouds. The colours were indescribable. beautiful deep greens and blues, transparent yet dramatically alive, as though burning with heavens fire, no flames but intensely spiritual. Like mighty cathedrals without beginning or end they dominated his senses, if it were a dream then he had fallen in love with it. 'My God, that was so beautiful, if this is just a fraction of what lays on the other side, then I shall fear no passing.' And with that the great man's eyes flowed with tears. In truth he had suffered concussion and who knows what doorways to perception are opened at such times? With the disappearance of the cyclopean landscape, the thumping, the high blood pressure within his head returned to a regulated rhythm. All was again back to normal, it was time to evaluate his immediate plight, to work out some plan of action. The discarded chemical suit had left him wearing only one undergarment, the official recognised boiler suit.

A mile up the road was the village of Peverell, haunted no doubt by plague mutants. Six or seven miles after that Appledore. To his right, some hundred yards away the old canal, where maybe, just

163

maybe, he might bump into Curtis. There was only two real alternatives open to him. One to cross the hundred yards or so to the canal, in anticipation that Curtis might appear. Or two, to risk a mile walk to Peverell and even if he got there, to infect himself further with the plague. Without his suit there was little protection against anything, besides the deep wound on his leg would reopen if he walked too far, and a heavy loss of blood would not help his situation. He didn't like the idea of sitting in the open either, the Mondemon could pick him out far easier by the roadside than down near the canal. 'Think, bloody think man!' Bronx was looking at the Bentley as his muttered thoughts zoomed in on an idea. I wonder, it's a chance, never known a woman not to? He slowly made his way across to the car, and trying hard not to look upon her facial features, he leaned in through the broken passenger side window. He smiled, the glove compartment had not been damaged in the impact. Pulling down the drawer, he quickly rummaged through her personal accessories. Handkerchief, nope, comb, nope, diary, nope, aha I knew it, bloody lipstick.' It was black lipstick but it would do the job. Using the only intact window and the two doors nearest the roadside, he quickly scribbled down a message, in the hope that any passing motorist could read. Short but to the point it read: 'Help, Ring 7776605551 Say Bronx by Canal A373!' It was of course an emergency number to Wonderland, the long dialling code would engage into a security exchange, which after recording any message transferred the information direct to Wonderland. Tired and hungry and in some considerable pain from his leg, Bronx crossed back to the canal side of the road. A glance at his watch showed the time as 10.45. He would wait for a couple of hours for the young combat, and then make a move towards Appledore, keeping close to the canal.

The horror of Transformation weighed heavily upon his mind, the normal incubation period was anything between six to eight hours. And then, well then there would be no Bronx, only a bloody miracle would save him, and that Miracle was in the shape of an Alien named Borcan. Bronx laughed as he trampled across the forest of mushrooms underfoot. The Mondemons shit, now dried and carried by the winds proved to be a source of nourishment for thousands of the fungi. Borcan has as much chance of finding an antidote as I have of meeting Curtis, thought Bronx. And an even less chance of discovering a virus which would eradicate the monsters. Still, he pondered, look on the bright side, I could soon be flying and enjoying a hearty meal, eyes, tongue, heart, liver, you name it and I will devour it. Ugh, where's Colonel Peterson? He can blow me away now. Stumbling a little because of his weakened leg, his eyes were suddenly brought to the attention of a cylindrical shaped object, lying on a flattened piece of grass close to the canal walkway. His heart began to race, was it possible, was it a combat torch? Bronx wasted little time in traversing the last ten feet of grassland, forgetting all about the injured leg, and the bloodflow, for he could hardly contain his joy on finding such an object. Nervously, picking it up from its fated place of rest, he turned the cylindrical body slowly around until he could read the engraved name. It read: 'Joshua Curtis, Combat!' Bronx held the torch as if in a trance, tears swelled in his eyes, it was a kind of fate or destiny? The car could of crashed anywhere along the road, but no, it was here near one of the few remaining oaks that the course of events had led him to. It was an omen, somehow he was going to survive, the inner light had not extinguished it was back and much brighter than before. Still holding tightly to the torch he took a few steps nearer to the edge of the canal. It wasn't very deep, then it never had been, the recent rainfall adding little to its overall depth. The outlet pipes from the town's sewerage systems giving an accurate guide to any rise in the water level. And on this occasion the outlet nearest to him was well above the surface water.

There was however a peculiar oddity to this outlet, the grating had been forced open, indicating something was either trying to enter into the drainage systems, or indeed had forcefully left? His eyes followed the direction of the canal towards Hatherton, there was no obvious sign of his friend Curtis, a chemical suit would have betrayed his position, even at a distance it wasn't hard to spot. Nothing on the embankment and nothing in the water, however after turning around to view the alternative route in the direction of Peverell, he espied movement. Clearly something had attracted much attention amidst the canal waters. It was hard to see what that attraction was, and even harder to imagine the sheer horror of rapid dismemberment by the Beasts. Bronx had no real alternative, it was man's instinct, some insatiability, to watch and record scenes such as this. The Dark Ages, the Witchhunts, burning at the stake, Guillotine and Hangmen's rope. The list was endless. The masses, the towns well respected citizens and the poor hungry starving wretches. They would flock in their hundreds to watch, to record, to shout, to scream obscenities at the victims, truly for them it was hell. He watched until they had finished their task, five of them some half a mile away, their wings flapping in some ecstatic praise to their accomplishment. One of them had turned, as though sensing an intrusion by watchful eyes, upon their macabre act. It then beckoned the others to turn, to cast aside their newly acquired flesh, and to observe a further source of nourishment. This nourishment was much larger than the rest and would therefore provide a bountiful supply of the rich red fluid. They took to the air, their black feathered wingspan propelling them to a couple of hundred feet, within minutes the Black Assassins as the Specials called them, were now coming for Bronx. 'Shit, fuck, this leg, I can't outrun them and there's very little cover, think man, think?' Bronx had little time to think however, a sudden rugby tackle unbalancing him and bringing him hard down onto the canal's pebble strewn walkway.

'What the, my God it's you Curtis, me boy, it's you.' Bronx lay still, hands over his ears as the SMG sent its message to the hovering demon. A second and last cartridge taking away the unholy face of one of them. As its remains fell the other four dropped to the ground. Bronx had reopened his leg wound, the makeshift bandage had lost its usefulness. Now completely soaked in blood, the acquired piece of skirt was removed, revealing the deep incision made by earlier talons. 'Skirts from her in the car boy, good looker too until she changed. Didn't think it would end like this boy, really didn't.' Curtis sat down by his friend, he too had exhausted himself. At least they would go together. Curtis recited the Lord's Prayer, he had reached, 'and forgive them whom trespass against us' when he thought he heard a voice, a voice inside his head, perhaps it was his Guardian Angel. It became louder and louder still, and then it dawned upon him. 'Shit' he cried 'It's Matthews, Sarge hit the deck, hit the fucking deck man.'

Bronx hit the deck, it was a command he would never forget, as volley after volley of intensive fire tore into the macabre forms. Both men froze to the spot, recognising the consistent sound of a carrier's mini guns. They waited, the young combat and the Sergeant, waited for a lull to the deafening onslaught of revenge, revenge perhaps for Turner? Time passed and at last silence. About the two men lay unfamiliar gore, pieces of undefinable matter scattered amongst Mother Nature's Earth. It was the unmistakable voice of Major Ansai which convinced them they were at last saved. 'Gentlemen, thank God for the calvary, if we hadn't stopped to investigate the abandoned car, then we would never have read Bronx SOS. Get to your feet Gentlemen, I have some very good news.'

BACK TO A STRANGE NEW WORLD

Room three housed the communal bar a waterhole for mixed pleasures. Usually it remained quiet and reserved, concentrating on disco weekends and the odd promotional party. Tonight though, the Ministry were providing the drinks, it was a time to celebrate to let one's hair down. Only the Alien Borcan would be in non attendance. For him the word Indulgence referred to enlightenment. There were a number of old grimoires he wished to study, before his return to Nilrem. Let the earthlings enjoy their strange fluid, that which overwhelms their thinking process and breaks the Illusory world temporarily. He Borcan had completed his mission, he had found a destructive antibody against the Beasts. It was strange indeed, that the form which crawls upon its belly in some hazardous movement, which conceals itself amidst the sands and rocks of the earthly deserts, would prove to be the benefactor of man's continual presence upon this sphere?

Miss Foster had called this form a 'Snake' or a 'Serpent'. She hated them, but at the same time admitted their 'Venom' had been useful as medicines in some areas of medical research. Borcan however had attached some kind of Affinity with them, finding them neither repulsive nor lacking intelligence. In fact he found these 'Snakes' possessed a communicative rapport with him, in other words he could understand their thoughts. Back in the Ops-lab he had,, without Miss Foster's permission, removed a poisonous variety of this form and without fear held its wondrous head in the palm of his hand, whilst its body had coiled tightly about his arm. It was called a 'King-Cobra' and its facial features could be quite mesmerising to the unprepared soul. It was the fated intervention by Miss Foster which caused the following chain of events.

'Borcan,' she cried, 'put that damn thing back. If it bites you who knows what affects the poisons will have upon your Alien Form?' Borcan smiled and looking deep into Miss Foster's eyes replied 'My fellow scientist, look here, is this not a bite, and here yet another? You should perhaps know I have visited your earth before, several times, and these snakes as you call them are not destructive to our biological make up. However, if our race were suffering from some life threatening virus then such bites would be fatal. Their toxins are similar to our own, and I think you would find that the 'Entors' which we use to cleanse any system, would be more than enough to remove such poisons from your own.' It was those last words that broke the spell, Borcan had not perceived such a simple bacterial form such as 'Entors' could be used in any other way. Until now. Putting the snake back into its cage, Borcan then quickly relayed an urgent message to Miss Foster, 'Please forgive me I must go to my ship, it's a chance, a miracle perhaps, but I think I know of a formula. On my ship are a number of Geddonian chemicals, from which I can create a batch of 'Entors'. Please be ready on my return with your dart gun, pray I'm right Miss Foster, pray I'm right.' And without further telepathic speech Borcan quickly made his way to the magnetic door and released its lock. It closed behind him. Annabel could just stare in disbelief, what was an 'Entor' and what had the snake to do with it? She pulled out some cigarettes from her apron pocket, the packet was a little crushed, but there was one or two unscathed smokes amongst the rest. Must have been that damn airgun, the butt must of damaged them every time she reloaded the barrel with a new dart. 'That thing must be full of bloody darts' she said hesitantly, whilst shaking loose a cigarette from the inflicted packet. She was tired, perhaps too tired to understand the significance of what Borcan had just told her? They had tried, they really had. Yet the damned monster was immune to everything. It was nearly 0900am and the Colonel's time was running out, he would have to be shot, there was no other way. Where was Richard, she needed to talk to him, just how much sleep did he need anyway? Gosh, she was a bit of a bitch wasn't she? Annabel felt like crying, she was stressed out, needed sleep, rest. What the hell was Borcan up to? The Beast was making funny noises, it frightened her.

Borcan did not congratulate himself, he should have perceived this answer to the plague, hours before. How simple time was, and yet here it would prove itself a Saviour, a God, whose intervention would save this earthly race from extinction. Earth was close to the Vortex, its Time level was therefore very fast. Metabolic reproduction would therefore also be very fast, and the introduction of 'Entors' into such a body would entirely deplete the natural defence of the system. True, Richard and Jefferson had ingested them before travel in the Time-traveller, but their ingestion had been in the Time level conducive to Nagosel existence. But here, the 'Entors' would rapidly consume any poisons and their Toxins, at an alarming rate. Any white cells inside the Beast's body would be used up by attacking the 'Entors' and the additional attack from the Earthly serpent venom would prove too much for the Beast's bodily defences. At least that was Borcan's theory.

It would take two darts to test his theory, the first containing a capsule of 'Entors' and the second some minutes later the deadly venom taken from the Cobra in the laboratory. If it worked, then a newly formed antibody could be extracted from the Beast's veins and used against the rest of the Mondemon. A small dose of the same being injected into Colonel Peterson's body, though the reaction of his now half human system may not respond accordingly. In any event he may surely die anyway. After carefully placing the newly formed phial of 'Entors' into his pocket, Borcan then quickly made his exit from the Traveller. Time was now an essence that could not be distilled. The transporter tube moved swiftly through the winding tunnel. Corridor eighteen soon revealed itself, there was no time to indulge in thought reading, the driver's mind would be read at a later date. Borcan's long legs still proved difficult in exiting the Transporter, the size of his feet causing considerable amusement to the driver. However, he Borcan was now privileged, had he not been given the pass key for the Ops-room door, at least Miss Foster regarded him with some respect, and taking no real dislikeness to his Alien form? Checking the phial was still intact, he punched in the security code. The magnetic lock now released, the heavy steel door now gave entrance. Miss Foster was sitting nervously at the far end of the ops-room table, her legs rather exposed, reminding Borcan of Amariel's delightfully endless legs. She stubbed out her last remaining cigarette, trying hard to hide her inner fears and her concern for the two missing combats, Curtis and Bronx. Borcan's telepathic voice soon calmed her fears however and his strange Alien smile prompted her spirit to fight a little while longer. 'These are the 'Entors' Miss Foster, I would suggest we use half a phial in the first dart, and after five minutes of your earthly time has passed, fire a second dart filled with the snake's venom. Please prepare the two darts for me whilst I put on the protective suit and mask, you have taken enough risks already.' The containment area remained intact, the Beast now a little subdued appeared to be studying the half eaten remains of the previous occupier of the rectangular room. The Mondemons never went short of food. 'Here Borcan' Annabel passed the light dart gun to Borcan, forgetting temporarily that her speech would not be heard by Borcan, but her thoughts most definitely would be. He smiled at her again, taking the gun and the second cartridge into the containment's airlock. Annabel checked on the beast again, it was doing something disgusting with the others remains, but at least its attention was not on the inner doorway. The red bulb flashed on the airlock's control panel indicating the air had been stabilised, and now would be the right time to open the inner door. Borcan was ready, he had raised the gun to shoulder height, preparing to fire the first dart, he too observing the Beast's every move through the strengthened door glass.

Annabel pushed down on the release mechanism, and watched as Borcan entered the room and fired the first dart. The outer door would remain closed until the Beast had received the second dart. Now the testing time would begin. She observed Borcan as he reloaded the other dart into the gun's chamber. He had a little difficulty in doing this, because of the Alien fingers, the circular ending appendages sometimes proving difficult in the easiest of tasks.

Annabel observed the Beast again, there had been no change, perhaps Borcan should have used a full phial of 'Entors'? No bloody change, no bloody change, she thought. She looked again at her wristwatch, six minutes had passed since the firing of the first dart. Shit, she waved to Borcan and at the same time released the inner door catch. Borcan raised the gun one more time and fired, hitting the Beast in one of his monstrous legs. This time the Beast recoiled, sprung to its feet and charged towards Borcan. The inner door appeared to be buckling under this new barrage, if it broke or the strengthened glass should crack, then Borcan would be trapped in the airlock. 'Oh hurry up and stabilise,' she muttered, glancing impatiently at the red stabilised button. At last it began flashing and with some urgency she pushed open the outer door release button. Her hands were shaking, it was hard to control her nerves now, quite hard.

Borcan removed the protective uniform and mask, disposed of it down a waste chute and made his way over to Annabel. His inner speech was quiet, he too was tired, all they could do now was watch and wait. The beast appeared more ferocious than ever, raining even heavier blows down upon the front observation glass some three feet away from Annabel and Borcan. Again Annabel looked at the time twenty minutes and nothing, she felt faint, perspiring quite a lot now around her forehead. In a last effort she called to God, 'Please forgive us Father, and show us thy might in our hour of need.' And as she spoke, Borcan's usually quiet voice now thundered into her head 'Look Miss Foster, look.' He was pointing directly at the beast's mouth, something was happening, something glorious was happening.

Annabel felt like crying, but was too overwhelmed. Borcan had done it, he had actually done it. She grasped hold of the Alien's hand, it was a spontaneous thing, she loved him in a funny sort of way. They watched as the serpent's power and the Entors ravaged the corrupt Mondemon's form. The beast began to sway from side to side, unsteady on its feet, it fell banging its monstrous head against the sharp corner of the restraining bed, its buckles snapped hours earlier by the beast. It gave out a hideous roar before choking on some internal manifestation, which poured its slime like qualities out from the jaws of hell, covering the floor with some evil abomination. Unable to breathe and under an attack from a force it could not defeat, the great beast fell again to the floor, its head smashing hard into the containment's area, hardened shell. Never to arise again.

'Quick Miss Foster, put on a protective suit and take a few samples from the beast's body. If we are in time, we may still save Colonel Peterson. We are both very tired but must act now to save the rest of Humanity. The Antibodies will be very virulent and we must prepare as many batches as possible for dispersement across your planet.'

And such was the chain of events which led us up to the present scenario!

Corridor 26 was indeed full to capacity today. July 4th 2017. Borcan and Richard would get a good send off. Borcan as a gift, left the magic box with Annabel, much would be learnt from its construction rather than its inner matrix. He in return had 'borrowed' a number of books from the library in the Briefing room, making a promise to return to Wonderland to exchange technology. Curtis had now been made Sergeant and Rosie Ansai replaced 'Candy' whom accepted an early retirement.

Richard would not be homesick, he looked forward to his new adventures, and besides he had a lot to talk about to Jefferson. He had promised one thing to Annabel at the party, he would endeavour to return with a picture of 'Sophiel'.

'Here take these boy' shouted an emotional Rosie, holding in his hand a fistful of large cigars. 'Don't know if they will be smokeable where you are going Richard, but it's worth a try, and tell Jefferson to move his fat butt back here one day, remember the time difference. I may not always be around fellas. Good luck.' He could say no more. Richard, clad in the familiar blue Nagosel uniform and holding face mask in hand, thanked Rosie. Promised the old man he would return, perhaps with a wife. 'Come my friend' Borcan's telepathic speech reassuring Richard that Nilrem was awaiting them both, and more importantly a night's union with Sophiel. Little more said the tall Alien and his human friend disappeared inside the Alien craft. The audible humming became unbearable and all present covered their human ears for fear of permanent damage. Annabel, watched fascinated, as the outer hull became alive, its density turning into vibration, into colour. In a moment they would be gone. There was so much to learn, so much to love. On Richard's return she would be so much older, and yet he would remain quite youthful. She turned away, back towards the transporter tube, after all Rosie Ansai and Bronx had promised her a party she wouldn't forget!

ELDER   SIGILS

'Allfhar'

To heighten conciousness to its highest level. To open doors to beyond. To protect against Evil . . .

'Aowoss'

An 'Entity', a magical current. Use Gold for any Amulet or Ceremonial work.

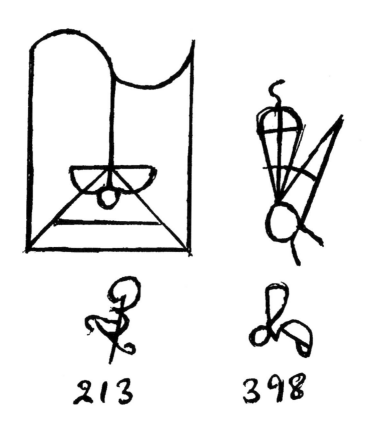

'Absilom – Abhornis'

'King of the Walking Dead'
One of the Shadows left behind by the Beast 'Naasbite'. Deep in the
bowels of the earth shall you find him. Call him forth to restore life.
Inscribe his Name on Gold.

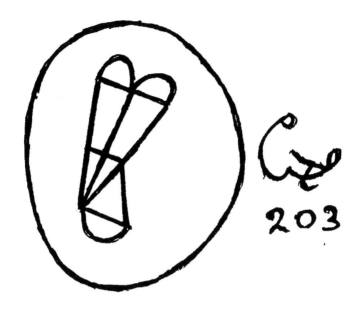

'Baalmedon'

(King of 'Demons')
A powerful Shadow left behind by the 'Master 'Naasbite'. He haunts the Deserts and Mountainous regions of your earth. Inscribe his Sigil on Glass. Useful in Dark Rites to enlist the help from Demons.

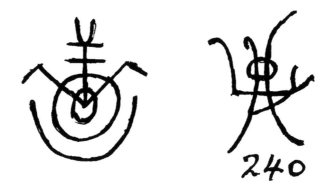

'Chulltoo'

'A Deep – One', The sigil and its device can be inscribed upon lead to discover underwater treasures.

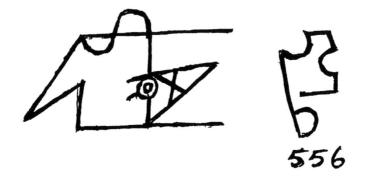

'Choronsax'

'King of 'Vampires'. This shadow was given his power by the master 'Naasbite'. He feeds upon the 'Essence' in blood and is dangerous to evoke.

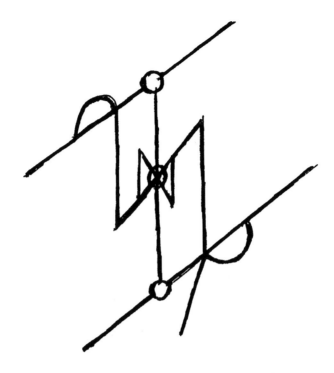

'Choronzon'

It is said he guardeth the abyssmal gate.
The 'Pylon' 'sehad' Is then a key
to his invocation . . .

542

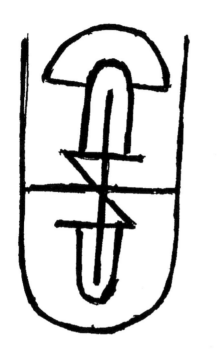

'Chutulzi' (A Deep One)

To be found in the Dimension to the right of 'Oshur'.

A magical current equal to 93. They possess great knowledge of time and its framework, and are best evoked near stagnant pools or ancient lakes. They can appear alarming at first sight. Their frog – like heads however should instill no permanent – fear.

'Eurynome'

Can call forth the greatest tempests. Can cause Asphyxiatian and still any fire . . .

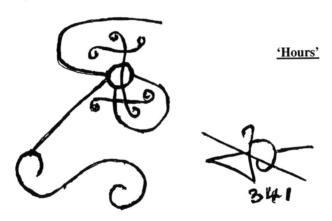

'Hours'

Brother of Zett.
A Sigil to call forth his light.

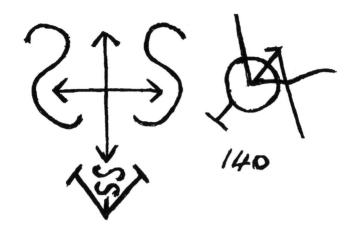

'Isis'

Infinite Stars in Infinite Space. The giver of Psychic – Gifts.

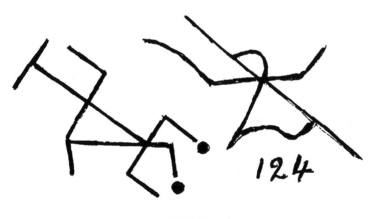

'Lillith'

She whom guardeth the third – gate of pleasure and understanding.

'Abrahadabra'

(A power word of Reflection)
This Sigil is an conductor of Star – energies. It will strengthen a
Ritual. . .

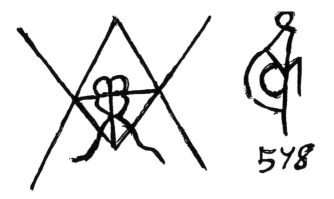

'Alaxbrasbra'

An Entity, a four – winged serpent. Its dimension is via Pylon
'Elsang'

'Merlin' (Nilrem)

He whom walked upon the earth after removing his third – eye. His Sigil giveth wisdom and Knowledge of Unknown things . . .

'Luviceerous'

(King of the 'Elementals' of the night). Powerful 'Sigils' to call forth the many 'Legions' under his command. . .

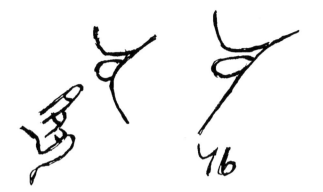

'Lham'

(An Ancient Elder). The 'Trigger', the 'Iggneytorr' of the 'Unseen' currents. chant his name thus, LHAM AYEGOSS, LHAM AYEGOSS.

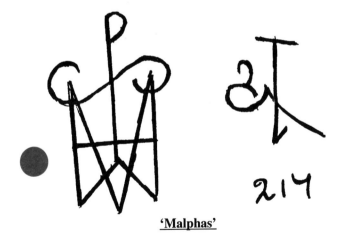

'Malphas'

Use his Sigil and devices to secure a protective amulet. Use also to open hidden doors.

<u>'Ne Gam Phor Mis'</u>

A 'Haunter of the deep'. Only those well practised in the arts should invoke his name.

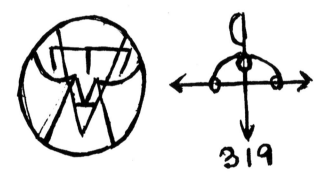

<u>'Omegra'</u>

A Powerful protection in all Occult workings. Use in an Amulet with thy name written around its circumference . . .

'Osireis'

For achievments and desires, inscribe both upon a Gold Talisman. Thy name beneath the sigil. Birth beneath its device. As the sun rises so too shall thy wish.

'Shaitan'

(A Dark One) Many desires can be achieved by calling him forth. But beware his dual – currents.

'Sabetasomec'

Usually only called upon by Dark – Magi. Dangerous indeed. But can give much power. Inscribe upon any 'Weaponry'.

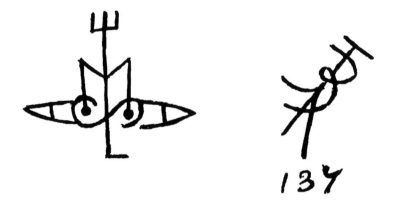

'Samael, an Elder'

Gives occult knowledge when called upon. Sigil for strength and obtaining occult knowledge. Use Silver or Lead Amulets.

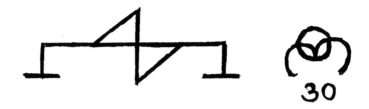

'Zett'

Usually worshipped in the desert. Useful on Talisman for Occult Quests. On Amulets for Psychic Defence.

'Shugal'

Male principle to 'choronzon' female aspect. The 'Matter energy – force.' Its other half being Anti – Matter.

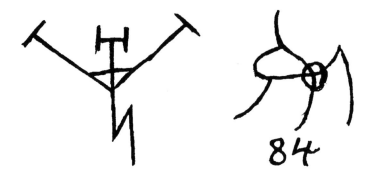

'Tanith'

(Light Serpent) A current that flows about our 'Astral – plane. Knowledge and occult symbols she will give thee. But thine Heart must be pure.

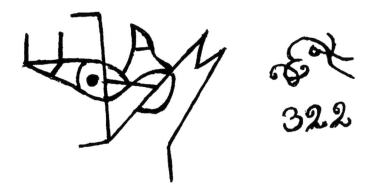

'Tasaramee'

A devourer of Astral – waste. A worm like 'Entity'. He has the power to open Gates to Treasure.

'Zazbavoo'

As a Denizen he is hard to contact. But Meditation upon his Sigil and gentle chants of his name, should awaken him. He is knowledge upon the frame work of space and beyond . . .

'Zommsfaron'

(His dimension is to the right of the 'Pylon' sehad.) His might is as great as Choronzon. He teachs poisons and black rituals.

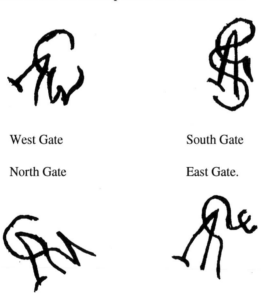

West Gate	South Gate
North Gate	East Gate.

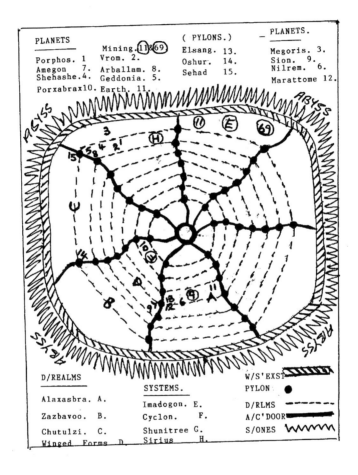

PLANETS

Mining. 11 & 69

Porphos. 1
Amegon 7.
Shehashe. 4.
Porxabrax 10.

Vrom. 2.
Arballam. 8.
Geddonia. 5.
Earth. 11.

(PYLONS.)

Elsang. 13.
Oshur. 14.
Sehad 15.

— PLANETS.

Megoris. 3.
Sion. 9.
Nilrem. 6.
Marattome 12.

D/REALMS

Alaxasbra. A.

Zazbavoo. B.

Chutulzi. C.

Winged Forms D.

SYSTEMS.

Imadogon. E.

Cyclon. F.

Shunitree G.
Sirius H.

W/S'EXST
PYLON ●
D/RLMS - - - - -
A/C'DOOR ▬▬▬
S/ONES ⌇⌇⌇

193

Wonderland Coding.

Arrows Unit	1	21	
Air – defence	1	4	First Figure
Briefing – room	2	18	Denotes;
Bacterial Exp	2	5	Corridoor.
Bedding – Store	2	19	
Complex/c/Bar	3	3	Second Figure
Clothing/Store	3	19	denotes;
Chemichal/War	3	23	Room
Chief Mech	3	13	
Decoding Fac	4	6	
Dental Treat	4	20	
Eating – hall	5	8	
Gunnery Range	7	18	

Wonderland Coding

Keep fit	11	6
Lazer Weap	12	23
Lunar/Maps	12	13
Medical/Blk	13	2
Maverick/RST	13	18
Officers/QTS	15	17
Officers/Bar	15	2
Power/STN	16	19
Research/OPS	18	●
Rifle/REQS	18	18
Saucer/Infil	19	9
S/Market Buy	19	2

Wonderland coding

(Specials)

Combat	19	3
Sgts Mess	19	19
Weaponry	19	23

Transporter repair	20	18
X-Ray Documents	24	4
Zenith Mapping	26	13
Zombie Cells	26	3
Zebra Zebra	26	26
Wonderland command	23	3
Earth Studies	5	19

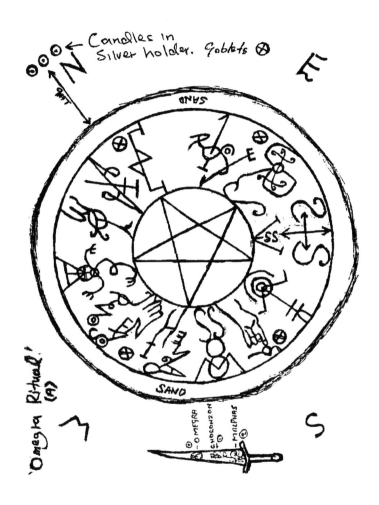

Candles in
Silver holder. Goblets ⊗

'Omega Ritual'
(A)

SAND

SAND

⊗ – OMEGA
– CHOLONZON
– MALPHAS

Illustration (B)
Alghar Ritual

S   W

CONCIOUSNESS

ABYSSMALL

goats skull

N

Black candles